Nell Grant

A Rainy Day in Cheltenham

This paperback edition published in 2025
© Nell Grant, 2025

Nell Grant has asserted her right under the Copyright, Designs and Patents Act, 1988, to be identified as the Author of this work.

Cover design by Dave Sneddon, Firehouse Design

All rights reserved. No part of this publication may be reproduced or transmitted in any form or by any means, electronic or mechanical, including photocopying, recording, or any information storage or retrieval system, without prior permission in writing from the author.

ISBN: 9798289627421

The author would like to express her sincere thanks to

Victoria Ellen Richardson
Hazel Gilmour
Emma Jane Wilson
Elizabeth Oates
Helen Rae
May Gilchrist
and
Lisa Nettleton

for their support and encouragement

Chapter 1

Codex, Carnival Bar, Citrus Clothing, Cocoa Bean. Victoria read out the shops that she could see from the window of the Queen's Hotel and wondered if the owners had agreed to start the names of their businesses with the letter C. Although why would they, it wouldn't boost sales or draw crowds. It was probably just a coincidence.

She decided that later in the day she'd go for a walk further up the street to see if the other shops in the row had names that began with C, just out of curiosity. Perhaps, she could take a look in Citrus Clothing to see if they had a sale rail with something nice that she could wear to dinner. Tonight was special, she would make it so. If Dan got called back for a second interview, then they would really have something to celebrate. It would be the fresh start they needed, far away from the issues that constantly hovered above both of their lives. On the other hand, if he didn't get the post, she would reassure him that it didn't matter, it just wasn't meant to be.

He had seen the advertisement for this job purely by chance, so imagine the possibilities if he had started looking earnestly for a new position. She was probably bias, but she believed that Dan was a strong candidate for this Head Teacher's role. He was currently the deputy head of a larger, more prestigious, school in the city of Edinburgh. Victoria reckoned that he could not only head up this little, independent school in Cheltenham with ease but could quite possibly take it to a higher level. He had so many attributes to bring to the post with his rugby and football coaching qualifications; not forgetting his musical talents, as few teachers nowadays could boast that they were grade eight pianists.

A thought niggled away at her, although she knew that she was being pedantic. This was a strict catholic school, and the application form had reflected that. One section asked about religion, and Dan had answered 'none'. The existing head may not approve of that. Then there was information required on his marital status, where Dan had written unmarried. No, they had never officially taken their vows before God, but they had lived a married life for fifteen years and had a wonderful son. Would the owner decide that he was living in sin, or would he suspect that an unmarried man in his forties would be gay; either way could be a negative in the eyes of the retiring head, whose father had founded the school. This was a classic case of her overthinking things, as usual. She needed to stop doing that.

The beds in hotels were always so comfortable, Victoria noted, nestling her head deep into the feather pillow. The crisp cotton sheets felt so good against her skin. Poor Dan, ahead of him was a stressful, full-on day and he didn't exactly have the best start to the morning. Sleeping through his alarm had been unfortunate, today of all days. An image returned to her mind of him running around searching for his shoes, then rooting around in the suitcase for his deodorant and ending up sorting his tie several times in the mirror before getting it right, it was a disaster. It would probably be something that they laughed about in the future, she decided.

Fortunately, she could look forward to a relaxing day doing a whole lot of not very much. Dan had invited her to join him on the trip because he said that he wanted some company, but she suspected he was also looking for a bit of moral support, although he would struggle to admit that. Regardless of the reason, it was a chance for them to get away by themselves, which they hadn't done since Artie was born. She suddenly missed Artie. This had been the first time she had left him. She had no concerns about leaving him in Dan's mum's capable hands, because she was an excellent substitute, and he loved her, but she just missed his little face and his funny ways. Maybe, she decided, when she ventures out to the shops later, she would pick him up something nice; he enjoyed surprises. *I hope Dan calls at lunchtime, to tell me how things are going*, she thought fleetingly, just before she closed her eyes for another sleep.

The dreams she was tormented by were always the same, suppressed hurts. In her waking hours, she could push them from her thoughts, but when she slept, they barged their way back in. Betrayal was a nasty crime, especially when it was not expected or deserved. It had only been one night, but the pain was equal to a hundred nights. Still, she had forgiven him and tried her best to forget, but unfortunately, her dreams kept reminding her every time she slept.

She awoke with the sound of rain pelting against the window. A troubled churning was already in her stomach, as it always was after the dream. When was it going to stop? When would she be purged of it for good? Her phone lay on the cabinet beside her, and she reached over to check for messages. It was too early for any news from Dan, but there was a possibility that he could have taken a break for coffee and sneaked in a quick text. There was no news, but she hadn't really expected there to be. Instead, she sent a message to Dan's mum to find out how Artie was. Leaving him overnight wasn't easy but many of her friends left their kids with grandparents regularly. The fact that he was excited to stay two nights at his gran's house made leaving him so much easier.

It had taken them almost seven hours to arrive in the heart of Cheltenham at the Queens Hotel, but they had taken a much-needed break at a Road Chef on the way. Dan had been exhausted when they arrived and maybe, in hindsight, she shouldn't have talked him into going for a drink in the bar downstairs. One drink had turned into four or five and it had been after midnight before they headed back to the room to sleep.

Guilt unsettled her when she thought about him sleeping through his alarm, then springing into action, rushing to get washed and dressed. He had even missed breakfast. Still, a bit of fasting wouldn't do him any harm, there was a little too much love on the handles around his waist these days. They had enjoyed a really nice evening and, to her mind, the late night was worth the whirlwind of a morning. Dan may not have agreed with her on that though. They had sat together talking and laughing, feeling comfortable together for the first time in years. It had been decided between them that they would get away together like that every couple of months, even if it was just for one night.

A text vibrated through her phone, which she instantly snatched up off the quilt. It wasn't Dan, it was his mum, Enid, informing her that Artie was a 'super boy' and was just getting ready for school. She told her that she would call them both later before Artie went to bed. 'I want all the interview news', she wrote.

Oh, please let it be good news. We need this fresh start, far away from everything. Come on Dan, Victoria willed. *Sell yourself. Show them what you are capable of.*

The rain continued to thrash unforgivingly against the window. The time was now half past ten, and she realised that she had missed breakfast. It didn't really matter because she didn't have much of an appetite lately. Pulling the white, toweling hotel dressing gown around her, she wandered to the window where all the C shops, with their unique signs, were lined along the street. Cocoa Bean sounded nice, so she would start the day there, then explore the rest of the street. She checked her phone once more before heading into the bathroom for a hot shower.

Her spotted rain jacket came in handy for the walk and, to think, she nearly hadn't brought it. A gap appeared in the traffic, so she took the opportunity to run across the road and into Cocoa Bean, where she spotted an empty table at the window. A quick glance at the sign on the counter told her that it was table service which meant that she could head straight over to take a seat, removing her wet jacket as she went. Was it bad manners to shake the rain off your jacket onto the floor, she wondered, looking over to see if the owner was looking. He was, so she casually laid the wet article over the back of the chair.

A young man in his early thirties, wearing a white apron, soon came over to take her order. He was the only staff member on the premises. Blue sticking plasters covered three of his fingers, which led Victoria to believe that he was probably the owner, waiter, chef, chief cook and bottle washer.

When the waiter/owner brought over her latte and croissant, he stopped to engage with her for a moment. There were only two other customers, and they had been attended to.

'I haven't seen you here before. It's mainly regulars I get at this time in the morning.'

'I'm only in Cheltenham for two nights. I'm staying at the Queens Hotel, across the street,' and she stupidly pointed, before realising that of course he knew the Queens Hotel was across the street; he saw it every day.

'Have you visited Cheltenham before?' he asked her, detecting a hint of Scots in her accent.

'No, this is my first time. My partner is attending an interview for The Bancroft-Hain School. It's for the post of head teacher. Do you know anything about it?' she asked. Inside information, good or bad would be great to tell Dan later.

The waiter laughed. 'Don't tell me old Bancroft-Hain is retiring. I thought he'd die on the job. I can't imagine him trusting his precious school to someone else.'

Victoria brightened up with the knowledge that someone knew the school. If they were going to be moving through in the summer, she wanted to find out everything she could.

'Did you go there?' she asked.

'Only for two years. I am ashamed to admit this, and don't judge me on it, but I was expelled. It wasn't strictly my fault. I had a best friend who came up with hilarious schemes and I'm the one who carried them out. It was a classic case of him loading the gun and me firing the bullets.'

There was a mischievous look appearing in his eyes that made her laugh. Something about this guy made it easy to believe that he had been a joker as a boy. 'So tell me about Mr. Bancroft-Hain,' she asked.

Pursing his lips, he drew in his cheeks, then began, 'Old Bandy Bain we called him, although I don't remember him ever being bandy. It just sounded good. He was a pompous old git, but to be fair, he really cared about the success of his students.' He paused in thought for a moment. 'Or did he?' He made a face at Victoria. 'I hadn't really thought about it until now, but maybe he cared about the success of his school more than the students. He was happy if the students did well, but that was probably because it reflected favourably on him and his little empire,' he laughed. 'No, I'm just being mean, he was a good sort, harmless. As far as I know, he never married. The school was his world.'

A sense of relief came over Victoria when she heard that he had never married. At least when he saw 'unmarried' on the application form, he wouldn't judge Dan for it. In fact, it may even work in his favour; kindred spirits and all that.

The young man continued down his path of remembrance. 'If your guy gets the job, look out for the painting in the front hall. It's old Bancroft-Hain's father although you'll swear it's him. Same tweed suit, same greased down hair, same starched collar. Bandy Bain's collar was starched so stiffly some days that it actually made his neck bleed from the friction. Oh man, you've really got me started on a thing. I swear, he used to live in private quarters in the school. He never left the building, so he had no idea how people were dressing in the outside world. I think he must have worn his father's clothes. A housekeeper came in daily to cook lunch for the pupils and dinner for him. It's quite sad really.'

In the job description, there was mention of a flat available for the new head teacher. Victoria had thought it unusual considering the pupils did not board at school, but on the other hand, for them it meant that they could rent out their existing home and live rent free. If they decided that they wanted to buy a property in Cheltenham, then the school accommodation would give them time to look around. That was her thinking but, as usual, she was getting way ahead of herself. Dan had to be offered the position first before they could make plans to relocate.

The young man introduced himself as Al, and she had been right, he was owner, waiter, chef, chief cook and bottle washer.

'Al, it's been very insightful talking to you, I'm glad I came in.' She rose to leave.

'Let me know if your man becomes the new Bandy Bain,' he laughed. 'Hey, remember to look out for that painting in the main hall. You'll get a kick out of it.'

The rain was still dancing off the pavement when Victoria stepped outside. Her rain jacket was no match for it, but she kept on walking regardless. The whole day was hers to do what she liked and there would be plenty of time left over for beautifying herself for dinner. It would be nice to get a new dress, something special to grab Dan's attention.

Shallow as it sounded, she wanted him to look at her and be delighted that she was his.

Three shops along from The Cocoa Bean was Citrus Clothing with its citrus-coloured dresses in the window. The bell above the door announced her arrival. An elegant woman in her mid-fifties welcomed her in with a fuss. No sooner had Victoria told her what she was looking for, but the woman had selected six possible dresses in her size. The assistant then entered the changing room and hung the garments on the hook. Like a ringmaster in the big top, she pulled the curtain over to one side, beckoning Victoria into the cubicle. She had no choice but to comply.

The bell above the shop door dinged her departure with a Citrus Clothing bag in hand. Although the saleswoman was a little on the pushy side, Victoria was delighted with the tangerine-coloured dress she left with. It hadn't been on a sale rail, in fact, there was no sign of any reduced items, but it was stylish and flattering and with a bit of luck Dan would think 'that's my girl'.

Her theory about the shop names all beginning with C, was found to be completely baseless when further up the street she entered the door of Flamingo. It didn't start with a C, but it was a shop filled with the prettiest toys and gifts. She browsed for a while before zoning in on the children's goods, all of which were hand painted, wooded, novelty items. Artie had a passion for collecting. He had collections of the most random items such as picture cards, pencil sharpeners, farmyard animals and dinosaurs, all displayed systematically in the cabinet in his bedroom. She looked along the shelves of colourful items until one caught her eye. It was a beaded wooden

12

giraffe that collapsed when the button on the base was pressed in. A chuckle escaped her when she saw it. She had something just like that as a child. With her thumb, she pushed in the base, making the animal crumple, she then released the button and it sprung back up. There was a certain satisfaction to be had from it. Up, down, up, down, she pressed it repeatedly.

'I think you're enjoying yourself there!' the gentleman serving shouted from the cash desk.

'It's taking me back to my childhood,' she told him, continuing to press the button. 'Do you have any other animals like this?'

'Give me a minute. I'll check through the back.'

With Artie's obsession for collecting in mind, Victoria left Flamingo with a collapsing giraffe, horse and mouse. It occurred to her that the proportions of the animals were way off. *Perhaps Artie will find it irritating that the giraffe is equal in size to the mouse.*

Across the street, a shop called 'Loud and Proud', caught her eye and she decided to pay it a visit. The rain was easing but it didn't matter now, she was drenched through. Her so-called rainproof jacket was quite literally a washout. If the raincoat company had only paid less attention to the pretty flowers and star shaped toggles on the drawstring, and focused on waterproofing the fabric, it would have worked out better all round. Things like that irritated her. After a row of cars passed, she made a dash across the street. There was no bell above the door, just the unsettling chords of thrash music blaring from more than one speaker somewhere. The long-haired youth serving, nodded as she entered. She nodded back but felt silly after she had done it. The boy made no attempt to make the environment more relaxing by lowering the volume of the music. He played it loud and proud, just like it said on the sign, and Victoria found it deafening. Her eardrums were pleading for mercy, and she turned to leave. A stand near the door caught her attention with its selection of shining metal key rings. Dan had been a big Led Zeppelin fan in his youth; he still was really, and as it happened, there was a Led Zep keyring directly at her eye level.

As the lanky, wannabe rocker wrapped the key ring, she couldn't help feeling that he didn't deserve the sale. He made no effort to strike up conversation as he bound up the key ring in bubble wrap. It was probably for the best, she'd never have heard him over 'Whiplash' being screeched from the multiple speakers overhead.

What relief she felt when she stepped outside, into the light rain. *That was hell. I must be getting old. I wonder if Dan will be embarrassed to put this key ring on his set of keys.* She tossed it into the Citrus Clothing bag and wandered back down towards the hotel. It was lunchtime and, disappointingly, there were no messages from Dan.

Before she entered the hotel door, she glanced over at Cocoa Bean. Al was serving the table at the window, but he happened to look over at the same moment. A wave was exchanged between the two before she entered The Queens by the revolving door. The plush carpet felt soft beneath her feet as she walked towards the stairs leading to the bedrooms. Her wet jeans clung to her legs, making it difficult to climb the three flights up to her room.

There was no lunchtime message from Dan, but perhaps he couldn't get a moment alone to call or text. It was understandable. She peeled off her wet clothes and stepped into the hot shower; it was heavenly. When she was finished, she decided not to redress, but instead, she scrambled beneath the sheets and let her head sink into the luxuriously plump pillow. She slept.

Once again, she awoke to the sound of the rain. It was now almost half past two and there was still no word from Dan. Relaxing in the comfort of the king-sized bed, a song began to play in her head. *Listen to the rhythm of the falling rain, telling me just what a fool I've been...*
The rain against the window made a perfect soundtrack. She had always liked that song. Her grandad played all the golden oldies to her as a child and somehow the words just stuck. Thoughts of what Dan may be doing at that moment came to her mind. Today was a group interview with the long list of applicants. She was unsure how many would be there, but she presumed it would be about seven or eight. Tomorrow would be the day for the short list and with any luck, he'd be on it. Surely, Dan would stand out among the stuffy types that would have applied. There again, Bandy Bain may like the stuffy type, it sounded like he was one of those himself. A smile came when she remembered Cocoa Bean Al describing him. That would be something to tell Dan over dinner later.
A text message vibrated in the silence of the room. Glancing at the screen on her phone, she saw that there was nothing there. Confused by this, she sat up and looked around the room. The sound had come from Dan's

side of the bed, it was his phone, still plugged into the charger. *Oh, no. No wonder he hasn't phoned.* She tapped the screen of his mobile, making it light up. A portion of the message was visible. It was from Julia Carson, a teacher from his school in Edinburgh. Victoria recognised the name, but she had never met her. She read the message aloud.

'With regards to what we talked about on Friday, I'm 100% in.' That was the only line showing on the screen but there was more to the text. *What did they discuss on Friday? Dan never mentioned any conversations of significance. She's 100% in? Sounds like she has no doubts about whatever plan they've hatched.*

There was a slight fear of this text ruining her evening with Dan, so she would have to ask him about it. If she didn't, then it would fester away like a weeping sore. His reaction would tell her everything she needed to know about whether the comment was innocent or not. Would he ever hurt her again? No, she truly believed in the depths of her heart that he loved her. *Have a bit of faith, Victoria. If we don't have trust, then we have nothing.* She rose from her bed and dressed in her jeans and jumper before heading downstairs to the bar.

The barman asked if she was having lunch when she entered. The bar was quaint and, with the help of an open fire, extremely cosy. Lunch hadn't entered her head until that moment, but the idea appealed.

'Yes, I think I will,' she told him.

'Take a seat and I'll bring you a menu. Can I get you something to drink meantime?'

'I'll have a glass of prosecco, and I think I'll also have a sparkling water.'

There was a woman seated at the table beside her, but apart from her there was no one else in the bar. The woman gave her a friendly smile when their eyes met.

'I've just had the soup and sandwich,' the woman announced. 'It was truly lovely.'

'Ah, thanks for the recommendation. I think that is just what I fancy.'

The waiter appeared at her table with her drinks and a menu.

'Thank you. Can you tell me what the soup of the day is and what sandwiches come with it?'

'The soup is leek and potato, and the chef can pretty much make any sandwich you like. Within reason,' he added, laughing.

'I will take the soup, and I will have a roast beef sandwich with horseradish sauce, if you have it.'

'I'm sure that will be fine.'

Victoria gave the woman a knowing wink. 'Thank you for that. I'm never very good at choosing from a menu.'

'Are you here on holiday?' the woman asked.

'Well, I'm here for a holiday but I'm with my husband who has an interview at the Bancroft-Hain School nearby.'

'I can't believe it! My husband also has an interview today at the school. I'm just here for the break. We arrived last night and booked tentatively again for tonight in case he gets through to the short list. This was the closest and the nicest hotel we could find. We've come from the borders. I'm Grace by the way.'

'Victoria,' she told her. 'What a coincidence. Have you heard anything yet?'

'No, Angus is not a texter or phoner. He prefers to give me the lowdown in person. Have you heard anything?'

'Well, Dan is a texter but unfortunately, he left his phone charging beside the bed. I think they are due to be back in about an hour or so. We just booked a room for tonight as well, we never get time away together. This is a bit of a treat.'

'If Angus is not successful, then we will just drive back to Melrose straight away. We can always pick up something to eat in one of those motorway places enroute.' She then added, 'I honestly feel that I won't be disappointed either way. A new challenge would be great for my husband. He has wanted a headship for so long, but I would miss my friends and family. I have to say though, Cheltenham is beautiful.'

'I feel much the same. A new start for both of us would be good but I am not pinning all of my hopes on it. Yes, I do agree that Cheltenham is really something. I've had a wonderful morning visiting the shops across the road. I've spent too much money, but it was great.'

Grace looked over at the rain on the window. 'I'm afraid I didn't have the desire to battle the elements this morning. I stayed in bed and watched T.V.'

When the soup and sandwich arrived, Victoria asked the waiter to carry it over to Grace's table. Lifting her glass of prosecco and sparkling water, she moved over to join her. Victoria told Grace all about Artie and the present she found in the shop called Flamingo. She also explained that one of the reasons she hoped that Dan would get the job was to send Artie to the school. He would benefit from being in a smaller class, sometimes she felt that he had become almost invisible in the large school he attended. All children are special but over the years they had noticed that Artie was a little different to most kids. It could be best explained by saying that he needed a bit of soft handling.

Having no children, Grace shared instead stories of her work. For her, the most enticing thing about moving to Cheltenham was the idea that she could give up her nursing job at the hospital, which was just outside Melrose. It wasn't the actual job she disliked; she just didn't agree with the hospital politics and the understaffing. She continued to talk at length on this issue whilst waving over to the barman for more drinks.

As the women were talking, the hotel receptionist's head appeared around the door.

'Mrs. Dinwoodie?'

'Yes, that's me,' Grace answered.

'I just wondered if you were keeping the booking for tonight or should I cancel it?'

'I am terribly sorry, but I won't know until my husband returns in about twenty minutes.'

'That's fine but if you could let me know as soon as possible, that would be great.'

Victoria looked at the clock on her phone. 'The men should be back any time now. I think I'll head up to start getting ready. I really hope that I see you in the dining room tonight. If Dan doesn't get the job, then my hopes are pinned on Angus.'

Chapter 2

The original plan that Victoria had hatched was for her to be all dressed up for Dan's return, but she was now cutting it fine. Talking to Grace had been refreshing and a great way to spend the last hour of her day without Dan. What a nice lady she was, so upbeat. Finding someone that you really connected with was a rare thing. It had been an incredible coincidence that both of their husbands were after the same job and they had booked into the same hotel; not only that, but they both happened to be Scottish. In the zipped compartment of her travelling holdall, she pulled out her hair straighteners and plugged them into the electrical socket at the mirror. When her hair was silky straight, she felt glamorous. Her thick, black hair was neither naturally straight nor curly, it just had annoying kinks that made it difficult to style. Straighteners were the best invention ever made, as far as she was concerned. Whilst she waited for them to heat, she applied her make-up. A ripple of excitement stirred her insides as she continued to make herself look pretty for Dan. Would he get a surprise? What would he say? What if he didn't notice? Second guesses passed through her mind making her realise that deep down, she was still insecure with him. What if the phrase, once a cheat, always a cheat, were actually true, she asked herself. No, she mustn't allow herself to think like that or it would ruin the night. Tonight it would be just the two of them, in a romantic setting, far from the stresses of life. Dan's mum had said that Artie would phone before bedtime; she couldn't wait. That little face of his could brighten anyone's day, and as for his comical ways, oh, she loved him so much.

Dan was so much later than she had anticipated. It was now after seven and he hadn't returned. This could definitely be viewed as a positive thing. The short listers were maybe kept behind for a further briefing about tomorrow. Of course, there was a slim chance that Bancroft-Hain had planned a dinner for the interviewees but surely he would have given them prior knowledge of this. Anyway, Dan would have found a way to get in touch with her to tell her.

The full-length mirror in the bedroom was undoubtedly flattering and Victoria knew this but still she couldn't help admiring herself in it because she was so used to seeing herself in jeans. The Citrus Clothing dress may have been more than she could afford, but it was worth it. It fitted her shape so snugly with its elegant cut. Tangerine was not a colour she had ever worn, but boy did she suit it. *If Dan doesn't notice how knock-out I look, then there is something seriously wrong with him.*

The dinner reservation had been for eight o'clock, but that had come and gone. It was now half past nine and Victoria was concerned. She had no idea what to do. Slipping on her shoes, she made her way down to the reception.

'Hi, I'm in room 32, my name is Victoria Richards. Have there been any messages for me? My husband left his phone behind this morning.'

The male receptionist turned to his senior on the desk and asked if she knew anything about this. The woman in charge, flicked through the notes that had been left from the shift handover.

By the look on her face, Victoria was hopeful. *Please let there be a message. Please,* she pleaded.

'No, I'm sorry. There is nothing for you.'

Feeling completely despondent, Victoria walked away but stopped suddenly as a thought entered her head. She hurried back to the desk.

'Could you tell me if Angus and Grace Dinwoodie kept their room booking for tonight?'

Again, the young man looked at his superior, probably checking if this was a breach of confidentiality.

'It's okay, we're friends. I thought we could dine with them tonight,' she said, squashing any doubts they had of ill intention on her part.

The woman in charge clicked away annoyingly on the computer keys, for what seemed like an eternity to Victoria. Again, as she looked at the screen, her face gave nothing away, which provided a fleck of hope.

'I'm sorry. Mr. and Mrs. Dinwoodie checked out at 6.25. The room was not required.'

What the hell was happening here? Victoria could not figure it out. Knots of tension began to tighten in her neck and shoulders. This made absolutely no sense. She walked away, not knowing what her next move would be. The bar or upstairs, she couldn't decide, what did it matter, Dan wasn't in either of those places. There had to be an explanation for this. The bar was her preferred option, at least she wouldn't be alone with her tormented thoughts in there.

'A glass of prosecco and a sparkling water please,' she managed to say.

'Take a seat and I'll bring them over.'

I have to think about this. It's, she glanced at her phone, *ten to ten. Grace's husband obviously didn't get through to the next round, so they have gone home. Dan has probably been selected, so they must be discussing what will take place tomorrow. But would Mr. Bancroft-Hain keep him until this hour at night? Surely Dan would try to get a message to the hotel, or to me for that matter, he knows my number. He could have asked someone if he could borrow their mobile or he could have phoned from the school office.*

Different scenarios were turning over and over in her head, all of them resulting in an explanation. The school wasn't far from the hotel, about three miles away. Was it possible that in the darkness, with the wet roads, Dan had crashed the car. He wasn't familiar with the area, so it was plausible. There had to be patches of flooding, it had rained all day long. She decided to wait until half ten, after which she would contact the police for information on any accidents.

As soon as the barman brought her drinks to her table, Victoria said, 'I'll have another.'

'Water too?'

'No, just more Prosecco,' she said, tapping the glass. 'Oh, can I ask you a question?'

'Fire away.'

'Are there many car accidents on the roads around here?' She felt stupid asking this, but she was desperate for any answers or any kind.

The barman turned thoughtful for a few seconds. 'I don't have any official stats or anything, but I would say it's just like any other town. It's not a hot spot for crashes, if that's what you're asking.'

It was obvious that he thought she was a nut. 'You see, I expected my partner back from a job interview hours ago and I've heard nothing. In saying that, he didn't take his phone. There are a few candidates that will get through to the short list and he must be on it.' She was totally rambling now, and she knew it, but she couldn't help herself. Her thoughts were spilling out of her mouth.

'Oh, that is a worry. If it were me going for the interview,' he said, trying to be helpful, 'I would probably ask the other guys if they wanted to go for a drink, you know, just to de-stress and unwind before I went back to the missus.'

'Yes, yes, that is a possibility that I hadn't thought about. Yes, that's probably it. Thank you.'

The barman smiled before promptly making his exit. Women regularly bared their souls to him, as though he were some kind of wise guru. In reality, he just served up the drinks.

Of course Dan hadn't invited the other candidates to join him for drinks; Victoria was sure of that. It just wasn't his style. Something was wrong, and she would have to find out what it was.

She physically jumped when her phone, lying on the table in front of her, played its irritating tune loudly in the quiet of the bar. Snatching it up promptly, she saw that it was Enid.

'Hi,' Victoria said, pretending to be happy. 'Where's my little boy?'

'I'm sorry it's so late, but we were watching the new Paddington movie, then he had toast and hot chocolate. If he can't have a late night at his gran's house, then it's a poor show. How are you both? Come on, give me all the news.'

Victoria searched for the most appropriate response. Should she tell her about Dan or make an excuse, what should she do? Was there any point in worrying everyone when there was probably a simple explanation and he could come walking through the door any minute.

'Enid,' she said seriously. 'Dan hasn't returned to the hotel. I am worried that he has had an accident or something. I'm sick to my stomach and I don't know what to do. I think I'm going to phone the police.'

'What's happened to daddy?' Artie began to cry.

'Nothing, sweet boy. Daddy will be fine,' she told him, cursing herself for blurting it out.

Enid was calm. 'Let's think about this, Victoria. He could still be at the interview. These kinds of things can go on all night on occasions.'

'You name a time when a job interview went on all night, Enid. Job interviews follow a tight schedule. They would never, ever, ever, go on all night. That is a ridiculous explanation.' She could feel her nerve endings getting irritated.

'No, you're right, job interviews never go on all night. I don't know what to think. I feel very concerned. Go and phone the police, then call me back. Say goodnight to mummy, Artie!' she shouted behind her.

'Goodnight mummy. Promise you'll find daddy.'

'I promise. Love you.'

Chapter 3

11.05pm

Victoria was unable to settle in the bar. Only a few hours earlier it had been a relaxed, happy place where she had chatted with a new friend and waited with excitement for Dan to return. It had now become a lonely place filled with strangers. Her excitement had turned to fear. She headed upstairs to the quiet of her room to give herself a chance to think about what she was going to do. By searching up answers on her mobile, she discovered that if she phoned 101, she could report Dan missing, even though 24 hours had not passed. It was better to alert the police sooner rather than later. Yes, she decided, it was time to report Dan missing.

The tremors in her hands were making it difficult for her to hold her phone. By switching to loudspeaker, she was able to rest her mobile on the bed, once she had dialed the number. While she waited, questions began torturing her. What if they say there had been a terrible accident? What if they think he's left me? What if they say, call back in the morning?

'Hello, my partner was due back around six o'clock and he hasn't returned. It is not like him to do this kind of thing, and we are here from Scotland. You see he had a job interview, and I came with him for company and...'. She stopped herself mid-sentence because she knew that she was babbling breathlessly.

The female switchboard operator asked her to calm down, then extracted the details from her. It was clear that the caller was in a highly distressed state, but they usually were, and she was fully trained in dealing with such situations.

'Most people who go missing return home or are found within 48 hours, so please try to keep a calm head. So, you think he has been missing now for five hours?'

'Yes.'

'Can you give me a description of him? You know, like height, hair colour, tattoos, what he was wearing when he left this morning...'

Victoria supplied the woman with everything that she thought was relevant. The model of his car and the license plate number were important, as was the address of the Bancroft-Hain School. It felt good to have the police on board, especially if he was lying injured in a ditch somewhere, unseen, crying for help.

'Please try not to worry. I have all of his details on record now. We will find out all we can. If he returns, please get back in touch immediately.'

The reality dawned on Victoria that there was no way anyone from the police station was going to go and look for Dan. They would probably just think he was out getting drunk somewhere or spending the night with some bit of fluff that he picked up in the pub. It was understandable, he wasn't a missing child, he was a grown man that was a few hours over his due back time. He was probably the lowest priority case they had on record. It was up to her now.

She decided to phone the nearest hospital, and the two closest public houses to The Bancroft-Hain School. Unfortunately, the phone calls did not uncover anything significant. Bar owners weren't in the habit of telling random callers if their partner was inside, they had too much loyalty to their customers.

The woman on the switchboard at the local hospital was able to supply her with information on a car accident that had occurred, but it had taken place on a stretch of road nowhere near the school or the hotel and the driver was a teenager.

Her last resort was to phone and speak to Mr. Bancroft-Hain.

The phone at school rang six times before switching to an answering machine.

'You have reached The Bancroft-Hain School. My most humble apologies from being unable to take your call. If you would like to leave your name and number and a brief explanation of your enquiry, then I shall endeavour to call you back.'

The voice on the machine was unquestionably Mr. Bancroft-Hain himself. Victoria had never heard such an upper-class, dare she say, pompous voice in her entire life. Cocoa Bean Al's description of him returned to her thoughts. The voice perfectly suited the picture that Al had painted of the headmaster.

Now at a complete loss, she climbed into bed and started to cry. Tears tumbled off her chin as she sent a quick text to Enid to inform her that there was no news. She was about to switch off the bedside light when an idea came to her. What if there was something on Dan's phone that would help. All she needed to do was figure out his pass code.

Dan's date of birth, Artie's date of birth, her date of birth, his mother's birthday, she tried them all, but to no avail.

Hysteria was setting in as she put in random combinations of numbers with no positive result. Feeling frustrated, frightened and angry, she threw the phone against the wall causing a noticeable dent in the textured wallpaper. *Dan! Where are you? Please come home.*

The rain battering furiously on the window awoke Victoria the following morning. Dan had not come home, and she had no idea what to do next.

Chapter 4

Lying in bed with her guts entangled, Victoria thought over the week leading up to coming to Cheltenham. Dan had been a little distant, but not noticeably so, to the outside world. Only she detected it, because she had become an expert on analysing his behaviour and facial expressions. Sadly, when a partner betrayed you once, you constantly looked for signs of guilt on their face that would indicate that they had done it again.

She saw nothing that would indicate that he had been with anyone, he was just reserved. It could have been the stress leading up to the interview. He probably wanted the job more than he made out. There was always a possibility that he had left her to start a new life, but would he really go to these lengths? He had insisted that she came with him to The Queen's Hotel, he could have easily come alone. None of it made sense.

A hot shower always took the edge off emotional discomfort for Victoria. She stood under the jets, deciding what her next move would be. At some point, she was going to have to go home to Artie, but she had no car, Dan had taken it the interview. Pulling on her red jumper and jeans, she then tied her hair in a top knot, slipped on her trainers and left. Her plan had been to go down for breakfast, at least to get a cup of coffee. Before she entered the dining room, on impulse, she changed her mind and left through the revolving, front door. Rush hour was at its congested worst on the road outside. The traffic was at a snarled-up standstill. Through a gap in the row of cars she ran over to Cocoa Bean. Al was the closest thing she had to a friend, and she needed to discuss this with someone.

Early morning coffee drinkers filled several of the seats in the café. Al served the tables with a joke and a smile. On seeing Victoria enter the café, he gave her a wave and a raised finger which she took to mean, 'I'll be there in a minute'. All she wanted was strong coffee, she still had no hint of an appetite. On the contrary, she was sure that if she put food in her mouth, she'd be sick.

'Well! You're still here so I take it that your man got through to round two.'

Victoria felt her bottom lip tremble. 'No, something has happened. Dan didn't come back to the hotel last night. I've phoned the police, the hospital, the pubs near the school, although that's not really his style. I even called 101 to report him missing officially. I just don't know what else to do.'

'Oh Man! I don't know what to say. Have you been to see Bandy Bain?'

'No, I called last night but there was no reply.'

Al looked off into the distance for a moment, before saying, 'I will give my sister a call and ask her to take over here. She lives nearby. I'll take you to the school. I presume you don't have a car.'

Tears spilled over in Victoria's eyes. This kindness ffom Al was pushing her over the edge.

Untying his apron as he walked, Al went behind the counter to make the call.

31

Chapter 5

It was Easter break for The Bancroft-Hain School, which meant that none of the usual parent and teacher cars were in the car park. There were, however, four cars parked in the visitors' section. Victoria presumed it was the cars belonging to the short listed candidates. Dan's car should have been sitting in one of the spaces, but sadly, it wasn't. Al pulled up outside the gates. 'Victoria, I would have suggested that I come in with you, but if he recognises me, he may not be very helpful. I sort of made the old duffer's life a misery.'

'No, don't worry about it. I just need to know if Dan said anything about where he was going last night.'

'Good luck. I'll wait right here for you,' Al assured her, switching off the engine.

'I'm so grateful to you.'

He waved off her comment.

Before entering the building, Victoria looked up at the magnificent architecture of The Bancroft-Hain School. When Dan had applied for the post of Headmaster, she had researched the area of Cheltenham. It was known as Britain's most complete Regency town and this school was no exception, with its white stonework and black wrought iron verandahs. Unlike many of the terraced style houses in the area, The Bancroft-Hain School stood alone on its tarmacked grounds. It would have been a wonderful place to bring up Artie, but any shred of hope that she had of Dan being there at the second interview, without first returning to the hotel, had long since dissipated. She was almost sure that he wasn't inside the school, chatting,

32

laughing and selling himself; he was gone. The very least she could hope for was that Mr. Bancroft-Hain had some piece of information that would help her find him.

There was no one around in the dark, wood-panelled entrance hall; however, she could hear voices in the distance. On the wall, beside the staircase, a large full-length portrait hung, just as Al had described. There was a stern, overly important pose from a man in a tweed suit, starched shirt collar and a gold pocket watch; Mr. Bancroft-Hain Senior. Down at the foot of the painting, she could see where someone had stuck a Beavis and Butthead sticker on the imposing figure's shoe. There was evidence that an unsuccessful attempt had been made to scrape it off. Kids could be so hilariously disrespectful; she couldn't help thinking.

A hum of male voices was coming from down the hallway, so that was the direction Victoria followed. Fear and nervous adrenaline shot through her legs and stomach, but the drive within her to find Dan continued to push her forward. For some reason, she found herself tiptoeing as quietly as she could. Passing the girls' toilets on the way, she felt a very strong urge to go in. No, she had to keep going. There must be someone in the gathering ahead that knew something. Dan was a sociable man; he would have exchanged words with possibly everyone at the interview. He must have said something relevant to someone.

The sound trail took her to the door of the gymnasium. Through a glass panel, she saw a man who was undoubtedly Mr. Bancroft-Hain, as he was identical to the man in the portrait. In front of him, with their backs to the door, sat four men in suits. *That must be the short-listed candidates. Why am I not surprised that there are no women interviewees. Should I wait until Bancroft-Hain stops talking or should I just barge on in.* Her heart banged some crazy irregular beats against her ribcage and her legs became so jelly-like that she feared they could give way any moment. *This is too important to wait. Dan has gone missing. After the count of three, I'm going in. 1, 2, 3…*

The door was heavy to push, and her strength had burned away on nervous energy. She pressed her shoulder against the door for extra weight. The door swung open, unexpectedly causing Victoria to fall her full length, face down on the polished wooden floor.

The men all turned around, rising to their feet. 'Are you okay?' one short lister asked.

'My, my, my, that was quite an entrance, my dear. You gave us all a considerable start. To what do we owe the pleasure of your interesting arrival?' Bancroft-Hain said, with a smile.

Her shoulder throbbed where she had landed on it. Giving it a quick rub, she composed herself.

'I apologise for interrupting your meeting, but I feel that this is an emergency.' She had the full attention of all present. 'My partner, Dan, left me at The Queen's Hotel yesterday morning to attend an interview here at this school.' Her emotions began to let her down as her eyes welled up, then spilled over. 'He did not return to the hotel last night and I have not seen him since. I have even reported his disappearance to the police. This is the last place he visited, and I wonder if you have any information as to where he was going after his interview. Thank you and again, I'm sorry.'

There was a slight muttering between the candidates and Mr. Bancroft-Hain stepped forward. His face was the picture of concern as he approached her. A comforting arm fell upon her shoulders while he guided her out of the gym hall and back down the hallway.

'Now, let's see if we can shed some light on this unfortunate conundrum. I have a record of everyone who attended my day of interviews yesterday.'

He led her through to the open office where he unlocked a drawer on the desk. Reaching inside, he brought out a leatherbound book that resembled a ledger, not unlike something Bob Cratchit would have used. She stood facing him, waiting to be shown the information. Instead, he held the ledger close to his chest and read from it.

'What did you say was the name of your spouse?'

'It's Dan McKelvie. We are not married.'

'I see. No, there was no Dan McKelvie here for an interview, I'm afraid.' He then promptly slipped the Bob Cratchit ledger back into the drawer. Outstretching his arm, he gestured for her to lead the way out of the office. His work here was done, and it was time for her to leave. After all, this was a very important day for the school's future leadership.

'I truly wish with all my might that I could have been more help to you. Do you know that there are several small independent schools in Cheltenham. Perhaps his interview was for one of the others. I hope you find him soon. If you need any further advice, do let me know. Good day to you, ma'am.' He made an awkward, out-of-practice smile and adjusted his starched collar to chaff on another side of his neck.

Sensing her cue to depart, she left without saying a word. What a ridiculous suggestion that Dan had an interview at a different school. Did he really think that she was that stupid and took such little interest in her husband's career. She left the building and made her way across the road to where Al was looking at his phone in the car.

'Well, did he tell them where he was going?' Al asked.

'Bancroft-Hain says that Dan was never there. He wasn't even on the list of interviewees.'

Al shook his head. 'What is going on here?'

'I have no idea. Would you mind taking me back to the hotel. I feel quite sick.'

Chapter 6

Back in her hotel room, Victoria took a call from the police. They were looking for an update on the missing person's report from the previous night. She explained that she had heard nothing, and that she had even visited the school where he was meant to be interviewed.

Did she detect a knowing sigh when she informed them that he was not even on the list of candidates; she wasn't sure. As she filled them in on the details again, she realised how much it sounded like she had been abandoned. He had gone out that morning on the pretense of having an interview and just left, running off to start a new life without her or, it suddenly occurred to her, to end his life. Panic set in at the suicide idea. He had been pretty withdrawn for the few days leading up to their trip to Cheltenham.

'I don't believe for one minute that this has happened,' she began by saying to the policewoman 'But have there been any reports of a body being found. You know, like a suicide victim or something.' Hideous visions of divers dragging Dan's body from the river flashed through her mind.

'No, not since last night. How did he seem when he left to go to the interview?'

'He was good, excited, hopeful even. We were planning a new life in Cheltenham, if he was successful. He said that he would be back around 5 or 6 at the latest and we would go for dinner in the hotel. He made the reservation. Would he think to do that if he were about to vanish, I just can't see it.'

'Leave this with me,' she said softly. 'If you could email a photo of him from your phone. Face on, non-smiling would be best. Are you certain that his interview was with Bancroft-Hain?'

'That's exactly what Mr. Bancroft-Hain asked. Of course I am. I may even have the letter at home confirming his interview, unless he took it with him to present on arrival. Yes, 100% yes, it was Bancroft-Hain School.' Sobs were blurted out between almost every word that she said.

'I will get back to you later today. Are you going to stay in Cheltenham, or are you heading back to Scotland?'

'I need to go home to my son. My mother-in-law is looking after him. This is the first time I've ever left him.' She didn't know why she told the policewoman that she'd never left Artie before, in a way she was concerned that the officer would think she was a bad mother, although that made no sense. 'I feel at a complete loss as to what to do. I haven't got a car, so I'll have to organise transport home.'

'We will keep in touch Ms. Richards and if I hear anything, I'll call straight away.'

The bathroom was filled with hers and Dan's toiletries. She began packing them away in the suitcases, along with the clothes that were strewn across the floor. Now she had her own suitcase and Dan's to take back to Edinburgh. Using her phone, she checked what time the next train left for home. She found that there was only one train per day, and it had left at 7.15am. The next one was at the same time, the following morning.

For Victoria and Dan, money had been tight, so checking into a high-class hotel for two nights had been an indulgence that they really could not afford. Now, she was going to have to find the money for another night at the hotel and a train fare home. How could Dan have left her to face such a mess? The words of the text on Dan's phone popped into her head. Julia Carson, his work colleague had said that with regards to what they had previously discussed, she was 100% in. It sounded guarded, even a bit cryptic. What if they had planned to run away together? They had obviously discussed something which seemed private, important and secret from her. Julie Carson had absolutely no doubts, after all, you can't be more than 100% certain. *I think I'm going to have speak to Julia Carson. I'll go and see her when I get home, if she hasn't run off with Dan.*

It was a flimsy lead, but it felt good to have a line of inquiry to follow. There was no way that she was going to sit back and do nothing. Dan had to be somewhere. People didn't just vanish into thin air.

At the reception desk, she waited in a three deep queue to book a room for one more night. It was only ten minutes until her check-out time, so it was her hope that she wouldn't be out on the street with two suitcases.

The movement of the revolving door caught her attention, she watched it turn full circle and to her surprise she saw Al walk out and into the lobby. It felt so good to see a friendly face. They had only met the previous day, but he had very quickly become her confidant and friend.

'I just came over to see if you were okay. My sister is still working with me, so I took the opportunity to slip away. How are you?'

More sympathy brought more tears. Somehow, when she was alone, she could hold things together emotionally, but as soon as she was shown kindness, she weakened. 'I was going to head home but the train to Edinburgh is not until tomorrow morning, early.'

Al stood alongside her in the queue, which now had only one couple in front of her.

'Thanks for checking in with me. You must be regretting the moment I walked into your shop.'

Al smiled. 'Not at all. I believe that everyone you meet in your lifetime is there for a purpose. When you think about it, we talked about your partner's interview. It turned out to be old Bandy Bain's school where I went as a boy. Then he disappears without a trace. Look, you don't know anyone in Cheltenham, so I can be your go-to person here.'

'Thanks. I'm hoping that the police will find something on CCTV, or his car will be spotted somewhere by the traffic cops. People can't just vanish these days. There is always a trail left somewhere…'

The receptionist was free to answer her enquiry. 'Hi, my name is Victoria Richards and I've been staying here for the past two nights. I was wondering if I could have the room for another night. My train home doesn't leave until the morning.'

'I'm very sorry Ms. Richards but the races are on, and this is our busiest time. I'm afraid every room is booked. There are other hotels around here, but you may find that it's the same story wherever you try. I really hope you find something. Are you ready to check out?'

The room had been prepaid, but there were items such as lunch and drinks to be settled. Using her credit card, she tapped the money that was due and asked if she could keep the keycard for the room long enough to collect her suitcases. As she returned her bank card to her purse, a thought entered her head. *Dan would need cash if he were running away. He must have used the bank card or maybe he's lifted a sum of money from the savings. I need to check the joint accounts online.*

'Thank you,' she said, walking away. Her focus was now on money or, to be more precise, missing money.

Al followed her upstairs to help her with the baggage. Walking ahead of him, she remained silent as her thoughts were now clawing and scratching at every possibility. There was just over £25 000 in their savings, it wasn't a fortune, but it had taken them a long time to save it. If it was gone then she'd know for sure. Surely he wouldn't take the money that they had jointly squirreled away together for the future. If it was missing, then at least she'd know the truth and she would be able to get on with some form of a life. There could be a line drawn under all the worry and torment. If he has left, she decided, there would be no searching for whereabouts or who withs, she had been tortured enough.

'Al, I had a thought when we were at the reception desk,' she told him as she stood at the door to the bedroom. 'I need to check our joint accounts. If he's taken the savings or spent any money from our working account, then I can presume that he has chosen to leave. I'm going to go onto my online banking on my phone before I check out.'

'I hadn't even thought about that. Of course he'll need money,' Al said, taking a seat in the high backed, velour chair. He looked out of the window at his coffee shop which had very few customers inside. He could see his sister chatting with an elderly couple who were sitting near the window. She was such a great girl, so reliable and trustworthy. What would he ever do without her.

'Right, that's me on my working account. Apart from me using the card to pay the hotel bill, it hasn't been used since I paid for coffee at Cocoa Bean, and before that I went shopping at Citrus Clothing, Flamingo, and Loud and Proud. All the spending has been made by me. Nothing has been spent by Dan. Now, onto my savings account.'

'Well, that's something…. I think.' He tried to read her expression. Was she happy about her revelation? He couldn't tell but at least she hadn't been abandoned. His attention strayed back to the window and his charming little coffee shop that was hemorrhaging money every day. There was nothing he could do to boost sales and bring in customers, he had tried everything. The Cocoa Bean branding was bold and professional, the frontage was open and welcoming, he greeted and chatted with all the customers, even when he didn't feel like it; what more could he do?

'Okay, I'm on my savings account and the money is all there. Nothing has been touched. I need to assume that he is missing, and not by choice.'

'Victoria, I don't want you to get the wrong idea here, but I have a spare room I can give you for tonight instead of going in search of a hotel. It would save you a bit of money. I won't be offended if you're not comfortable about it.'

Victoria's phone rang with 'Enid' illuminated on the screen.

'Hi Enid, how's Artie?'

'He's good. He has left for school. Any news?'

'There's been no news, I'm afraid, but I just checked both bank accounts and no money has been lifted or spent,' Victoria told her.

'Did you honestly think he'd lift money and run off?' she asked, sounding surprised and even disappointed.

'No, of course not. I just needed to know if he had used his card for food or petrol.'

'Yes, that was good thinking. Have the police come back to you?'

'Only to say that they'd do what they can.' Inside she felt a sense of hopelessness but outwardly, for Enid's sake, she adopted a positive disposition.

'Oh yeah, sure they will. My missing son will be filed away in the bottom drawer of the couldn't-care-less cabinet.'

'No, Enid, that's not fair, the policewoman was really helpful. I do believe she wants to help. Listen, I have to stay another night because the train back to Edinburgh doesn't leave until tomorrow. It will get me home around lunchtime. Meanwhile, if I get any news, I'll call right away.'

The two suitcases sat side-by-side, upright at the door. Al insisted on wheeling both of them to the lift. 'So, do you want a bed for the night, or would you like me to take you to try a couple of hotels that I know nearby.'

Victoria had already formulated her answer while she was speaking to Enid. 'I'll take you up on your kind offer, if you're sure you don't mind.' She followed him out of the hotel and across the road to the coffee shop.

'I thought we could get a coffee before we drop your cases off at the house. Come in and meet my sister Amanda, you'll like her. Maybe we can all put our heads together and try to come up with some ideas about what to do next.'

'I'm so grateful to you. It's nice to know that I'm not alone.'

Chapter 7

As soon as the coffee shop quietened, Victoria got a chance to talk over theories with Al and Amanda. Leads and next-step options weren't exactly plaguing her, but it was good to talk things through and get the opinions of others. The way she felt when she was with Al and Amanda was like being with long-term, trustworthy friends. They were good people, but she wondered if perhaps in times of difficulty, relationships become intensified. It was, essentially, a case of taking a leap of faith or be left to handle things alone. Had everything gone to plan regarding the trip to Cheltenham, she would be at home in Edinburgh with Dan and Artie, and she would never have met this brother and sister duo, but she was becoming increasingly glad that she had.

Victoria tried to bring them up to speed. 'I met a woman at the hotel whose husband was also attending an interview at The Bancroft-Hain School. She came from a town called Melrose in the borders. By the time I discovered that Dan was missing, the woman and her husband had checked out. He obviously hadn't made the short list. I know their names are Grace and Angus Dinwoodie and I remembered that Grace mentioned she was a nurse in the hospital outside Melrose. Angus probably didn't see Dan, but I would like to track them down to ask him about it.'

Amanda nodded in agreement. 'I think at this stage, it's worth talking to anyone who was there. Al, show her what you've got.'

Al reached into his back pocket and took out his phone. He clicked on the colourful photo icon, then scrolled through until he found what he was looking for. Turning the screen to face them, he said, 'It's probably pointless, but I took this photo of the cars that were in the car park of the school. They presumably belong to the short-list interviewees. There are four men who may remember something about the previous day. If you could find out who the owners of the cars are, then you could ask them if they saw anything at all. Even if you showed them a picture of Dan and his car. You just never know.'

'Can I just put in a car registration number to a computer and find out who the owners are?' Victoria asked.

'No, you can only find out previous owners. So, if the couple in Melrose know nothing, then we may be able to acquire the names of the short-list car owners, but that's if nothing else turns up.'

'How would you be able to do it if the information is not available?' She was confused.

Amanda sat forward. 'I may be able to help with this. Jack, my ex-boyfriend, is a cop. He cheated on me, and I dumped him.'

Victoria made a face, she knew what that felt like. 'You can't possibly ask him now, can you?'

'I can if I have to. He will do anything to get me back. I would never go back with him, but he doesn't know that. I'm not keen on contacting him, but I will if I need to. Ask the people in the borders first and if that turns up nothing, then give the car registration numbers to the police, they may investigate. If I am being totally honest, I don't hold out a lot of hope that they will have the manpower to track

46

the people down, interview them and follow any leads. Maybe I am being unfair, but the police are stretched to the brink.'

Al agreed with his sister. A middle-aged man driving off one morning and not coming back just didn't scream urgency. 'Does Dan have a best friend that he may have contacted?'

She thought for a moment. 'No, he plays rugby and football with a bunch of guys but no one that he's close to. I am probably his best friend… Oh, and he is very close to his mum. She knows as little as me; she is worried sick.'

'Are the police going to interview Bandy Bain?' Al asked.

'I don't think so, but I might mention it when I next speak to them. There is one other thing that is a bit of a mystery. Dan slept through his alarm yesterday which meant that he was running around like a headless chicken trying to get ready. He forgot his phone.' She felt a sense of betrayal telling them that she was suspicious of him, but she continued, nonetheless. 'A text came through that morning after he left. It was from a work colleague called Julia Carson. I can't get into Dan's phone, but I saw the beginning of the message. It basically said that further to something they had discussed on Friday, she was 100% in. I don't know this woman, I've never met her, and Dan didn't mention any serious conversation that had taken place at school. There again, he may not have thought that it would interest me. I just don't know what to think.'

'You definitely have to speak to this Julia Carson,' Amanda told her. It had been suspicious texts that had blown the lid off her partner's infidelity.

They fell silent for a moment before Al asked, 'Have the police picked up his car anywhere on CCTV?'
'I haven't heard. I think I'll give them a call later.' There had to be footage on a camera somewhere of Dan's car driving to The Bancroft-Hain school around eight-thirty yesterday morning, so she would mention that on the call to the police. Finding out what time he left the interview would also be helpful and in which direction he drove.
'Any other theory or loose end?' Amanda asked. 'Or have we exhausted the subject?'
'Six months ago, Dan had an affair,' she blurted out. If everything was going to be out on the table, then she had to share this. 'When I say an affair, it wasn't like a full-on affair, more a one-night stand with a woman who lives in our street. He regretted it and never spoke to her again, or so he said.'
'I'm so sorry,' Amanda said, touching her shoulder. 'It's agony, I know. Chances are, he hasn't spoken to her again.' She wasn't sure if she believed this or not, but she hoped it gave comfort to Victoria. 'When you get home to Edinburgh, I think you should have a word with this individual too.'
Victoria sat back on her chair. 'That conversation won't be easy, but I do agree that I need to explore everything. Dan has to be out there somewhere and I really, really need to find him.' She began to cry. 'I'm sorry. I won't be any use to anyone if I'm going to be a big bubbly baby.'
Al laughed. 'Yeah, stop being a big, bubbly baby.'

Chapter 8

It was nearing lunchtime when Al took Victoria to his house. They drove to the far side of town and during the journey, Victoria found herself looking down every side street for Dan's red car. The busy streets turned to leafy avenues with high-wall privacy, which left her wondering where Al's house could be. It was not until he drove through tall gates and along an extensive driveway, that she realised that this was it. At first, she thought it must be a portion of the grand Victorian home that stood alone on private grounds. It was, in fact, larger than The Bancroft-Hain School with all of its outbuildings.

'Home sweet home,' Al announced.

'Is this whole house yours?' she asked.

'Yep,'

'Do you live alone?'

'Yep.'

'I hope you don't mind me saying but the coffee shop business must be booming.'

This comment made Al laugh out loud. 'The coffee shop business is costing me a fortune. It loses thousands of pounds every year.'

Turning to look at him, she tried to figure out what was going on. 'You are a mystery, Al.'

'Come on in. You can take your pick of the rooms.'

Victoria followed Al as they climbed up the wide staircase which was as grand as she would have expected of a house of this calibre. Al opened the door of a bedroom on the second floor and told her to go in ahead of him. It was painted in a calming shade of wedgwood blue and although it was the first one that Al showed her, she was sold right away. It was superior to the room that had cost a small fortune in The Queens Hotel. There was no need for him to show her any others once she'd seen it. The two windows gave views of the front and back gardens which were somewhat overgrown but pretty in a wild kind of a way. Everything about the place felt soothing and homely, and she had no feeling of awkwardness about it being the house of what was ultimately a perfect stranger.

'I'm afraid there is no ensuite for this room, but the bathroom is the door with W.C. on it, almost directly opposite. I'll get you some clean towels and I'll put fresh bedding on the bed. It's been a long time since anyone slept in it, so it may need freshened up.'

'No, please, don't go to any trouble for me. I will be leaving early tomorrow morning to ensure I get to the station in plenty of time.' At that moment, her phone rang, prompting Al to leave the room, presumably to give her privacy, pulling the door shut behind him. Gestures like this didn't go unnoticed by Victoria and she really appreciated how considerate he was.

'Hi Enid.'

'It's not Enid,' a little voice said. 'It's me, Artie. Have you found daddy?'

'Not yet, sweetheart but I will, I promise. How was school?

'It was quite okay. I wasn't the star writer, and I didn't get to be the monitor this week but maybe next week. Philip Sampson wants me to go and play at his house after school on Friday. Can I go, please, please?'

'Of course you can. We'll talk about it when I get home tomorrow. Are you being a good boy for your gran?'
'Am I being a good boy, gran?' he shouted in the background. 'She says that I am.'
'Well, I'm very glad to hear that.'
'Can we get pizza for tea tomorrow?'
'Yes, cheesy pizza with a bit of pineapple, just the way you like it.'
An incoming call appeared on the screen of her phone. It was the police.
'Artie, darling, I'm going to have to go now but I love you very, very much and I will see you tomorrow.'
'Bye, bye mummy.'
Victoria's heart physically hurt for her son and for Dan. Her family was being ripped apart, and there was very little she could do. She connected the call with the police.
'Victoria Richards?'
'Yes.'
'Just calling to find out if your husband is still missing or did he return.'
This was disappointing, because she hoped that they would have news for her, not the other way around. Also, this was a male police officer calling, and she would have preferred the continuity of keeping the same female cop as before. 'No, he hasn't returned. Have you checked CCTV footage for yesterday at 8.30? You have the car colour, model and license plate. There has to be evidence of him leaving The Queens Hotel and driving to The Bancroft-Hain School. Also, could you interview Mr. Bancroft-Hain, because he says that Dan wasn't even on the list of interviewees, but that is not true.'

'Yes, as discussed with you yesterday, Ms. Richards, we will do all that we can. It hasn't been 48 hours yet, so we will give him time to turn up. In the meantime, if you do hear from him, let us know.'

Well that phone call had been a useless, box-ticking exercise, she decided. It would have been fruitless to ask them to search and interview the owners of the four cars in the school car park. She sensed that they couldn't care less about Dan. As far as they were concerned, he was a big boy that should be able to drive from A to B without disappearing and if he couldn't, then he had vanished on purpose. All the leg work would have to be carried out by her, with more than a little help from her new friends.

Victoria hadn't realised how tired she was, until she awoke to a dusk-coloured sky outside. The bedroom was such a silent, calming place, and although the bed was a little musty smelling, just as Al had said, it was so comfortable when she lay on top of it.

At first, she had no clue where she was until she saw the suitcases side by side near the door. *Dan is missing*, was the first thought that crashed in on her. Here she was lying on a bed in a man's beautiful home, wondering what to do next. After splashing her face with water from the quaint, clam-shaped sink in the room, she headed downstairs, all two flights.

Music was playing from somewhere, so Victoria took it as an indicator as to the whereabouts of her host. She followed the sound through the ground floor until it led her to the back of the house. Sure enough, Al was in the kitchen, singing along to the music, cooking up a storm in the frying pan. The smell in the air was unbelievably good, making Victoria instantly hungry. She looked around at the classic Victorian kitchen which was fitted with outdated looking units that smacked of excellent quality. This house was in a league of its own which made Victoria intrigued.

'Are you hungry?' Al asked.

'Starving. I didn't mean to sleep so long.'

'It's fine, you must have needed it. Take a seat.'

Among the many contents of frying pan, Victoria could recognise potatoes, onions and tomatoes. When she tried a forkful, she thought it was probably the tastiest concoction she had ever eaten.

'What's in this?' she asked, shoveling in another spoonful. 'It is so good.'

'Secret recipe, sorry.'

He lifted the frying pan and held up the spatula when she had finished. 'More?'

'Yes please.'

Taking the corkscrew from the cutlery drawer, Al opened a bottle of red wine and sniffed the cork. Without asking, he filled two crystal glasses almost to the brim and handed one to Victoria.

Victoria thanked him, then proceeded to tell him all about the pointless conversation that had taken place with the police officer. 'I've asked him to speak to Mr. Bancroft-Hain and to check CCTV footage for Dan's car from that morning, but I couldn't bring myself to ask for the identity of the short-listed car owners from their license plates.'

'I'll give Amanda the green light to check with her ex if nothing turns up from the borders' couple. What's your first port of call when you get home?'

'I'm desperate to see Artie, but he will still be at school when I get back, so I'll go and see Enid, Dan's mum. I will also make an appointment with Julia Carson, to see what she's got to say for herself.'

'Good. Keep checking your bank accounts, you never know, he may dip into them at a later date.'

They finished the bottle of red wine as evening closed in and Al decided it would be a good idea to open another. He invited Victoria to sit through in the formal lounge where it would be more comfortable, but she declined.

'When my friends come over for the night, we always stay in the kitchen. It's kind of cosier, if you know what I mean.'

'Fine by me. Just say if you want coffee, something else to eat or if you're cold…'

'Al, everything is just perfect,' she interrupted. 'I'm so glad I'm not stuck in a hotel room, alone.'

Almost two bottles of wine later, Victoria had to ask about the house. How could a young man with, in his own words, a failing coffee shop, afford such an opulent abode. She simply had to know, and the alcohol had made her a bit brazen.

Topping up his wine glass, he began telling his story. It began when he was a boy, and his parents were diplomats in Saudia Arabia. Originally, he and Amanda lived out in the middle east with them. They were housed on the luxurious British Diplomats compound, and he attended school in Dhahran.

It did Victoria good to listen to the well-told tale of Al's life, because it took her mind to somewhere other than Dan's disappearance. As she listened, Al continued to top up her glass with the remaining dribbles and take her on the journey which held the answer to her question; how could he live in such a beautiful home.

He explained that middle eastern life had been one of privilege, which he didn't fully appreciate until recent years. Every need was taken care of, and every task was carried out by staff. There came a point, he admitted, when he was a young teen, that he was an unpleasant and obnoxious boy. 'I became disrespectful to teachers and my peers. I genuinely thought that I was superior to everyone around me.' He shook his head, shuddering at the memory of this revelation. 'Eventually, the principal of the school sent my parents a letter basically telling them that I was no longer welcome at the school.'

Feeling slightly drunk from the sheer volume of wine, Victoria laughed. 'So, that's two schools you've been expelled from.' She saw by Al's face that he didn't find this funny, quite the contrary, he walked away, busying himself at sink. The alcohol had made her insensitive, and she felt terrible. 'Al, I'm so sorry. I was only joking. I shouldn't have said that.'

'Oh, don't be silly. You didn't offend me. Let's face it, it's true, I was expelled from two schools. It's what followed later that upsets me and I often wonder if I could have prevented it.'

'Go on,' she urged him. 'I'll keep my mouth shut this time.'

Al continued to describe how he was sent back to England. His aunt moved into the family home, which was the house they were now sitting in. Aunt Alicia took care of his needs but somehow he felt alone, adrift, abandoned. His parents decided to enroll him in The Bancroft-Hain School, which they did by phone. All he had to do was turn up on the first day of term, by himself. This had been such an unhappy time in his life, and he could feel the dormant emotion rising unexpectedly within him. He hadn't discussed this period in his life with anyone. Perhaps the alcohol had unlocked grief's door.

'Are you okay? If it's painful to talk about this, you can stop now. It was none of my business, I shouldn't have asked,' she told him.

Wiping his eyes on his sleeve, he carried on from where he left off. 'I got friendly with a boy, who now looking back, I think had sociopathic tendencies. He spent so much of his time creating plans to ruin other kids' lives, just for the sake of it. I was vulnerable and easily led and as I told you before, he hatched the plans, I put them into action. I hurt a lot of people, and I feel quite tormented about that now.'

Victoria took the opportunity to speak when he paused. 'I think everyone has regrets about how they behaved in their youth. No one will remember any of it. These children are not still at Bancroft-Hain, crying over what you've done to them. They are adults with their own careers and families.'

'Yeah, I know. I just wish that I had been better.'

He reached for the kettle and began filling it with water from the tap. 'Coffee?'

Victoria nodded.

As he spooned the granules into the cup, he talked more about his life. After all, he hadn't even touched on her original question.

It wasn't long before he got the news that Amanda couldn't settle in Saudi without him. She wanted to return to the United Kingdom to live in the house with him and Aunt Alicia. This made him feel less alone, especially because she also enrolled in The Bancroft Hain school. 'Having my sister around gave me confidence and brought out an even cockier side in me. My sociopathic pal and I started getting into all kinds of trouble, although I was always the one who got the blame. The next thing I knew, I was out on my ear and my parents were so disappointed in me. I was sent to the local high school where I never really fitted in. Let's just say that it was a humbling experience and certainly knocked the arrogance out of me, quite literally.'

'That must have been tough. Did you ever go back out to see your mum and dad in the middle east?' Victoria asked. She couldn't help second guessing where the story was going.

He shook his head. 'I always knew that my mother and father were important people. They had a kind of superior air about them, although that was probably just my kids-eye view of them. I did notice that people pussyfooted around my father in particular. They were very sociable in their lifestyle, you know, like functions, dinners and parties most weekends. In Saudi, alcohol is forbidden, but not to the diplomats. They had the finest of everything and my father consumed it in abundance. I was young at the time but, looking back, I recognise that when he had too much to drink, he could be highly outspoken, insulting even. My guess is that this sealed his fate somehow. I might be wrong.'

'Did he lose his job?'

'No, you probably won't remember this, but it was all over the news. When my sister and I were living with Aunt Alicia, I was sixteen, we got a call to say that they had been found dead. They had not returned home to the compound after some important meeting and dinner that they had attended. Their bodies were found the next day. Dumped like garbage. That's all we were told.'

'Oh Al, that is so shocking. I am so sorry.'

'My theory is that my father had been drinking and became obnoxious. His filter disappeared with alcohol. I think he must have offended someone. Next Tuesday, it will be sixteen years since it happened.'

Al stopped talking and finished making the coffee. He sat the milk and sugar on the table because he didn't trust his voice box to ask if she wanted either. Tears were close and he feared he was going to break down in front of this wonderful lady who had more than enough grief of her own to contend with.

Once his emotions had settled down, he added a fake, sing-song tone to his conclusion.

'So, I got this beautiful big house, and Amanda got a stylish apartment in the centre of town. I was left the shop in the will, which had been leased to a butcher. My father probably thought that I wouldn't amount to much, so a shop would be perfect for me. The joke is, I haven't amounted to much. I turned the premises into Cocoa Bean and did everything in my power to prove my success, but it hasn't worked out that way. So, there you have it, the long-winded version of why a man like me lives in a house like this.'

'What made you ever think that you could have prevented this tragedy from happening?' she asked.

'Lots of reasons. I could have tried to make him proud of me instead of being an embarrassing disappointment. Maybe he drank to forget what a failure his son was. Also, if I hadn't been sent home, he possibly wouldn't have gone out so much. My father was a family man first and foremost, and he enjoyed when we were all together and happy. I broke up the family and because of me, he was out in the middle east without his children. That must have been a real blow to him. Things just didn't turn out the way he would have hoped. I don't know why I couldn't have been better, nicer and more appreciative of everything.' Hiding his face in his cupped hands, he shed silent tears for his parents.

'Al, most teenagers disappoint their parents at some point, but they don't hit the bottle and get murdered. The teenage years are a dark tunnel of insanity, and parents know that they have to ride the storm. My mum used to say, if they enter the teenage years as a good kid, then they come out the other end a good adult. What happened to your parents has absolutely nothing to do with you.'

Outside, the daylight was spreading across the lawn, and the chorus from the birds was relentless. It was hardly worth Victoria's while going to bed as she would need to leave in just over an hour to catch her train. It had been a good evening in many ways and, surprisingly, she had almost forgotten that her partner and father of her child had vanished off the face of the earth.

Chapter 9

The journey home on the train home was long and reflective. The events of the past couple of days whirled around and around in Victoria's mind as she desperately sifted through them for answers. Dan was gone and she was leaving Cheltenham without him. If only she could have looked into a crystal ball and seen the heartbreak ahead of her. Al's story had stayed with her, and it had made her wonder how many people out there were left with no answers to the blows that life had dealt them. Seeing Artie was the first thing she wanted to do when she got back. She would never forget his words to her, 'Have you found daddy?' Her promise to find him seemed hollow now. Find him? Find him where? There was nowhere to even start looking.

Taking her phone from her handbag, she called the police, explaining who she was.

'Have you looked on CCTV for his car around 8.30? Have you spoken to Mr. Bancroft-Hain?'

After being asked to hold for a lengthy period, she was then informed that these tasks would be carried out later in the afternoon. *Yeah, sure. Did my phone call prompt them to act? Probably.*

'Okay,' she told them. 'Could you call me later today to let me know the outcome... no, second thoughts, I'll call you.'

The response from the cops really highlighted to her that she would need to pester them relentlessly if she wanted them to help in the search for Dan. The irony was that the longer he was missing, the more likely they were to help, but the longer he was missing the harder it would be to find him.

It took almost six hours for the train to arrive at Waverly Station in Edinburgh and from there she took a black cab to Enid's house. Artie was at school, but she only had an hour to wait to see him. There was a warm welcome hug from her mother-in-law when she arrived, and it wasn't long before she had a cup of coffee in her hand. Enid asked her for a breakdown of the events of the trip from arrival until the disappearance. Victoria furnished her with every minute detail, including conversations, Dan's mood and his body language. The only part she purposely left out was spending the night at Al's house. Yes, she knew it was an innocent necessity, but she was wise enough to know how it would be perceived.

'I think I'll phone Dan's school and ask to meet with Julia Carson first thing tomorrow. Enid, would it be okay if I borrowed your car to drop Artie to school and I will head straight over to meet her afterwards?'

'Of course. In fact, I can do better than that. Bob's car sits in the garage doing nothing, take it. Since he got his free bus pass, he never drives anymore. Between you and me, he had a bit of a bump with another driver, and it was his fault. He also seems to have lost the great sense of direction that he used to be blessed with. I think he has lost his confidence on the roads, but he'd never admit that. I'll get the key, and you can do a practice run, with me beside you, to pick up Artie. I think it will need petrol.'

'I am so grateful to you.' Tears sprung into her eyes. 'Where can he be, Enid?' she suddenly blurted out. 'I don't know what to think. Do you think we'll ever find him?'

'I don't know, I really and truly do not know,' Enid told her with heartbreaking honesty.

Artie ran out of the school gate and up into his mother's arms. His hands clasped tightly around her neck.
'Did you find daddy?'
'No, not yet but I promised I would, so I will.' She put her hand into her coat pocket and took out the wooden giraffe, which she hid behind her back. 'Pick a hand.'
He chose the left hand which held nothing. Pointing at the other hand, he tried to sneak a look behind her back.
'You big cheater,' she told him.
She held the giraffe out in front of him, making his face light up.
'Tell the giraffe to faint,' she told him with her thumb ready on the base button.
A look of confusion spread across his face, furrowing his eyebrows. 'Faint!' he shouted.
The giraffe collapsed on demand. This made Artie bend over double with laughter.
Victoria, once again, reached into her pocket, this time hiding the horse behind her back. 'Pick a hand.'
The look of excitement on Artie's face was precious. He picked the correct hand first time.
The horse stood on its stand in front of him. 'Tell it to play dead,' she told him.
'Play dead!' Artie shouted at the top of his high-pitched voice.
The animal played dead.
'Last one,' she told him, bringing out the mouse.
She held it up but noticed that Artie's face drooped.

'It's not right,' he cried. 'How can the mouse be the size of the horse and giraffe. I don't want that one.'

The oversized mouse was returned to her pocket. *I suspected as much. I was stupid to buy it.*

That evening, when Victoria tucked Artie up in his own bed, she read him his favourite story. It was the same story he requested most nights. She then turned out his light and made to leave the room.

'Mummy!' he shouted, for her to come back. 'Arthur Simpson's dad left his home for a different lady. Do you think that daddy wants a different lady?'

'Of course not, silly.' *I hope with all of my heart he hasn't met a different lady.*

With Artie safely tucked up in bed, she sat at the kitchen table and took out her phone.

'Hi, my name is Victoria Richards, and my partner is missing. I am looking for information that one of your officers said they would acquire about CCTV footage of his car and an interview with the headmaster of The Bancroft-Hain School. Could you supply me with this please?'

'Hold the line.'

Please have some information, please, please, please.

'Hello Ms. Richards, I'm sorry, Officer Reynolds took your call earlier and I'm afraid that he is off duty now. He will call you back in morning.'

Chapter 10

Driving Dan's father's car through morning rush hour traffic was a pretty hairy experience. The gears crunched, and the engine stalled several times. Victoria was used to an automatic; in fact, it must have been about ten years since she had driven a manual car. She parked as close as she could to the school gates, then walked with Artie along to the lollipop lady who ushered them across to the school side of the street.

'Have a lovely day, little man. Remember to work hard and be kind.' She kissed his cheek, then high-fived him with the left hand, then the right. They did exactly the same routine every day at the same spot, just inside the gate. The last part of their ritual saw Victoria standing waving until Artie entered the building. He turned around four times to wave back. Victoria didn't question this regime, she did it because it made Artie feel safe. The alternative was a meltdown and that was something to be avoided at all costs.

On the way to Dan's school, Victoria decided that the worst-case scenario for her would be that this Julia Carson woman would be missing too. The very idea that they were both '100% in' on something, made her feel sick.

It suddenly dawned on her that no one had called to tell the school that Dan was missing. They must have thought that he hadn't shown up for work and couldn't be bothered letting them know.

Perhaps a detour past the headteacher's office to inform him would be a good idea. She would also be able to ask directions to Julia Carson's room whilst she was there.

The headteacher, Mr. Kennedy, acted suitably concerned when he was told about Dan. On impulse, she asked him if he had any information about Dan's sudden departure. She was aware of a slight hesitation on his part before he answered with a firm no. Did she imagine that he knew something relevant, she couldn't be sure.

'If you do know anything at all, even if it seems unconnected, then please tell me,' she pushed him. 'Our family are in pieces over this. I've even had to bring in the police.'

The word *police* jolted something in his conscience, or perhaps it simply highlighted the seriousness of the problem. She detected an inward struggle in him as he looked down at the floor. His body was visibly tense.

'I can assure you that I don't know anything about where he could be, but he has a very close relationship with our biology teacher, Maggie Morton. I think that if he had told anyone about where he was going, it would be her.'

Did he just put a heavy emphasis on 'very' close relationship. Did he drag the word out with a hidden meaning behind it? Yes, I believe that he did. I have never even heard Dan talking about Maggie Morton, but there again why would he if they had a 'very' close relationship.

'Would it be possible to speak to Maggie Morton after I speak to Julia Carson,' she asked, through slightly gritted teeth.

'I'll try to arrange this. Come and see me after you speak to Miss Carson.' He then pointed her in the direction of Julia's room before reaching for the school phone to contact Mrs. Morton.

Victoria knocked on the door of the classroom. Moments later, Miss Julia Carson answered her knock, telling her to come in. Victoria could have thrown her arms around her neck and hugged her when she saw her, because she was quite the most unattractive women she had seen in a long time. Her long, grey wispy hair was severely tied back in a straggly ponytail. The woman was in her sixties, for sure, and the years had shown her no mercy. High colouring and liver spots adorned her wrinkled face. Victoria knew that she wouldn't need to take much of this elderly woman's time, but she had to say something; after all, she had asked to meet with her.

'Miss Carson, I will make this brief. Dan has disappeared. He left in the morning for a job interview in Cheltenham and he didn't return.'

Julia Carson's hands automatically sprung up to her face in sheer horror.

Victoria continued. 'He left his phone behind and a message from you came through, although I could only see the beginning of it. It said that you had discussed something and that you were 100% in. I was just wondering what that might have been about, you know, just in case it was helpful in my search for him.'

Miss Carson composed herself, visibly shaken by the news. 'I am so, so sorry this has happened. Have you contacted the police?'

'Yes, yes, the police are involved.' *Just answer the question so that I can move on to the next teacher.*

'Dan and I coach the rugby together. The team's kit is past its best and really quite dated looking now. Every team we compete against always looks so smart and our school is like the poor relation. We've asked Mr. Kennedy, the Head, for new kit but apparently there is no money available. Last Friday, Dan asked me if I would be interested in doing a fundraiser to get cash to kit the boys out. He asked me if we could think about doing it on the last Saturday of the month. I said I'd let him know. I checked my diary, and I was free, so I said that I was 100% in.'

'That explains it then. Thank you so much for your time. Could you point me in the right direction for Mrs. Morton's room, please.'

The door of Maggie Morton's room was a few inches ajar. Victoria knocked whilst entering.

'Hello. Excuse me, Mrs. Morton,' she said, hearing the noise of someone in the cupboard.

'Hi. Come in,' said the most beautiful, smiling face.

Oh no, oh no, oh no. She is gorgeous. Too gorgeous to be a friend of Dan's. I feel sick.

'How can I help you?' she asked, guiding Victoria over to a chair.

'I believe that you and Dan are good friends?'

'Yes, we are. Kindred spirits really. We share the same views on many things.'

'Dan is missing. I was wondering if you knew anything about where he might be.'

'Oh, my word. That is so terrible. Have you contacted the police?'

Of course I've contacted the ruddy police. I really wish people would stop asking me that. 'Yes, he has been reported missing. I have no leads whatsoever and neither do the police, it would seem. I am looking for something, anything, that would help me find him.'

Maggie Morton fell thoughtfully quiet for a moment. 'He did confide one thing to me before he went to Cheltenham, but I would rather not divulge what it was because it was nothing whatsoever to do with him disappearing. I think for several reasons, I would rather keep the information to myself. It is not my secret to tell.'

'Do you understand the severity of this matter, Mrs. Morton? My partner, Dan, is gone. There is no trace of him. I may never see him again and you have the cheek to keep a secret about him from me.' Victoria felt her face reddening. This woman in front of her was becoming more and more unlikeable, and it started with her outstanding good looks.

'I'm not trying to cut you out of anything, it's just that I promised. If you knew what it was, you'd understand.'

Rising to her feet, Victoria fought back tears. 'Well I don't know what it is, so I don't understand,' she snapped.

That was quite enough of that conversation, she decided. Leaving the classroom and banging the door behind her, she then hurried at speed along the corridor and out to her car, or Dan's dad's dreadful car for that matter, because her own had car disappeared along with her partner. Speaking to Dan's teacher friends had just distressed further, if that were possible.

Later that afternoon, she received a call from Officer Reynolds at the police station.

Hello Ms. Richards, Officer Reynolds here. I phoned to inform you that we have picked up some footage of Dan's car on our CCTV. His car is seen leaving The Queens Hotel at 8.37 am. He then drives down the main thoroughfare. Seven minutes later, he is seen turning into a road which is parallel to the road that The Bancroft-Hain School is on. There are no cameras on the side streets, so we have no indication as to where he was going. I checked roads leading out of Cheltenham but there was nothing. His car does not show up again on any footage, I'm afraid.'

'How do you explain that, Officer?' she asked, struggling to keep her emotions in order.

'I can't. I will, however, check with local businesses in the area to see if they have any security camera footage.'

'Did you get a chance to speak to Mr. Bancroft-Hain?' she asked.

'Yes, but it was a dead end. There was no Dan McKelvie on his list of interviewees. He even checked back in his paperwork to find Dan's application as he wondered if Dan maybe thought he had an interview or if he was sent an invitation to attend by mistake but, unfortunately, he did not receive an application from Dan. I'm sorry I don't have better news for you.'

Victoria deflated like a burst tyre. How could that be? Dan had read to her the answers he had written in the application. It wasn't possible for a person and a car to vanish. She phoned Enid to give her the devastating news. A text came through her phone while she was delivering the details of Dan's non whereabouts. It was a text from Al. This lifted her spirits somewhat and she hurried Enid off the line. 'I have to go Enid. I'll call you later.'

Al: *Any news?*

Victoria: *No, nothing on the cameras of importance and Bandy Bain didn't even have an application from him. If Enid can look after Artie, I'm going to track down the couple in the Borders.*
Al: *Tell me when and where and I will meet you there for moral support. Amanda can look after Cocoa Bean.*
Victoria: *You don't need to do that. It's so far for you to travel.*
Al: *I insist. A day out will do me good.*
Victoria: *I'll take you up on your offer then. Details to follow.*

It was totally unnecessary for Al to drive up from Cheltenham to meet her, but she was relieved not to be going it alone. If Enid could take Artie, she would head to Melrose on Saturday. Today, she would face the source of unbearable pain, Orla Francis, the woman who pulverated her heart, the woman who distracted Dan from his family, the woman who shared intimacies with her sweetheart. Orla Francis, the woman who taunted her in her dreams. It was going to be tough, but every stone had to be unturned, and every door peered behind until she found what she was looking for - Dan.

Chapter 11

Al looked out at the traffic passing the window of Cocoa Bean. In the shop, at the back table, a lady with deep set, sorrow wrinkles sat alone, staring into her tea as though it contained the secrets of life. Near the window a couple of student types sat together laughing. The same thought entered his head, as it did most days; is this my life? Was this all there was? Empty seats and long dragging days, while outside the world was simply passing him by.

Talking about his parents the previous night had really ignited something within him. He realised that it was possible to bury unwanted thoughts and memories but that sooner or later, they rose from the dead, haunting your thoughts day and night. Whoever killed his parents was still out there, living, breathing, enjoying life. For the first time ever, he developed a burning desire to find out the truth. What really happened on the night both his mother and his father were executed.

A young couple entered the shop, snapping Al away from the turmoil going on in his head.

'Welcome,' he said smiling. 'Take a seat and I'll get you some menus.'

'No need, mate. We are just in for coffee.'

This kind of thing was starting to really irritate Al. Every morning he bought fresh cakes and pastries; now, more and more often, people were treating the place like a Costa or a Starbucks drive through.

'No problem. What kind of coffee would you like?' He didn't know how much longer he could go on like this.

His mind drifted to the weekend and although he knew that Victoria didn't need his supportive hand-holding in Melrose, he wanted to go. He wanted to help her find Dan, he also wanted to see her. Since meeting her, she had awakened something within him. It was like climbing down from the hobby horse to ride the rollercoaster. Something was beginning to flow through his veins, and it felt so good; in fact, it had made him take a long hard look at how shit his life had become. Yes, she had definitely been good for him and for that he was grateful. A weekend in the borders was something to look forward to.

The annoying coffee people left, as did the students. The sad lady at the back had nursed the same cup of coffee for almost two hours. *Oh, what the hell*, he decided, as he made his way over to her.

'Excuse me madam, would you like a refill? On the house.'

'That would be lovely,' she told him, handing over her cup.

Taking her cup from her, he headed to where the coffee machine sat. 'How about a piece of apple strudel, on the house?'

A beaming smile lit up the elderly woman's face. She gave him a nod.

When the sad, lonely customer finally left an hour later, Al shut up shop. Enough was enough. Opening his laptop, he searched hotels in Melrose. A nice one caught his eye, called The Thistle and Rose. He booked himself in for two nights; might as well make a trip out of it, he decided. Then drumming his fingers on the counter, he thought about what he would do next. *I think I'll treat myself to a haircut.*

Turning the sign on the door around to show *Closed,* Al locked the shop and made his way on foot to the Turkish barbers that he liked a few streets away. As he strolled through Cheltenham, he thought about Victoria. He was excited to see her, not in a romantic way; well, maybe if it was another time, another place, but no, it was her company and, most importantly, the fact that she needed him. When was the last time he felt needed? Never. No one ever truly needed him. Amanda loved him and enjoyed being with him, but she managed perfectly fine without him.

Chapter 12

It was just over an hour until Artie's school came out, which gave Victoria plenty of time to speak to Orla Francis, if she was home. Miss Francis lived on her street and as she drove towards the house, she began wondering how she and Dan met. Dan had never shared any of the details of their brief encounter; the subject had been closed. Guilt had forced him to confess and perhaps a fear of Orla spilling the proverbial beans. Dan must have felt so much better after his admission of infidelity, the problem was that all the suffering was loaded straight onto her. Ignorance may have been a more blissful option. Still, she forgave him, they moved on from it and she didn't bring it up again. There was no point in burying the hatchet if you were going to mark the spot.

Indicating to turn left, she drove into her street. It was a neighbourhood made up of bungalows and semi-detached houses. She and Dan could only afford one of the semis and even then, they had to borrow the deposit from Enid. All the houses in the street had red roofs, a garage and a decent front and back garden. Al's unbelievable property crept into her mind. Oh, what she would give for a beautiful Victorian house, nestled in the middle of a mature garden with sprawled out lawns at every side. Her envy was short lived when she remembered the reason why he was alone in that perfect house. He deserved it and she was happy that he was at least cared for financially.

She parked the car outside Orla's house, which happened to be one of the bungalows. For a few moments, she sat in the car, quietly giving herself a pep talk. *Come on Victoria. You can do this. You can do it for Dan. She is just some silly woman who caught his eye, but I'm the one he loves. Be strong and keep your cool. Just ask if she knows anything and if she doesn't, then leave.*

In the absence of a doorbell, she knocked heavily on the red front door. There was no reply. She thudded again harder, then harder still. Stretching up onto her tiptoes, she stole a peek in the living room window. A cat on the windowsill gave her a judgmental stare and she found herself mouthing *sorry*. Looking past the watchful creature, she saw that in the living room there were no signs of life. In a way, she was relieved not to have to engage with the woman. She walked back through the gate that badly needing oiling, to her car.

'Hello!' a voice shouted from a few metres away. 'Were you looking for me?'

Victoria spun around, and the relief she had felt when Orla wasn't home quickly dissipated, causing her stomach to somersault. Her emotions moved from anger to jealousy to wounded betrayal. She walked over to meet her, not smiling, nor scowling, just looking.

'Hi, I'm Victoria Richards,' she began.

'Yes, I know who you are,' Orla replied, sensing trouble.

'I am sorry to intrude but I was wondering if you had any information that could help me.'

'Come on inside. There's no point in standing out in the street.'

The situation was surreal, but Victoria tried not to do her usual over analysing. Instead, she followed the woman, who had slept with her partner, into the house where they did it. She was led into the front room where the cat watched suspiciously from the windowsill. The room was stylishly tasteful, so much so that Victoria made a mental note that when Dan got home, they should change the décor and perhaps look at new sofas.

The two women sat anxiously across from one another, both feeling equally uncomfortable.

Orla was the first to speak. 'You said that I may be able to help you with something?'

'Yes, yes, I did. You see, Dan has gone missing, and I wonder if you know anything about this. He had a job interview in Cheltenham, and he didn't turn up. He hasn't been seen since. The police are involved but there isn't any trace of him or his car. Did he say anything to you?'

Orla felt truly ashamed. 'Listen Victoria, I think that you must imagine that what happened with Dan and me was more than it was. I haven't seen or heard from him since that night. I am so sorry about everything, please believe that. I know it must have hurt you terribly, but it was honestly nothing.'

'It tore my heart out,' Victoria told her, unwilling to cut her any slack.

'Can I tell you what happened?'

That was a difficult question. Would the details of the affair make it better or worse. Was it more or less than she imagined. She found herself nodding her answer.

'I was at my Christmas night out with my work colleagues. I had way too much to drink, but we were having such a good time. I got the last bus back from the city centre, and I saw Dan sitting on a seat at the back. I had never spoken to him before, but I knew he was my sort of neighbour. He had also been at his night out from work, and he was pretty drunk. I introduced myself to him and we chatted some slurred nonsense all the way to our stop. We walked along the road together until we got to my house. I asked if he wanted to come in, he said no. I then told him to come inside because I had something to show him. I was inebriated and lonely. Once he was in the house, he didn't stand a chance.'

The honesty from this woman was quite remarkable and Victoria found herself relaxing somewhat.

'After the clumsy, fumbling deed, he fell asleep on my bed. He awoke in the morning in a complete panic, and I could see that he was filled with regret. He ran out of my house, no goodbye, thank you or let's do it again sometime. We haven't crossed paths or contacted since.'

'It sounds awful, not at all what I imagined. I came for answers about where he might be, but I can see now why you wouldn't know anything. Still, in a way, I'm glad I came round. Thank you for your honesty.'

'Again, I'm so sorry.'

Chapter 13

Heavy rain suddenly poured down in sheets just as Victoria left Orla Francis's house. It was almost time to head over to pick up Artie, but she had time to run into her house and grab a jacket from the coat hooks in the porch. The downpour of rain fell so hard that it brought with it a loud roaring sound. It was like nothing Victoria had ever seen or heard before.

Inside her front door, hanging on a hook was her showerproof jacket that she had worn in Cheltenham and which had turned out to be a non-showerproof failure. Flicking it up to one side, she looked for a more substantial covering underneath. She reached up to loosen off Dan's jacket, the one he wore for rugby training. It made her feel sad, but on the other hand, it felt nice to slip it on. She slung the hood up and made a run for it to the car. The windscreen wipers on their highest speed were no match for the force of the torrents. The drive to school was treacherous, combining the inclemency of the weather with the unskilled driving of Victoria in a manual car.

The windows of the car steamed up when Victoria switched off the engine to wait for school to come out. Feeling cold and wet, she pulled Dan's jacket tightly around her. *Dan, where are you? Please come home. We need you.* Her mood was best described as wretched, and she could not stop herself from crying tears of desperation. Her hands felt so icy cold that she thrust them into the deep pockets. Her fingers caught a slip of paper, which she pulled out. Straightening out the corners, she saw that it was a receipt for £940 from Elmsley Jewellers in town.

What the heck, was all she could think. She had never received any jewellery from Dan, let alone something at that price. They simply didn't have that kind of money to throw away. What did he buy, and more importantly, who the hell did he buy it for. Her face burned with anger, hurt and every negative emotion that came with finding out your partner had been buying extravagant presents for someone. A knock on the passenger's side window startled her. She opened the window to see what the pleasant lady standing in the pouring rain wanted.

'Hi, I'm Philip Sampson's mum. I think the boys have organised a playdate today at my house. They cooked it up between them, but we would love to have Artie over if it's okay with you. He can have dinner with us, and I can drop him home later.' She gave a kind, mumsy sort of smile.

Victoria found it hard to resist. At the back of her mind somewhere, she did remember Artie asking her about going to Philip's house. 'Thank you. That would be very kind of you. I'm sure Artie will love that.'

Philip's mum ran over to the gates in the torrential rain to wait for the boys. She gave Victoria a backward, I'll-take-it-from-here wave, and Victoria drove off. In a way, it was a good thing that Artie still wanted to go on playdates and stay with his gran, as it showed her that he felt secure enough to be away from home and confident enough to live his own little life, doing things that made him happy. This gave Victoria great comfort.

Being alone in the house for a few hours without Artie would give her a chance to have a thorough look through Dan's pockets. It might also give her time to check the bank accounts again and contact the police for an update. It had been an emotional morning, and her nerves were strung like a piano. Maybe a medicinal glass of red wine would be on the cards too. It suddenly occurred to her that she was using alcohol as a crutch to help her cope with everything that had been thrown at her, but she decided that when it was all over, and Dan was back in his own home, she'd give up drinking altogether; well, maybe not altogether.

Chapter 14

A text came through Victoria's phone when she arrived back home. It was from Al. She was pleased.

Al: *I'm heading down to the borders tonight. I thought it would save me the long journey in the morning. I'm staying at The Rose and Thistle, just ask for me at the reception when you arrive tomorrow.*
Victoria: *Al, I'm so grateful to you. I'm sorry you are giving up so much time and money to help me.*
Al: *Don't be silly; this will be my yearly holiday. I've never stepped foot in Scotland before, so it's a first for me.*
Victoria: *You've really missed out on life! You won't want to leave. See you tomorrow.*
Al: *I hope we uncover something.*

When the messaging with Al was over, Victoria found herself smiling. There hadn't been much to smile about lately, so it felt good.

Now, it was time to check out the bank accounts. Opening her laptop, she went straight to online banking, first one, then the other. They were untouched since the day in Cheltenham when she bought a dress, toys, a Led Zepelin keyring and a few coffees at Cocoa Bean. That day seemed like a lifetime ago. How everything could change in the blink of an eye. A thought returned to her, where did Dan get the money for the expensive piece of jewellery? Did he have a different account that she didn't know about? It was definitely time to start digging a little deeper.

In the hall cupboard, on the top shelf, Dan kept a box which contained insurance policies, birth certificates, the mortgage agreement and his contract from work. Using a chair from the dining room, she reached up and slid the box from the shelf. She carried it to the bed, where she could sift through the contents.

First, she removed the policies, setting them to one side. Birth certificates for her, Dan and Artie were next, then the passports. She was surprised to find an order of service for Dan's grandad's funeral. He had been good to Dan growing up and looking at the photo of him on the front of the booklet made her feel quite emotional, even though she hadn't known him long. It was nice that Dan had kept the memento from the service. Delving into the box further, she found Artie's hospital band that had been around his wrist when he was born. Now, that really set her off. She allowed herself a wailing cry for this sentimental find. Alongside the band was a photo that had been printed from a printer, perhaps from his phone. It was a picture of her in a hospital bed, holding newborn Artie. She looked dreadful but happy, Artie looked cute, but he was crying. The certificates that were awarded to Dan for completing the rugby and football coaching courses were laid next to the policies. It really was a box of Dan, and it made her incredibly sad.

Leaving the contents strewn over the bed, she headed to the kitchen to pour herself a glass of wine. *Dan, where are you? Are you safe? Have you started a new life? Please just give me a sign. I'm lost.* Her pleas were just that of a desperate woman as she held out no hope of receiving a sign. Was this what life was going to be like from now on, just her and Artie alone, never knowing what had happened.

With her wine in hand, she headed back to the box to look for something, anything. At the bottom of the box was a set of paper receipts clipped together. There was nothing untoward about them when she flicked through them, until she came to a large receipt which was folded in four. Slipping it out from the rest, she opened it up. It was handwritten and from a jeweller in the city, but she didn't recognise the name. Items were listed in a column, a gold watch, a gents gold signet ring with diamond, a gold medal from Dunkirk and a gold chain. At the foot of the receipt were the words, *One thousand pounds paid in full.* The receipt was dated three months previous, which was around the time Dan applied for job at The Bancroft-Hain School.

Victoria sat on the floor with her back against the bed. The items that had been sold to the jeweller were Dan's grandfather's. They had been left to Dan in his will. Why had he not told her that he had sold them? She was now starting to believe that there had never been a job interview and that his intention all along had been to disappear without a trace. Perhaps he had met a woman online or someone from his distant past that got in touch. Whoever she was, she must be someone pretty special for him to sell his precious grandad's belongings. Dan was a hoarder of sentimentality, selling keepsakes was totally out of character.

When Victoria heard a car stopping outside the house, she realised it must be Artie getting dropped off. She packed away Dan's things into the box and put on a happy face.

That evening, after Artie's bath, Victoria tucked him up in bed. She explained that he was going to spend the day with his gran because she had to go out to a town called Melrose to look for clues about daddy.

'Can I come too?' Artie asked.

'No, sweet boy, it won't be any fun for you.'

'Can I sleep in your bed with you tonight?' he asked.

'Of course you can. Now, what story would you like me to read?' She headed over to the bookcase in Artie's bedroom.

'I want Stick Man because he gets lost too, then he finds his way back to his family.'

It felt like a hand had clutched Victoria's heart and squeezed with all its might.

Chapter 15

Please let Angus Dinwoodie remember something about Dan, she willed, as she drove in the direction of the borders. By now, she believed that it was more likely that he didn't even have an interview at Bancroft-Hain school, but the part that foxed her was, why he took her with him. He had insisted that she came on the trip. It would have saved a small fortune if he had gone alone. Two nights in the Queens Hotel was expensive; why not just set off to his new life from Edinburgh. It was a totally unnecessary pretence; in fact, it was downright cruel. Her mind replayed the conversations that took place with the teachers and Orla Francis. That woman Maggie Morton must have seen how tortured she was and yet she told her that she had a secret with Dan that she couldn't share. Victoria wondered what kind of person could stick a dagger in deep like that. If that was the sort of person he was *kindred spirits* with, then she really didn't know him at all.

A call came through her phone whilst she was driving. It was from the police; she took it on loudspeaker.

'Hello, Ms. Richards, this is Officer Reynolds.'

Her heart skipped two beats before thudding hard against her chest. 'Hi,' she said breathlessly.

'It was just to let you know that there is no news this end. No sightings of Dan or his car. Anything your end?'

'No.'

'Well, if you hear anything, please let us know.'

She ended the call and screamed loudly with frustration. 'Bloody useless!' she shouted.

Her mind continued to question what she knew. If Dan had left to start a new life with a woman, or a man for that matter, or even alone, the police would have seen his car. Would he really have gone to the lengths of buying a new car to keep from being found. Who did he think would hunt him down? This was a new theory that began birthing in her thoughts. Was there someone after him? Was he in trouble? Had he committed a crime? Maybe, he had really angered someone, someone dangerous. If that had been the case, surely he would have somehow messaged her. Now she began wondering if he left his phone on purpose because he was being tracked. Admittedly, she did watch a lot of crime dramas, but the fact of the matter was, Dan had vanished.

When Victoria drove into Melrose, she had to admit that it really was the prettiest town. It had been a place that she had always wanted to visit. Dan would travel through on occasion to take his school rugby team to the Melrose Sevens tournament, but he had never thought to invite her along. Now, arriving in the heart of the town, on a beautiful, sunny but cold day, she was glad that she was seeing it at its very best. How different her mood would have been if the weather had been wet and miserable. She drove on through the main street, keeping her eyes scouting for Al's hotel. When she saw a woman walking along carrying shopping bags, she decided to pull over beside her to ask for directions.
'Excuse me.'
The woman stopped and smiled, setting her bags down on the pavement.

'I'm looking for a hotel called The Rose and Thistle. Can you point me in the right direction?'

The woman gave a small laugh. 'I can do better than that. I can show you it.' She pointed over to Victoria's left where a large granite stone house stood on the hill. 'That's it there, dear.'

'Thank you. That has saved me a lot of time searching.'

'Just follow that road over there beside the church and it will take you straight up to the grounds.'

The hotel sat elegantly overlooking the town. Victoria couldn't help smiling at the thought of Al making a holiday out of the trip. There were probably dozens of places that he'd rather be visiting on holiday, but she was thankful that he gave up everything for her.

A phone call up to Al's room brought him bounding down the carpeted staircase. Instinctively, he ran at her, hugging her and planting a kiss on her cheek. He was really pleased to see her.

'Go into the lounge and order a coffee on my tab. I'm just going to go up to my room and finish getting ready. I didn't expect you so soon. I'll be no more than ten minutes, then we'll head to the hospital.'

'Okay,' she told him, laughing at his, what could she call it, excitement.

True to his word, Al appeared, groomed and shaved within the promised ten minutes. The directions to the hospital were already set up on his phone, so they headed off in her car to see what they could find out.

On the way there, Al laughed at Victoria's driving. He winced at the gear changes and tried to ignore the countless times she stalled at the traffic lights.

She said nothing until they arrived at the hospital car park, then she whacked his leg, saying, 'I can't help it, it's not my car. My car is missing, remember.'

'Sorry,' he said, making an adorably cute face.

This made her laugh.

Victoria asked Al to wait in the car whilst she went into the hospital reception area.

'I wonder if you can help me?' she asked the male receptionist. 'I really need to speak to a nurse by the name of Grace Dinwoodie. It is very important.'

The young man checked a sheet of paper on the desk in front of him before making a call, probably to the department that Grace worked in. He then hung up the phone. 'Nurse Dinwoodie doesn't start her shift until 2pm, I'm afraid.'

'Can you supply me with her contact details?' It was a big ask and she wasn't hopeful for this request.

'No, I'm sorry. If you want to leave me your name and number, then I can ask her to call you when she comes in.'

That was a good option, but only if she remembered meeting a Victoria Richards in Cheltenham.

Back at the car, she explained the situation to Al. It was only ten o'clock, so they had a fair bit of time on their hands to kill. This was Al's first ever trip to Scotland and Victoria wanted it to be something more for him than a day of support in the search for Dan. Subconsciously, she felt responsible for Al enjoying his two-day holiday because he had taken time off to help her out. A bit of sightseeing would make his trip a little more memorable. She suggested that they find out what was worth visiting in the area.

Al took out his phone, making a few clicks on the screen. 'Okay, things to do in Melrose. First up, we could go to see the home of Sir Walter Scott, it's called Abbotsford House. Are you up for that?'

'Yeah, that sounds great. I actually know a thing or two about Sir Walter Scott,' she laughed.

'Oh, do you now. That's something for me to look forward to then,' he told her with a twinkle.

They drove across town to the baronial mansion with its renowned landscaped gardens. They decided that as it was such a beautiful day, they would explore the grounds and not bother with the tour of the house.

Together they walked through the pathed glades which showcased an extensive range of exotic and indigenous trees that had probably been planted on the instructions of Sir Walter Scott himself. Although the sky was cloudless, the weather was far from warm, but Victoria was cosy in Dan's heavy jacket.

Al announced that he didn't feel the cold, and since he was walking around with a short-sleeved shirt, she believed him. They ventured down a smaller path which led into a denser wooded area. When they passed a weather-beaten wooden bench, Victoria suggested that they sit for a minute just to take in everything around them. Life had been so stressful since Dan's disappearance, and every waking thought and dream had been consumed by it. To stop in the stillness of the woods with the sun filtering through the pines was the pause button she so desperately needed.

'I don't know much about this geezer Sir Walter Scott. Did he write Ivanhoe?' Al asked, breaking the bird-cheeping silence.

'I think so,' she told him, then remembered something she had learned in her youth. 'I studied a Walter Scott poem for an exam at school. I wonder if I can still remember it. Do you want to hear it?' Clearing her throat, she didn't wait for an answer, she stared down at the pine needles on the ground and began reciting.

'Look not thou on beauty's charming;
Sit thou still when kings are arming;
Taste not when the wine-cup glistens;
Speak not when the people listens;
Stop thine ear against the singer;
From the red gold keep thy finger;
Vacant heart and hand and eye;
Easy live and quiet die.'

A huge smile of accomplishment spread across her face, and she gave a small head bow.

Al applauded loudly, causing a clap of echoes to repeat through the trees. He had no idea of the poem's meaning, but he admired the skill of being able to recite a poem at will. Victoria's accent sounded pleasing in his ears and somehow, she managed to add emotion to the words. His flesh had tingled as she spoke, and goosebumps had miraculously been raised on his arms.

'I don't know what you just said, but it was truly awesome.'

'I can't believe I still remembered that after all these years. Can you recite any poems?' she asked.
Of course, I know hundreds of poems,' he lied.
'Say one then.'
'Okay, if you are going to push me into it.' He adopted a serious expression on his face and clasped his hands tightly together.

'Doctor Foster
Went to Gloucester
In a shower of rain
He stepped in a puddle
Right up to his middle
And he never went there again.'

'That's really, really good, Al,' she told him sarcastically. 'Did you learn that in nursery?'
'Yes, I bring it out once in a while at dinner parties.'
The funniest thing for Victoria was not the poem, but the feigned earnestness with which he had delivered it.

Chapter 16

They left Abbotsford House having had a very enjoyable walk and a light lunch. It had been a welcome distraction from the reason she was in Melrose with a man who until less than a week ago she had never met. There was still some time left to pass until two o'clock, when Grace Dinwoodie would begin her shift at the hospital. Chances were, she may not call straight away, she may wait until her tea break. Victoria tried not to think about it. Under the circumstances, she was having a really nice time.

The next tourist attraction on Al's list was Melrose Abbey. He didn't know much about Robert the Bruce, but he noticed on the blurb that the abbey was the final resting place of his heart.

'Are you a fan of Robert the Bruce?' Al asked on the way to the abbey.

'Oh yes, I have posters of him all over my bedroom wall,' she joked, then felt bad about being sarcastic. 'I wouldn't say I was a fan. I do prefer William Wallace, but I like any story in history where the Scottish beat the English.'

Al being fully English, simply shook his head, saying, 'Victoria, you're not using your words nicely.'

She laughed. 'Did you also learn that in nursery?'

The abbey's ruins, which were surrounded by crumbling walls, were steeped in ancient history. Wandering round the grassy graveyard with its headstones from previous centuries, got Victoria thinking about how life was merely the blink of an eye in comparison to time. One minute your life was plodding along on an even keel, the next thing you know you're tossed into the eye of a storm. The time was now three minute to two, according to her phone, so hopefully, Grace Dinwoodie would call soon.

'This sign here says that there is a gargoyle of a bagpipe playing pig somewhere around here,' Al told her.

Victoria's phone rang with an unknown number. 'That'll be her. You go and find your pig with the bagpipes.'

'Hello Grace, you may not remember me...'

Grace interrupted her mid-sentence. 'Of course I remember you. Did your partner get the job?'

'Oh Grace, I'm so pleased that you knew who I am. No, no, Dan didn't get the job, in fact the whole thing has turned into a living nightmare. The reason I contacted you was to see if Angus remembered seeing Dan at the interview...'

'Slow down, lass. I'm not following you. Take your time and tell me what's happened.'

Victoria couldn't hold back her sobs. 'I'm sorry, I didn't want to cry. Would it be alright if I came over to your house to speak to you both, as soon as possible. I wouldn't ask if it wasn't important.'

'Of course you can come over, but I can't arrange it until tomorrow evening. You see, Angus bought himself a Harley Davidson and he has gone off to the highlands on a jaunt with some other old cronies on their bikes. I think he's trying to relive his youth. He won't be back until tomorrow around five. Come then. I'll text you my address. I'll make dinner. How does that sound?'

'That sounds perfect,' she said, feeling a terrible disappointment about the wait. 'Would you mind if I brought my...' she searched for an acceptable description, 'cousin?'

'I don't mind at all. I'll see you both tomorrow night.'

Victoria relayed the conversation back to Al, who stood nodding. Now she would need to return to Edinburgh, only to drive down again the following day. Al explained to her that he had the room at The Rose and Thistle for one more night and it was conveniently furnished with two single beds. Tempting as it was for her, she thought about how it would be perceived; spending the night with another man while searching for her missing husband. No, that did not look good at all. However, driving all the way back to the far side of the city, only to return the following day, wasn't an appealing option. She was left in a complete quandary as to what to do for the best. Enid wouldn't mind taking Artie for another night, but how would Artie feel about the disruption to his life over the past week; he disliked change. What if Angus Dinwoodie didn't see anything that day at The Bancroft-Hain School, then it would have been an unnecessary rabbit hole she had travelled down. A bitter cold wind blew up and she pulled Dan's jacket tightly around her. *Where the hell are you, Dan? I don't know what to do for the best.*

Maybe staying at The Rose and Thistle would be the easiest option. There was a Tesco in the heart of the town where she could pick up a toothbrush and a few other items necessary for an overnighter. The problem was, she just wasn't sure.

They made their way back to the hotel where they sat in the bar and ordered coffee. Victoria was preoccupied with thoughts of Artie. Was she neglecting him whilst she searched for Dan, or was finding Dan the best thing she could do for him; it was hard to know. Talking with Grace on the phone had felt good, probably because she was there, in the same hotel, waiting for her husband to come back from the same school. They had everything in common in that respect, except that her husband came back.

Al could see how troubled she was. He understood that, on paper, the situation wasn't ideal, but for convenience, it was perfect.

'I'm going to call Amanda and ask her to go and see Jack, the cop. Even if Angus Dinwoodie saw something, it's good to also get the views of others.' He decided to go ahead with this idea on impulse because Victoria looked like she needed another ledge to cling to. Looking across the table at her furrowed brow and wringing hands, he realised that if he ever went missing, he would want someone like her searching for him. Someone who would follow every lead and stop at nothing to find him.

Al suspected that Victoria was going to stay the night if her mother-in-law and son gave a thumbs up to the idea. It was understandable that she had to clear things not only with them but with her own conscience. No matter how much he wanted her to stay, he didn't coax or encourage her. The choice was hers to make, and hers alone. There were no words to describe how thrilled he was when she announced that she was staying.

When they sat together in the dining room, Victoria said something to him that pierced him, like a bullseye to the heart. They had been talking about his childhood and the devastating demise of his parents.

She had listened to him intently, then when he fell silent, she asked, 'Have you never thought about contacting relevant government officials to reopen an investigation? Someone out there murdered your parents, and they need to be brought to justice. Apart from that, you need answers. Maybe you owe it to your mum and dad to dig as deep as you possibly can.'

Victoria's suggestion had twanged a nerve in him. He gave no response, but the comment continued to writhe around in his head. Why hadn't he taken things further? If he didn't fight for answers, who would?

Chapter 17

It had been a relaxing evening of easy conversation and several good laughs, but things turned somewhat uncomfortable when it was time to retire to the room for the night. The easy banter turned to polite chit-chat.

'After you,' Al said, holding the door open.

'Thank you,' she replied.

'Feel free to use the shower first if you wish,' he offered.

'I may just do that. Thank you.'

Having no pyjamas to wear meant that Victoria had to sleep in her shirt and pants. She kept her socks on but discarded them once she was cosy under the duvet. When Al climbed into bed, she couldn't help but notice that he wore brightly coloured boxer shorts with Ralph Lauren written around the waistband. They lay quietly, side-by-side in their separate beds, looking over at one another. A few months ago, if someone had shown Victoria a future snapshot of this moment in her life, she wouldn't believe that it was true.

'Thanks again for this, Al,' she told him, before putting out the bedside light.

'No problem. I'd have bought some new boxers if I'd known I was sharing a room.'

Al watched Victoria nestling down to sleep. The full moon conveniently shed some light across her bed allowing Al to see her without being noticed. She really was a very special lady. An event like this may never occur again, so he decided to just lie awake for a while to watch her sleep until the moon left the window.

In the morning, Victoria awakened first. Giving a quick glance over to Al, she saw that he was lying on his back, fast asleep, with his bare chest exposed. Her cheeks blushed when she analysed the situation she had found herself in. If Dan had walked through the door, he would have wondered what the hell was going on. There again, would he have the right to be angry with her? Her situation was completely innocent and circumstantial, whereas his had been a drunken episode. No wonder he didn't want to talk about it. The way Orla described it made it sound like it was best forgotten. Why was she still giving that infidelity issue thinking space, she wondered. It was time to let go, now more than ever. All she wanted was to get Dan back home safely and move on.

Quietly, she reached for her phone to send a text to Enid. Artie had been her first thought when she woke. Was he distressed about her not returning home? She needed to know. The thought of him crying or, worse, suffering in silence so as not to upset his gran, was torturous to her.

Hi Enid, just checking in on Artie. Was he okay last night?

Enid was a prompt texter, as she kept her phone with her at all times, so while Victoria waited for the reply, she once again checked her online banking to look for money missing. Instantly, she could see that nothing had changed in either of her accounts. As soon as Al woke up, she'd call the police in Cheltenham to see if there was any news there. She knew for sure that they wouldn't have found him because you had to be actually looking for someone in order to find them.

A reply text vibrated in from Enid. It put her mind at ease when she read that Artie was absolutely fine. Enid told her that they were heading off to spend the day at a farm park. That was exactly what Artie liked, seeing animals and being outdoors. Knowing that her little boy was happy, allowed Victoria to focus her attention on finding out what she could about Dan's movements on that fateful rainy day in Cheltenham.

Victoria rose out of bed whilst Al was asleep, which ensured that her modesty stayed intact. They had an entire day to while away before their visit to the Dinwoodies' home. Once she was dressed, she would plan somewhere for them to go for the day. After all, Al had never visited Scotland, so she wanted to make his first time memorable. Grabbing her bag from the armchair, she headed into the bathroom for a quick shower.

By the time she emerged from the bathroom, Al was just awakening. When his head appeared out from under the duvet, he seemed incredibly pleased to see her. Having someone with you who is genuinely happy to see you in the morning was such a nice way to start the day. It wasn't that Dan was unhappy to see her each morning, it's just that the stresses of life swallowed up the little morsels of joy, like greeting one another with a smile.

As soon as Al was washed and dressed, they headed down the staircase to the formal dining room for breakfast. They both ordered a full Scottish breakfast from the menu and ate toast and drank tea until it arrived. Victoria told Al that she had planned a sightseeing day for them, explaining that it was a secret, and all would be unraveled when they got there.

Al was nominated as the driver for the day and Victoria designated herself as the navigator.

'Okay Al, drive that way out of the town centre, then turn left at the top of the road,' she told him, when they finally left the hotel.

'Are you going to tell me where we're going?' he asked, studying the roads signs.

'Not yet.'

'Do you know that I find it highly annoying when people do that,' he told her.

'Good,' she laughed.

'Can you at least give me some clues?'

'Okay.' She thought for a moment. 'The finale of a very famous book and film is set there.'

'Is this another Walter Scott, Robert the Bruce kind of a thing?'

She laughed. 'No, in fact the author is American.'

'Is it something to do with Mel Gibson and Braveheart?'

'No. Mel Gibson didn't write Braveheart, and it was loosely based on fact. I'll give you another clue. The author said that he thought this place was the most mysterious and magical place in the world. This tourist attraction is a feature point in the quest for the holy grail.'

'Got it! Is it Dan Brown's The Da Vinci Code?' he shouted. 'But where are we going?'

'We are going to Rosslyn Chapel. Well done for working it out. Now, keep going along the road until you see the sign for Roslin Village.'

They took a tour of the chapel, which was so worth seeing, followed by a bowl of soup in the adjoined restaurant. The final part of the visit was a walk through Roslin Glen where they saw the partially restored ruins of Rosslyn Castle. Victoria tiptoed and leapt through the thick mud that covered the pathways through the trees. Unfortunately, the only shoes she brought on the trip couldn't have been more unsuitable for the terrain.

It had been such a lovely way to spend a day, but now she was anxious to get to the Dinwoodies' house to speak to Angus. If he remembered something, anything to connect Dan to The Bancroft-Hain School, then it would have been worth coming to Melrose, even if it meant leaving Artie.

Unlike the car journey to the chapel, which had been filled with jokes and punchy banter, the trip back to Melrose was silent. Victoria stared out of the car window, her mind focused on one thing, getting some kind of lead about Dan.

'I've had a really nice time,' Al said. 'This has been the first trip I've taken anywhere in about ten years, so thanks. I haven't forgotten why we're here and I hope with all my heart you come away with some news tonight.'

'Thanks Al. Me too.'

Chapter 18

Victoria drove to the Dinwoodies' house in her car, while Al made his own way there. It was easier this way, as they would both be heading home in opposite directions once the evening was over. The satellite navigation woman directed Victoria right to the front door of her destination. A quick glance in her rear-view mirror and she saw that Al was close on her heels. The street where Grace and Angus lived was much like her own, a blend of semis and bungalows. The Dinwoodies were fortunate enough to have one of the bungalows.

The front door was opened by Grace, smiling a most welcome greeting. Angus was not at all what Victoria had pictured. Somehow, the image she had of him had been of a small, portly man with clown-style balding hair. It just went to show that it was never right to make assumptions about people, she thought, as she stared at him. The real Angus that stood before her was tall, his hair was thick and shoulder length with no sign of thinning. Under his leather waistcoat, she spied the face of Robert Plant, lead singer of Led Zeppelin, staring out at her. Is this a sign from Dan, she wondered. Now she wished that she had brought the Led Zepplin key ring to give to Angus. She couldn't help wondering if he had toned things down a bit for the interview at Bancroft-Hain School. There couldn't possibly be two more different men than Angus and Mr. Bancroft-Hain. Her guess was that the pompous headmaster didn't approve of this man, but she thought he looked fantastic. *Dan would love this guy.*

'Come in, come in,' Grace beckoned, holding the door open wide.

Victoria stepped into the hallway. 'This is my cousin, Al.' By the confused look on Al's face, it occurred to her that she had forgotten to tell him that he was her cousin.

Al nodded with a smile.

'How was your trip?' Victoria asked Angus, when they were seated in the lounge.

Grace answered the question for him. 'He's exhausted and sore all over. No wonder, gallivanting all over the highlands on a Harley Davidson Fat Boy. I'm not sure if the name describes the bike or the biker,' she laughed, reaching over for his hand.

Angus then answered for himself. 'It was excellent. A great chance to get peace from the wife for a while.' He took Grace's hand up to his face and kissed it. 'Al, what do you do?'

'I run a coffee shop. It's nothing grand, it just ticks away.'

Victoria sensed that Al was embarrassed, although he had no need to be. In the short time that she'd known him, she had picked up on his low self-esteem and figured that it was something that he had dragged with him since childhood. He needed bigging up.

'Al is too humble,' she told the couple. 'His coffee shop is stylish, and the coffee and cakes are the best. It's in a prime location in Cheltenham, right beside the Queens Hotel.'

'You know, Al,' Grace told him earnestly, 'Having my own café, restaurant or coffee shop has always been a big dream of mine.'

'It's not all it's cracked up to be,' he told her. 'There are too many big competitors like Starbucks and Costa. It is impossible to make a decent living from it. I own the premises, which makes it a bit easier, but I don't know how small businesses pay the extortionate rents and make money.'

Angus stood nodding. 'I'm with you on that, Al. I think small, independent businesses will simply die out. Take a card shop for example, how many cards would you need to sell every day to cover the costs of staff, rates, utilities, it would be impossible.'

The men stood discussing this and various other topics until Grace told them that dinner was ready.

They were led through to the dining room where the table had been set in an informal way. Victoria followed Grace to the kitchen to help out. From the kitchen, she could hear Al and Angus talking and laughing, they were clearly getting on really well. The fact that Al fitted in so effortlessly and seemed to be having a really enjoyable time, pleased her. It had been a pleasant way to round off his two-day holiday.

'So, Victoria, Grace tells me that you want to ask me something about the day of the interview in Cheltenham. I'm all ears,' Angus said, running his fingers through his thick locks.

Taking her phone out of her handbag, Victoria found the best photo of Dan that she had. She also searched for the only photo of their car, which was in the background of a picture of Artie.

'On the day of the interview in Cheltenham, Dan didn't return. He hasn't been seen since, neither has his car. I met with Mr. Bancroft-Hain, but he told me that he didn't have Dan McKelvie on his list of interviewees. He even said that he had never received an application from Dan. The police have done what they can, but they have no information whatsoever.'

Grace and Angus sat open mouthed, desperately trying to make sense of what she was saying.

'Show me your photos,' Angus said, reaching his hand out for her phone.

'This is a recent photo of Dan.' She handed over the phone to Angus.

He gave it his full attention for some time before saying, 'No, I didn't see this man at the interview. I am positive.'

Victoria took the phone from him and flicked the screen to reveal the photo showing their red, Volkswagen Scirocco.

Angus took hold of the phone but this time, he didn't need to think long and hard about it.

'Yes, I saw that car in the car park of the school. There was no one inside it. I am absolutely positive about that. The reason I remember is because about thirty years ago, I owned one of the old style Sciroccos, so I like to look at the changes to the new model. I saw that red Volkswagen parked in a space near to the entrance of the school on the day of the interview,' he concluded, with firm certainty.

Tears formed in Victoria's eyes as she looked across at Al.

Chapter 19

There was no reason for Victoria to feel elated about this latest revelation from Angus, but she did. It didn't answer all of her questions but what it did do was eliminate some of the variables. He hadn't just run off that morning, leaving her to find her own way home. The new information didn't mean that Bancroft-Hain was lying, chances were, he hadn't even meet Dan, but his car had been in the car park and that had been confirmed.

They left shortly after they had eaten dinner. Both had a long drive home, although Al's was considerably longer. It was a pleasant evening but more than that, it was a step in the right path to finding Dan and Victoria was so glad that she had gone. It was now time to go home to her little boy, whom she had missed terribly.

Saying goodbye to Al was surprisingly emotional. They had spent forty-eight hours in each other's company and under the circumstances, it had been fun. His company was easy, even the silences. Would she ever see him again? She wasn't sure. He was, however, going to contact her as soon as he found out who owned the cars in the car park on the day of the shortlist interviews. Perhaps one of the candidates not only saw the car, but also saw Dan.

On the drive back from Melrose, Victoria thought about what a great couple Grace and Angus were. They had so obviously knitted together tightly over the years, without having to sacrifice who they were. Would she and Dan ever come to a point in their relationship where security and trust were never an issue? She hoped so. From the first moment she met Dan, she knew that she wanted to spend the rest of her life with him. People always laughed when she told them how she met him.

'We met at the frozen food section in Morrisons,' she would tell people when they asked. It made her smile to think about it. He had lifted a bag of frozen corn on the cob, and she had advised him to buy fresh. Fresh corn was sweeter, tastier and much better for you, she had told him. It was probably the one and only time he ever listened to her advice. At the checkout, she saw him in the queue. He looked over at her, then reached into his basket to wave the fresh corn on the cob at her. It could have been the first and last time they ever met, but she visited the freezers in Morrisons ever day at the same time for a week. It had paid off, because a week later, he walked in.

'I've just come in for some frozen corn,' he told her. 'Some stupid woman told me to buy fresh and it was rubbish.'

They had both laughed, then introduced themselves.

'Can I have your number?' he had asked.

It was getting late when she pulled up outside Enid's house and, to her utter delight, she saw a sweet little face watching from the window.

Artie ran out of his Gran's house to meet his mum. He had missed her so, so much. There had even been a few tears shed at bedtime. It stood to reason that if your daddy could disappear without trace, then so could your mum. Gran had read Stick Man to him before he snuggled down to sleep, it had become his new favourite book, and the ending gave him comfort. Now, his mum was home safe, and this made him happy.

Enid had already packed Artie's things into his backpack which she handed to Victoria. While Artie was through in the lounge saying goodbye to his grandad, Victoria took the opportunity to tell Enid about what she had found out from Angus Dinwoodie.

'So, he definitely was at The Bancroft-Hain School that morning,' Enid commented.

'Yes, definitely. Whether he went inside or not is another story but at least we know that he arrived at the school. It's not much information, but to me, it's a whole lot. I have another avenue to wander down regarding the candidates that were at the second interview, but I'll tell you about it nearer the time.' She hugged her mother-in-law and thanked her for taking Artie. She then shouted through to the lounge, 'Artie, it's late, let's get home.'

They headed home, just the two of them.

'Mummy, why is grandad strange?'

'Strange in what way, Artie?'

'He asked me who I was.'

They were no sooner in the door than Victoria's mobile rang. It was the police station in Cheltenham. Artie was sent to the lounge to give her privacy when she took the call.

'Victoria Richards?'

'Yes,' she said, suddenly feeling unnerved by the seriousness of this new officer's tone.

'This is just an update on your missing person's case. Your partner's car was picked up on a doorbell camera across the street from The Bancroft-Hain School. The footage shows him indicating to turn into the drive. There is no other footage of him leaving the school, although the owner of the camera did say that it was temperamental and did cut out on occasions, which is very unfortunate. I'm going back to speak to Mr. Bancroft-Hain tomorrow afternoon. Anything your end?'

'Not really,' she told him, feeling delighted that they were active on the case. 'Much the same as you. I tracked down one of the candidates that attended the interview. He said he didn't see Dan at the school, but he positively identified his car in the car park.'

'Any money missing from your account?'

'No.'

The officer didn't say anything for a few moments. 'It doesn't quite add up. I'll be back in touch after I've been out to the school.'

'I am so grateful to you. Thank you.' She cried after disconnecting the call.

Artie came wandering through to where Victoria was standing motionless in the hall. Possible scenarios spun around and around in her mind but all of them led to a dead end. There was simply no plausible conclusion she could follow through that made any sense.

'Are you coming through to sit with me?' he asked, pulling on the waistband of her jumper.

'Artie, I know it's late, but I am hungry so I'm going to call the pizza place in town and ask if they will deliver two nice pizzas for us. What do you think?'

'Yes, yes! Gran gave me dinner hours ago. Then will you come and sit with me?'

'Of course I will, I just have a couple of quick things to do. I think that you should go and get into your pyjamas, then give your face and hands a big wash. By that time, the pizza will be here.'

The order for pizza was placed and Artie skipped off to get ready for bed. It was way past his bedtime, but Victoria didn't care, she needed to spend time with him. She could hear the tap running in the bathroom, so she took the opportunity to go through to the bedroom to root around Dan's things. She needed to know that she hadn't missed anything from her previous search in the box. Sitting herself down on the bed, she looked around the room considering where to start. The unpacked suitcase in the corner, near the window, caught her attention. Dragging it to the middle of the floor, she unzipped it and flipped it open. It contained Dan's casual clothes, as he had left that morning dressed in his suit. His good navy-blue shirt was folded neatly; she pulled it out and sniffed it. This was her favourite of all Dan's clothes; he really suited it. It had been washed and ironed but there was still a pleasing trace of aftershave remaining on the fabric. *He must have brought this shirt to wear to dinner. He knew that I liked him in it.* Tears spilled over onto the shirt. *I am so glad that he wanted to look as nice for me as I did for him.*

The zipped pocket in the suitcase was slightly open, so she reached her hand inside and it closed around a velvety feel bag which she pulled out to take a look at. The drawstring top was pulled tight. Using her fingers, she prised the bag open, tipping the content into the palm of her hand. She studied the small box that sat there. *It couldn't be, could it?* she asked herself. Flipping open the lid, she screeched aloud. In fact, it was so loud that it brought Artie running through to find out what was happening.

Nestled beautifully within the velvet inset, was a three-diamond engagement ring. So sparkly, so pretty, so her. Exactly what she would have chosen for herself. And yes, the tears flowed, full on, but happy tears were allowed. Was this why he insisted that she came with him? Had he planned the night to be even more special than she could ever have hoped for? This was obviously the item he bought from the jewellers, most likely with the money he got from selling his grandfather's items. It was all more than she could bear. Another connected thought sprung to her mind. *Is this the secret that Maggie Morton knew about? I was so mean to her for keeping something from me, but what if she had told me and then Dan came back the following day. She was right not to say anything; it wasn't her secret to tell.* Perhaps she should send her a quick email to verify, then apologise.

Victoria and Artie ate the cheese and pineapple pizza when it arrived. The time was charging on, but she wanted to cuddle up with her son on the sofa to watch the animated version of Stick Man. Her fingers automatically ran through Artie's soft, thick hair. What a precious, little boy he was; he was her heart.

'Watch this part, mummy,' Artie told her, nearing the end of the film. 'This is when the daddy Stick Man finds his way back to his family.'

The finding of the ring had filled Victoria with a sense of joy and security, but the truth of the matter was, Dan was still missing.

Chapter 20

On the long drive back to Cheltenham, Al played his favourite soul music. His thoughts were full of Melrose, Walter Scott, Rosslyn Chapel, and Victoria lying there sleeping next to him. She was the first woman he had ever met that he felt completely comfortable with. Spending time with her was not only easy, but it was fun and addictive, addictive in the sense that the more time he spent with her, the more he craved to see her when they were apart. Would it be so wrong for him to wonder if there was a chance for them to be together if Dan was never found. On the other hand, would there always be a part of her that couldn't let go of him. Oh, why was he thinking this way, he was a friend in need, nothing more. After a quick comfort and coffee stop at one of the many service stations, Al was on the home stretch. It was a long way, but the roads were pretty clear in the evenings, giving him a straight run at top speed. Marvin Gaye was singing about how he heard it on the grapevine, and this made Al think of his father. It had been his dad who shared his love of artists such as Otis Redding, Marvin Gaye and Stevie Wonder, who were his favourites. Victoria's words about finding out what had really happened to his parents returned to his mind. There was a big part of him that wanted to shake the tree to see what would fall out, but where would he start? Who could he contact? There was no way the authorities would ever reopen the case unless there was new evidence. Casting his mind back, he remembered a young man from Bangladesh who had worked for his father in Saudi. What

was he called? The name just wouldn't come to mind. He mentally thought through the entire alphabet just to find the first letter of his name. G, yes it was definitely G, Ga, he thought. Then another letter revealed itself to him, it was Gad something. He glanced at the clock on his dashboard, wondering if it was too late to phone Amanda.
'Hi Amanda, I know it's late, but I need you to jolt my memory. What was the name of the young man from Bangladesh who drove dad around in Saudi? I think it was Gad something. Oh, wait a minute, I've got it, Gadhar something. Do you remember?'
'Al, you do know that it's almost midnight. I am in bed, and I was actually asleep.'
'I know, I'm sorry. I just got to thinking about mum and dad. I feel that we were never given any real answers and...'
Amanda's tone became harsh. 'Al, drop it. The reason we were given no answers is because there were no answers to be given, now let it go. Move on and find happiness. How was Scotland?'
'It was great. Victoria found out that Dan's car was at the school on that day. I know it's not the best time to ask you this, but could you contact Jack and ask if he could find out about the license plates? If one interviewee saw the car, then another may have seen Dan.' His head had been so full of thoughts of one kind or another, it hadn't occurred to him how selfish he had been, phoning so late.
'Okay, I'll do it for Victoria. Do you need me to open the shop tomorrow?'
'No, I'll do it myself. Thanks for everything. Now, go to sleep. What are you doing up at this time!'

'Goodnight, Al. Oh, and before you go, Gadhar's surname was Banik.' She disconnected the call.

Chapter 21

Artie was quiet as he sat in the back seat of the car on the way to school. All he knew about his dad's disappearance was what he managed to overhear in phone conversations. He couldn't be away looking for a different lady because his mum was great. Stick Man got separated from his family by sheer chance and all he wanted was to find his way back. He folded the index finger on one hand, over the middle finger, then did the same with the other hand. Good, now that his fingers were crossed, he shut his eyes. *Daddy, I'm sending out a message to you with my mind. I don't know where you are, but we miss you. Mum keeps having to leave me at Gran's so that she can look for you. I think the man on the phone to mum said that your car showed up on a doorbell camera. I thought that was very interesting. Try to find your way back to us. Stick Man didn't think he would see his family again, but he did.*

'Are you alright in the back there, Artie?' His lack of chatter was highly unusual.

'Yes, it's okay, I'm fine. I'm just sending Daddy a secret message using my mind. What do you call that again?'

'Telepathy. That's good sweetheart. Could you tell him from me that I love him, and I will find him.'

'Did you catch that, Daddy?' Artie said aloud.

Their usual routine was carried out at the school gate. High-five left, then right, followed by Victoria standing at the gate waving until Artie entered the building. Artie turned around four times to wave back before he reached the door. Once he was safely inside, Victoria headed back to the car. She drove to the top of the road and an unexpected impulse took hold of her. Turning left instead of right, she headed to Dan's school to ask Maggie Morgan if the big secret they shared was the ring.

This time around, the head teacher was not as sympathetic towards Victoria when she walked into the office. He gave the impression that she was becoming a pest. When she asked if she could have a quick word with Ms. Morgan, he was reluctant, to say the least. Perhaps she had informed him how rude Victoria had been at the last meeting, or maybe they were just busy running a school. Regardless of the reason, she found herself almost pleading for a brief, thirty-second meeting, nothing serious. He caved.

Maggie Morgan was on guard when Victoria entered the classroom. The big boss man must have phoned ahead to warn her to take cover.

'Firstly, Ms. Morgan, I'm sorry for the way I spoke to you the last time I was here. I'm not making excuses but it's just that I am at a loss as to where Dan can be. I don't even know if he is dead or alive. Also, I just wanted to ask you a quick question. Was the secret you shared with Dan an engagement ring?'

The taut muscles on Maggie Morgan's face visibly relaxed. A pleasing smile spread across her mouth, bringing with it a sparkle to her eyes. She really was a beautiful woman. It had been jealousy that had encouraged Victoria to form a negative opinion of this lovely lady.

'You found it then?' Ms. Morgan said. 'Isn't it a beauty?'
'It is exactly what I would have chosen for myself.' Victoria felt the sting of tears.

'I'm proud to say that he showed it to me first for approval. I gave it a ten out of ten.'

Victoria was touched that Dan wanted to get it just right. Her eyes were watery, and the words she wanted to say struggled to come out. Maggie Morgan wrapped her two arms around her and hugged her tightly.

'Victoria, you will find him. People don't just disappear. And, when the big wedding comes around, I want an invite.'

'That's a definite,' she managed to say. 'Thank you for your kindness.'

Chapter 22

It didn't take Al long to find Gadhar Banik on social media. It was most definitely him and actually, he hadn't changed a bit. He had, however, moved up in the world. Al was quite astonished to find out that Gadhar now worked in the Bangladesh High Commission in London, which he read was the diplomatic mission of The Peoples Republic of Bangladesh to the United Kingdom. *How did this guy, who was a driver and errand runner, end up with a gig like that?* Thinking back, Gadhar did have a certain confidence about him. His father had relied on him for everything. *My father would probably have been more devastated about Gadhar Banik leaving the country than he was about my departure.*

He sat staring at the screen for a while, deliberating whether or not to reach out to this man from the past. Victoria entered his thoughts, not for the first time. The way she searched for Dan was inspiring. She didn't sit back and wait for the police to do the leg work; she was out there finding answers for herself. It was thoughts like these that made him connect with a short message to Gadhar.

Hi Gadhar
You probably don't remember me, but you used to work for my father in Saudi, he was a British Diplomat.
My name is Al Montgomery, and I left Saudi around 17 years ago.
If you have a recollection of me and you are up for a chat, let me know. Al

There, it was done. It may yield nothing, or it may uncover something. Either way, Al somehow felt better having done it. Just sending that short message endorsed the fact that he was actively searching. He had no idea where he would take it from there.

The customers weren't exactly lining the streets waiting for him to open the coffee shop. But he unlocked the door, put on the lights and music and made the place as inviting as possible. The fresh cakes and pastry man arrived with his tray of sweetmeats balanced on his shoulder. Al shouted his usual 'thanks' to which the cake man would always reply 'enjoy' as he walked out the door. Al never touched the cakes; had it been cheese and biscuits then that would have been a different story. The truth was that the cakes and pastries ended up in the bin if there was no one to gift them to. Maybe he should cancel all deliveries, he had pondered, but that would be the very time that some old dearies would come in and ask, 'What cakes and pastries do you have?'

The day was no busier or quieter than usual, it was just the same old, same old. He found himself staring out of the window looking for a red Volkswagen Scirocco to drive past. Were Victoria and her missing partner becoming an obsession to him, he wondered. Everything had changed since that day Victoria walked into Cocoa Bean and now he couldn't change it back, but there again, why would he want to. A spotlight had been shone on his life and, by all accounts, it was pretty shit.

In the late afternoon, Amanda walked through the door of the coffee shop, and she was smiling.

'You look like the cat that stole the cream. What's made you so happy?' Al said, pulling out a chair for her to sit on.

'I sent Jack a text after you called me the other night. He replied, then I replied, then he replied... We ended up talking all night. I've agreed to meet him.' There was no disguising her pleasure.

'Do you mean you're going to meet up with him to get the car registration contact details?' Al asked, feeling quite surprised by her change of heart.

'No, I got those this morning.' Reaching into her handbag, she took out a piece of paper with information listed on it. 'One of these reg plates was a hire car. The guy lives abroad, I think. There is an address for a man in Wales and there are actually two right here in Cheltenham. Anyway, to answer your question, no, I am just meeting Jack because I've missed him.'

'Wow, you are full of big surprises today, Amanda. Be careful with him. Don't forget how much he hurt you. Anyway, thanks for this,' he said, waving the piece of paper containing the details.

Al told Amanda to sit by the window to make the shop look busy. They sat together drinking coffee and chatting about matters in their lives.

Amanda asked nothing about Gadhar Banik and why Al would be interested in him after all this time. This was a relief in a way because he wasn't ready to share his intentions with anyone.

Chapter 23

A text came through Victoria's phone while she was driving and there was a great temptation to reach into the bag beside her to see who it was. Artie was in the car, so she decided not to do anything dangerous. There was no way she was going to take any chances with her precious boy. Had she become even more protective of him since Dan went missing? Yes, she probably had. There were times when she mentally made plans for the future that didn't include Dan, but on the other hand, since she found out about the engagement ring, she couldn't stop her thoughts from straying into the territory of weddings, dresses and honeymoons. Her mind had become a place of chaos and disarray and until Dan was found, her thoughts would remain out of control.

Artie unclicked his seatbelt and ran ahead of her into the garden. She stayed behind in the car to reach into her handbag to retrieve her phone. Her heart trilled a little when she saw Al's name on the message. Chucking her mobile back into her bag, she decided she would wait until she was in the house to read what Al had to say. A barely noticeable smile formed on her lips; she liked hearing from him.

'Mum, can I get a biscuit and a drink?' Artie shouted from the sofa, as he watched his favourite programmes.

'Yes, I'll bring them through, but don't make a mess.'

Once Artie had been attended to, she took time to read the message from Al.

Hi, hope you're okay. Any news?

Amanda spoke to her ex. I have the details of the interviewees. Two are from right here in Cheltenham. Do you want me to speak to them?
Al

This was great news for Victoria, even if she only questioned two out of the four men. Could she depend on Al to speak to them, or would she prefer to do it herself? She wasn't sure. Travelling down to England meant leaving Artie for another night or even two, and it also involved driving that terrible car of Dan's father on such a long journey. There was a high probability that she would venture all the way to Cheltenham, interview the men and come home with no information. But when it came down to it, at least she'd feel like she was doing something, even if it was a waste of time.

That's great news, Al.
If you don't mind a lodger for a night or two, then I would prefer to come down and speak to the men myself. Please thank Amanda for me. I know it couldn't have been easy contacting her ex.
Let me know when would be a good time.
V x

Once she had checked availability with Enid regarding Artie, she would plan her one… no, two-day visit, to Cheltenham. It was going to feel strange going back to the place that set her life spinning out of control, but she had to do it. Every lead had to be chased, just in case something was there to be uncovered. Thoughts of Al pushed their way into her head. Wasn't fate an unfathomable thing, she pondered. She had only known Al for such a short time, and yet he was the only person she was interested in hearing from. By rights, she shouldn't know him, he was just a man that owned a coffee shop that she had visited, but now he had become her closest confidante and lifeline. There was nothing untoward about her going down to Cheltenham to stay at Al's house, but it was best that she kept her lodging arrangements quiet from everyone.

She placed a call to her mother-in-law.

'Are you sure you want to drive all the way to Cheltenham, Victoria? Can't you ask the police to interview the men? I'm not sure that Bob's car will get you there,' Enid explained.

'I have to go. I got the contact details through a source; I'm not really supposed to have them, so I can't ask the police to do it. I'll hire a car for a couple of days. Enid, if I don't chase this lead, then I have nothing else. The police have nothing either. I have to do it for Dan, surely you can see that.' Tears burned in Victoria's already raw eyes. What was she supposed to do?

'I know, I understand, I'm worried sick too. I just don't want anything to happen to you. You know we could hire a private investigator to check things out for us.'

'I had already thought about that, but they can cost anything up to £85 per hour, for a reputable one. This is not a surveillance job, Enid, it's a missing persons' case, with zero leads. It could take weeks for a P.I. to come up with something. I can't afford it even if you helped with costs. If Dan is never found, then I am going to have to support Artie on my own. I need to chase this myself before I think about hiring a professional.'

Everything Victoria said was true and Enid knew it. If she was able to help with the childcare, then that was her contribution to the search. Artie was no trouble; in fact, she actually enjoyed his company. His little quirks ranged from comical to challenging at times, but she was working through it and finding strategies to cope with the meltdowns. She noticed that many of Artie's traits were identical to Dan's when he was a boy. The neat, random collections were Dan to a tee. Somewhere, up in the attic, there were boxes full of action figures, coins, commando comics and tickets from everything and everywhere. The memory of it made her cry for her son. He had also been an interesting, unusual little character with a head filled with facts about animals, oceans, continents and world records. What she would give to go back for one day to see that young boy one more time.

Worrying about Dan and Artie had been a distraction from the other problem she was facing, which was Bob's memory. Her husband was displaying all the signs of dementia. She was constantly reminding herself not to mention that he was repeating the same statement several times. He was losing his glasses and keys on a daily basis and forgetting whether he had eaten dinner or not. It was breaking her heart to watch the decline of such a witty, intelligent man. The doctor had advised her to pretend it wasn't happening. 'Don't make a thing of it when he forgets, repeats or misplaces. It will distress him.' It was solid advice but not easy to follow. Dan's disappearance hadn't come up in conversation and she had decided that it was best left that way.

Enid sent a text message to Victoria telling her that Thursday and Friday were the best days for her, with regards to looking after her grandson.

Chapter 24

On the tediously long drive to Cheltenham, Victoria asked herself whether it was absolutely necessary for her to make the trip. Al was sharp, and he could have interviewed the men for her; he had offered. No, this was her search for her partner, and she had to carry it out on her own, with Al in the background for support. The voice on the satnav broke into her thoughts to tell her to stay on the A74/M6 for two hundred and thirty miles, which was soul crushing. Why did Cheltenham have to be so far away? The only consolation was that the rental car was brand-spanking new, and it was a joy to drive. Never before had she sat behind the wheel of a new car, with the smell of the interior leather in her nostrils.

The arranged plan when she arrived in Cheltenham was to meet Al at the Cocoa Bean and get a coffee, before heading to his beautiful house on the outskirts of town. She had already decided that she would choose the same room as before. The blue on the walls calmed her mind and helped her to think clearly.

With half an hour to go before reaching her destination, a phone call came through the speaker in the car. It was Artie.

'Are you there yet?' he asked.

'Not yet, sweet boy, but very nearly.'

'Is it the same place that you went when you came home without daddy?'

'Yes, I'm afraid it is. I'm just having another look for him.'

'Could you bring me back three more animals with the push up bottoms that make them faint?'

Victoria laughed. 'Of course I can. I'll ask the shopkeeper what other animals he has.'

'Just don't get ones that are the wrong size, okay?'

'Don't worry about that, I've learned my lesson. You be a good boy for Gran. I'll phone tomorrow. I've just arrived. Love you.'

'Love you too.'

Victoria headed to a car park that Al had advised her to go to. It was a short walk to the coffee shop, and she was happy to stretch her legs. She had completed the journey in one sitting, without a stop. The drive had been a killer but at least she had a full day of no driving before she had to do it all over again.

As she walked along the street in Cheltenham, she couldn't help thinking that Dan must be somewhere nearby. The CCTV had no sightings of him leaving town, which meant that he was still around. The question was, could she feel or sense his presence, was that even a thing that was possible. For a moment, she thought she could, but soon dismissed it as wishful hoping. She approached the entrance to The Queen's Hotel and memories of that rainy day flooded her thoughts. It had been, by far, the worst, most stressful day of her life. A sick churning manifested in her lower abdomen as she hurried on past the place, without so much as a glance into the doorway. The Cocoa Bean was across the road, and she found herself hurtling in the door to get away from the hotel that triggered so much anxiety in her.

By the look on her face and her body language, Al could see that she was distressed. He was undecided as to whether he should make a joke about her entrance to lighten things up or to simply say nothing and hug her. The latter was the preferred option. Coming out from behind the counter, he rushed over, enfolding her in his arms. It felt good to hold her close but that was not why he was doing it. Her hair smelt gorgeous, piney and herbal; quite intoxicating if he was being honest. For a few moments, they stood locked together. Al felt that if he had let go of her, she would have dropped like a stone. When she started to cry, he tightened his hold.

The door of the shop opening forced them apart. Al laughed awkwardly as he pointed out the tearstained patch on his shirt. 'Look at the mess you've made.'

'I'm so sorry, Al. I think I must have had some kind of panic attack when I passed the hotel door. This has never happened to me before. The drive was so long, and I didn't stop, so my legs are a bit on the shaky side.' She took a handkerchief from her handbag to wipe her eyes. 'I'm sorry about your shirt. I'm just a big state.'

Al instructed her to sit down, then walked over to serve the couple who had come in with their baby. The baby was staring up at Al with big chocolate button eyes. Using his index and middle finger, he tickled the baby's chin. 'That's a sweet baby you have there,' he told the couple. 'I'll just get you some menus.' As he walked over to the counter, he gave Victoria's shoulder a squeeze as he passed her.

Shortly after the young family left, Al turned the sign on the door to closed.

'Here, you clean the tables and the counter, and I'll mop the floor.' He handed Victoria the antibacterial spray and a clean cloth. Otis Redding was turned up to an acceptably loud volume whilst they prepared the shop for opening the following morning.

It was good for Victoria to be busy; it took her mind away from the negative thoughts she was experiencing about finding Dan. Being far from Artie and her home had weakened her reserves and her guilt burden was weighing heavy. She had to be strong, or she would be no good for anyone. Hearing Al singing loudly to the soundtrack made her smile, and her mood began to lift.

'We need to talk,' Al told her, pulling a chair out from the table.

She joined him.

He sat forward, leaning his elbows on the table. 'Okay, so there are two men in this area that we would like to speak to. I think we should rule out the guy who lives abroad and the one in the London area. Agreed?'

'Agreed.'

'I don't have any phone numbers for these men, only addresses. One of them is about two miles from here. Just say if you're not up to it, but I think we should go cold calling on him tonight, like right now. What do you think?'

Victoria's body became tense. She didn't think she would have to face talking to anyone tonight. But realistically, it was better to use her time in Cheltenham wisely and strike sooner rather than later. 'Yes, I agree. Let's do it.'

Chapter 25

Mr. Graeme Wright-Martin lived in the suburb of Prestbury, close to the centre of Cheltenham. The position of Head Teacher at The Bancroft-Hain School had seemed like an ideal escape from the stresses of the real educational world. The state school he had headed up for almost eighteen years had, over time, become nothing more than a powder keg ready to blow. Lack of discipline options and zero back up from the parent body, had slowly changed the job from educator to babysitter. His nights had become sleepless, his libido had all but left him and he found himself counting calendar days to the next school holiday. His dream job had become a life of dread. A pleasant little private school, full of well-behaved children, seemed like a perfect transition to ease him into retirement. As far as he was concerned, he had paid his dues and now he was owed a softer option.

There was a knock at the front door just as Mr. Wright-Martin sat down in his armchair to watch *Pointless*. His wife had prepared him a wonderful feast of mince, potatoes and scoop of Heinz beans; it was his all-time favourite.

'Graeme!' his wife shouted from the hallway. 'There's a couple here to see you.'

'Who are they?' he shouted back.

'They want to ask you a few questions.'

Grudgingly, he laid the remainder of his dinner on the coffee table, mumbling angrily at the inconvenience.

There was no invite to enter, but Victoria stepped forward onto the doorstep.

'Mr. Wright-Martin, my name is Victoria Richards, and my partner Dan was due to attend the same interview as you, at The Bancroft-Hain School. He didn't return to the hotel after the interview; in fact, Mr. Bancroft-Hain informed me that he was not even on the list of applicants. I wonder if it would be possible for you to look at a photo of Dan and also a picture of the car he was driving. I just need to know if you saw anything.' Tears bubbled in her ducts, but she fought to keep them there.

Mr. Wright-Martin nodded. 'I remember you. Didn't you fall in the door of the gymnasium on that second day of interviews?'

'Yes, that was me. I was in a bit of a state. There have been no sightings of Dan or his car since the day he left me at The Queen's Hotel. Would you mind taking a look?'

Standing aside, he invited Victoria and Al into his home. He led the way into the lounge where he eyed the last few mouthfuls of his meal and wondered if it would be bad manners to tuck in.

'Oh, I see you were having your dinner. I am so sorry. Please finish it before it gets cold,' Victoria told him. She had spotted him glancing furtively at it.

She scrolled through her photos slowly, giving Graeme Wright-Martin time to polish off his dinner. As soon as she saw him laying down his knife and fork, she conveniently found the photo of Dan.

'This is a recent picture of Dan. The likeness is good.'

Graeme wiped his hands on his trousers, then slipped on his glasses. 'Betty! Put the big light on.'

Betty had been standing in the doorway. She reached over to flick the light switch.

With Victoria's phone in his hand, he studied the photo. 'Yes, I saw this man. I brought a pad of paper and a pen to take notes at the interview, but I accidentally left them in my car. I excused myself during the introductory coffee session and dashed out to the car park. This man ran in the main door as I was leaving. He said hello and rolled his eyes in a frustrated, kind of harassed, gesture. It was definitely him.'

When he returned the phone to her, Victoria mentioned the photo of the car.

Once again, he donned his reading glasses. 'I can't be sure about the car. I think there was a red one beside mine, but I can't say for certain that it was this model. There again, I can't say that it wasn't.'

'Did he join the rest of the interviewees?'

'No,' Graeme said, shaking his head. 'I saw him at the door, and I didn't see him again.'

Tears spilled over with emotion. 'I am so grateful to you for this information. It has been incredibly helpful. Did you get the job?'

'No. In the end, no one did. Mr. Bancroft-Hain decided not to retire.'

Chapter 26

Al and Victoria dissected the information that Graeme Wright-Martin had given them when they returned to the car. Dan had been at the school after all, so why did Bancroft-Hain say he hadn't. Did he really not know anything about Dan or was he hiding something.

Victoria made a call to Enid.

'Enid, Dan was at the school. The candidate that we went to see positively identified him from the photo. He didn't just think he saw Dan, he was certain he saw him. He was there, Enid, there at the school. However, he wasn't seen at the actual interview. I can't make sense of it, why turn up but not go through with it?'

'I think you should go to the police with this information,' Enid told her sternly.

'What's the point, Enid. If they interview Mr. Bancroft-Hain he'll just say the same thing that he said the last time, that he had never even heard of Dan McKelvie. Maybe it's true. What if Dan took cold feet about everything in his life including the job interview and decided to do a runner.' Her voice was starting to waver. 'I don't actually believe that, but I'm starting to second guess everything. Can I speak to Artie?'

'Artie, your mum is on the phone,' Victoria heard her shout in the background.

'Hi mum, have you found daddy?' Artie asked excitedly.

'No, lamb, not yet, but I'm getting closer.'

Artie handed the phone back to his gran. There was no point in talking about anything else.

'I have to go, Enid. I'll let you know how we get on with the other interviewee.'

'We, who's we?' Enid asked.

Oh shit. What will I say? 'I meant… we, the man I'm speaking to and me.'

'Oh,' she laughed, 'I thought you were in Cheltenham with someone. I'll talk to you tomorrow.'

'Yes, I'll keep you updated.'

'By the way, which hotel are you staying in?'

Victoria heard the question but ended the call as though she hadn't. Guilt gnawed away at her, and her stomach began a spin cycle. *I'm here in Cheltenham with another man and I am staying at his house. It sounds so awful, especially to Dan's mum.*

Al sensed her tension. He knew exactly what she was thinking and feeling. Yes, to any onlooker, it seemed like a betrayal, but he was her friend, and he wanted to help. As far as he was concerned, fate had brought them together to find answers.

When they pulled into Al's drive, the incredible property smacked her with the same impact it had the first time she visited. It was hard to believe that her friend Al owned such a beautiful home, but she was delighted that he did. Being able to stay two nights in the house instead of a hotel was saving her a fortune. It didn't matter how things looked, she needed Al and all the help he could offer. As long as she could sleep easily at night knowing that their friendship was innocent, that was all that mattered.

They sat together drinking wine, discussing and following through possible scenarios which all ended abruptly. She pondered on the idea of calling the police to tell them what they had uncovered, but it was pointless. Dan was low priority, and she got the feeling that while she was out with her big magnifying glass hunting for clues, they sat back and simply used her information to update their case. Whenever they called, instead of supplying her with new details, they opened by asking if there were any further developments.

It was late when they headed to bed. Victoria was exhausted, mentally and physically. Al showed her up to her room, which really was beginning to feel like *her* room. The bed covers had been changed and two fluffy towels sat folded on the chair at the window. On the dressing table, sat a small glass vase with pretty wildflowers displayed haphazardly. The idea of Al going out to pick flowers to dress up her room touched her more than she could say. What a guy he was. In fact, he was just a big onion with a new surprise under every peeled layer. She could never have done any of this without him; he gave her strength.

Before leaving the room, Al ruffled Victoria's hair in a playful manner. 'No rush to get up in the morning. If this next guy we want to speak to is already in education, he won't be working on a Saturday. We'll head over to see him about twelve. His name is Ben Gibb. He sounds a bit like a Bee Gee, doesn't he?'

'Ha ha ha ha, stayin' alive, stayin' alive!' Victoria's high-pitched impersonation was decent enough to raise a laugh from Al. 'Good night. Thanks for everything you do for me.'

Al smiled. 'Thanks for everything you do for me.' He left her room, shutting the door behind him.

As she lay in her bed with an aroma of fabric softener coming from the bedding, Al crept his way into her thoughts, and not for the first time.

Chapter 27

Ben Gibb had been a deputy head in a large comprehensive school. He had worked under the direction of the head teacher, Mr. Givens, for almost twenty years and he despised the very bones of the man, as well as the air he breathed. Everything his superior did made his nerve endings squirm and writhe. The way he talked, the way he ate, his sneeze, cough, laugh, even his resting, doing nothing face. He hoped with every fibre in his being that the old codger would keel over so that he could move straight into his shoes, although he even found his shoes highly annoying. But no, the old fella just kept going and going and going.

Eventually, Ben Gibb decided that he, himself, would probably die before Givens, and the way his stress levels were going, it could be sooner than he thought. It was time to visit fresh green pastures, far away from the cause of his anxiety. When he saw the post of Head Teacher in the Bancroft-Hain School, he thought it was the ideal position for him. He breezed through the interview and was called back for the short list. Then in an ugly twist of fate, old Bancroft-Hain decided not to retire after all. In Ben Gibb's mind, he saw himself in that school, sitting on the leather swivel chair, barking orders to all around him.

With his golf clubs slung over his shoulder, Ben opened the front door, only to be met by a young man and woman.

'Mr. Gibb?' Victoria asked with the song, ha ha ha ha, stayin' alive, stayin' alive, playing in her head.

'Yes.'

'I've come about my partner Dan, who has been missing since the day of the job interview at The Bancroft-Hain School. Can I show you a photo of him, just to see if you recognise him?'

'Sure,' Gibb said, maybe a little impatiently; his weekends were precious, after all.

He studied the photo of Dan McKelvie. 'No, I did not see this guy at the interview.'

'It was a sock to the guts for Victoria. 'How about this car, in the car park?'

'I'm sorry, I don't remember the cars that were there.'

'Can you tell me anything at all about the start of the interview, you know the introductions and coffee time. Anything at all.'

Ben Gibb suddenly remembered something which he thought may or may not have been of significance. 'Yes, there was something a tad odd. We all stood around chatting, drinking the coffee which was available from one of those big... what do you call them again, metal tank things with the tap on them.'

It was irrelevant to the story, but Victoria wanted to hurry him along. 'An urn, I think you mean.'

'Ah, yes, an urn. So while we drank coffee from the urn, Bancroft-Hain sat behind a desk with his laptop open. He was so preoccupied with something on the screen that he didn't join us. He was fixated. He then stood up and shot out of the room, apologising for having to leave us. According to him, it was an emergency. At the door, he shouted, 'Talk amongst yourselves. I shall return as soon as possible.' I would say that it was about half an hour before he rejoined us. It was fine because it was a good chance to get to know the other applicants, or should I say weigh up the competition. Anyway, apart from that, it was a completely normal interview.'

'Did he give any explanation as to what had happened?' Al asked.

'No, but his cheeks were flushed, and I noticed beads of sweat on his brow and around his stiff collar.'

'Interesting, thank you for sharing that. Well, we won't keep you from your golf any longer. You have been really helpful.' Victoria slid her arm through Al's as they left Ben Gibb's property in the direction of where the car was parked.

What they had just heard from Mr. Gibb was somehow significant to Dan's disappearance, Victoria could sense it. Call it gut instinct, but she now suspected that Bancroft was a liar.

After the meeting with Ben Gibb, Al drove them both over to the coffee shop where Amanda was running the show. It was surprisingly busy, but it was a sunny Saturday. Al caught Amanda's attention before taking a seat with Victoria at the only table left. He knew his sister meant *one minute,* when she held up one finger. It was a common worldwide language when the words couldn't be spoken.

Bancroft-Hain was not what he seemed, Victoria thought, whist she sat with Al at the table. Dan was seen entering the school at roughly the same time Bancroft-Hain seemed to have been faced with an emergency. What could he have seen on his laptop that would make him bolt for the door? It was a mystery. The question was, where could they take it from here? On sheer impulse, she reached for her phone and called the police.

Al left her to make the call. Amanda looked like she needed help with clearing tables and preparing orders. It wasn't fair to leave her to do it by herself. The problem was, he was losing the inclination to come into work at all these days. Maybe it was time to reinvent the shop into something else or even sell it. When Amanda saw him helping with the duties, she made a sign where she wiped her brow with the back of her hand. Al knew this to mean, *Phew, I could do with the help.*

Victoria listed the new information to the officer on the other end of the line. It was a woman this time, but not one that she had ever spoken to before. The female officer asked her to hold the line and Victoria suspected that she was going to check if there had been any new developments. Of course, there weren't. It's difficult to find what you're not looking for, she thought cynically. After a bit of back and forth, toing and froing, the officer agreed that someone should go to the school and interview Mr. Bancroft-Hain once again. By now, she was experiencing a passing wave of DeJa Vu. Had they not told her last week that they were going back to speak to Bancroft?

The coffee shop calmed down to a manageable level, and all customers were served and happy. Al made his way over to the table and he beckoned to Amanda to take a break and join them. He could see that her cheeks were flushed, and wisps of frizz had escaped her ponytail. What would he have done without her over the years, she was rock solid and the most uncomplaining person he knew.

Around the table, Amanda listened as Al explained the new details they had discovered from the witnesses. Victoria could just see Amanda straining to slip off her shoes under the table. Running the shop on her own had been a big ask but she had done it willingly. The relationship between the siblings seemed unshakeable, they were there for one another through the good and the bad. Victoria had no one in her life except Dan and Artie, and this had always been enough for her, until now. Having no one of her own to turn to had left her feeling alone. But now, Al and Amanda had become like her family, and she thanked God for giving them to her in her desperate hour.

'I've got an idea about what our next move could be. Let me explain, then tell me what you think,' Al announced. He had been chewing on the idea since the previous night.

'Okay,' Victoria said. 'I'm open to anything because I am at a loss as to where to go next. The policewoman said they'd send someone out to the school, but I'm not holding my breath.'

'Right, hear me out. You've met Bandy Bain,' Al said, looking at Victoria. 'So you can't go back there, or he'll get suspicious as to what this is about. He knows Amanda and me, but he hasn't seen us since we were teenagers. What if we booked an appointment to take a tour of the school to potentially send our daughter there. Don't laugh at this bit because I'm deadly serious, I think we could wear disguises.'

Victoria couldn't help laughing out loud at a mental image of this, which set Amanda off.

'No, don't laugh. I mean believable disguises. Amanda, you could wear one of those old wigs of Aunt Alicia's. They are in a suitcase in my loft. I could lay off shaving for a few days and wear a baseball cap.'

'Okay, that sounds plausible. What will you do when you get in there?' Victoria asked.

'I thought if you could phone me at a pre-arranged time, I could leave the tour to take the call. I won't take the call because I'll know it's you, but I will go into the office to get a look at that ledger you told me about. I could see if Dan's name was on it. I could even have a nosey around for anything that might be helpful. I know it's flimsy, but we've got nothing else.'

By the look on her face, Victoria could see that Amanda was nervous about all of this. It was never her intention to involve Al, let alone his sister, in Dan's disappearance. Already, Amanda had contacted her ex-boyfriend for inside information from police records. She felt awful, but when you were desperate, you could tuck guilty feelings away to the back of your mind. Quite frankly, you would do just about anything for answers. When Amanda agreed to go through with Al's somewhat hairbrained scheme, Victoria put up a threadbare fight, insisting that there was no obligation to be involved, but secretly she was delighted that the plan would go ahead. As Al said, it was a flimsy plan, but it was all they had.

It was agreed that Al would phone the school on Monday for an appointment. He would ask for a tour after school hours, to ensure that other staff members, especially in the office, had gone home. Al and Amanda would give themselves new names and an agreed back story. They all shared ideas about the lives of this young, incognito couple and their make-believe child. Al jotted all the ideas down on an order pad from the counter. Strangely, he found himself feeling quite excited and invigorated by the risky little operation. He hadn't felt this thrilled since he was a boy; funnily enough, tormenting Bandy Bain.

By the time they were finished joining the dots of their plan, it was no longer flimsy; in fact, they felt it was pretty watertight. There was no need for Victoria to stay in Cheltenham, she could leave the following day as planned. Her only role in pulling off the plan was to phone at the designated time to allow Al to leave Amanda and Bancroft-Hain.

At closing time, they all helped in cleaning and stocking up for the following day. Al then turned to Victoria to get ready to head back to his house.

'Amanda, why don't you come over tonight and have some wine?' Victoria asked.

Great disappointment washed over Al. This surprised him because he loved his sister very much but his time with Victoria was precious and would be short lived. Tonight he wanted her all to himself.

'That would be great,' Amanda told her. 'Al, are you okay with that?'

'Of course. You are always welcome.' *Always, apart from tonight.*

Chapter 28

The evening was relaxed, and the company was fun. It was so easy for Victoria to forget why she was in Cheltenham in the first place. Alcohol made a great anesthetiser. Amanda became witty and animated and just about everything she said made Victoria laugh. However, it hadn't gone unnoticed by her that Al was more withdrawn than he had been the previous evening. A yearning came over her to see Artie, as they sat chatting and laughing. This was a very difficult time for him without his daddy around and the changes to his routine couldn't be helping matters. She decided that she would make it up to him when she got home. A thought suddenly stuck her, she hadn't visited Flamingo to buy him any wooden animals. From her bag she took out her phone, apologised for her bad manners then researched wooden animals. If she ordered a few for his collection, they may come within a couple of days.

On seeing Victoria on her phone, Al took it as a sign that it was acceptable to take his phone from his back pocket. He had felt the buzz of a notification, making him curious. No one ever phoned or sent messages to him, simply because he had allowed all of his friendships to dwindle away. Of late, his only friends were the two women seated around his table.

He glanced at the screen of his mobile and saw that it was a social media message. His adrenaline spiked when he saw that it was Gadhar Banik.

Al, I certainly do remember you. If you are anywhere near London, why don't we hook up for a couple of drinks?

Al's mind raced. This was big news. Gadhar was the closest confidant his father had, although he had no idea why. It was an unlikely friendship, but his father relied on Gadhar for everything. Hearing about the events of the evening his parents died, from a different perspective, would possibly bring him the closure that he sought. He wondered if his feelings of disconnection from the world around him stemmed from losing his parents in such a brutal way. There had been no resolution for him; in fact, at the time, he was told nothing more than they had been murdered.

He had nothing to lose by arranging a meeting with Gadhar. London was a two-and-a-half-hour train journey from Cheltenham, and he could even book an overnight stay. For now, he'd say nothing; Victoria had enough to contend with, and Amanda would simply worry about him. He sent a brief message back to Gadhar saying that it was great to hear from him and he'd be back in touch to arrange a date.

Amanda stayed overnight in what had originally been her family home. She took the floral room on the first floor, which, back in the day, had been her bedroom. It was agreed that she would help Al open the shop, whilst Victoria set off on the long drive home to Edinburgh.

Chapter 29

Artie ran out to meet his mum as soon as the hire car pulled up at the kerb outside his gran's house. 'Did you get the animals? Did you get the animals?' he shouted, before she left her car seat.

'Yes, but I don't have them here. The man in the shop is going to post them.' This was a little, white untruth because she had actually ordered them from Amazon. 'He didn't have them in stock, so he is posting them out to our house. You can expect a parcel, all for you, from the postman in a few days.'

'What did you get me?' he screamed excitedly.

'I got you a zebra, an elephant and a monkey.' *Dear God, let them be good. Please let them be good.*

His little arms wound around her and hugged her tightly. 'I can't wait, I can't wait. Thank you. Did you find daddy?'

'Not yet. Come on, get your stuff and let's go home.'

Enid's front door closed, and the house fell deafeningly silent. Would things ever be the same again? Would she ever see her precious son's face again? It was heartbreaking and mystifying at the same time. She knew beyond all doubt that he would never just up sticks and walk out on his family and, even if he had, he would have found a way to contact her; she was his mother. The image of his body lying in a ditch somewhere returned to her mind. She saw the same vision every time she shut her eyes. It was torture. If she believed in such things, she would have gone to the Sir Arthur Conan Doyle Psychic Centre in Edinburgh to find out if they could contact Dan.

But that was all claptrap, and she wasn't about to resort to desperate measures. No, she would turn her focus to prayer. She was going to make a pledge to God that if he returned her son to her, she would commit to attending church for the remainder of her life.

Things had gone unusually quiet in the front lounge. Enid had left her husband watching television with a tray of dinner on his lap. She had a fear of him wandering off somewhere. Lately, he'd been taking bus trips around town, but there had been a day the previous week when he hadn't returned at the expected time. Fortunately, she was able to track his whereabouts from his phone. She found him in Portobello, not only distressed, but trying to hide his confusion. According to him, it had been the bus driver's fault. He really was causing her great concern but not more so than the disappearance of her wonderful son.

Bob McKelvie was not in the lounge when his wife entered to check on him. The television set was switched off and the tray that held his dinner had been placed on the seat of the armchair. Enid panicked and began shouting his name throughout the house. She ran around frantically, checking every room. Tears welled in her eyes as she looked under the bed in their room, and the two spare bedrooms. 'Bob! Bob! Please shout if you can hear me, darling. Please tell me where you are.'

A faint creaking sound came from the airing cupboard in the hall. It was only audible when she stood silently, listening. She opened the door only to see the most heartbreaking sight. Bob was cowered in the floor of the cupboard; his head hung down. He used his hands to cover his wet trousers.

'I thought this was the toilet, Enid. Did we move it?'

When Artie was bathed and in his pyjamas, Victoria tucked him under his duvet. 'What story would you like me to read you tonight, little guy?'

'Stick Man. I'm very tired, so just read the part where Stick Man goes back to his family.'

A text message hummed through the back pocket of her jeans. *That will be Al, checking that I got back safely.* This brought a happy smile to her face.

'What are you smiling for, mum?'

'Oh, nothing really. I just feel happy that you are my little boy.' She flicked the pages over in the book to reach the part of the story where Stick Man arrived home.

'Now, you snuggle down and have lovely dreams. I love you.' She swept his soft hair back from his forehead and kissed it. He was already asleep. Ever so quietly, she tiptoed to the door.

'Mum, I love you too.'

Her little boy was going to be okay, as long as she stayed strong and kept his life as normal as possible. Perhaps she would invite his friend Philip over next week; he could stay for his dinner.

Hurling herself onto the sofa, she stretched her shoulders back and raised her arms to loosen her joints. The drive from Cheltenham had been grueling, but boy had it been worth it. Somehow, the key to everything was at The Bancroft-Hain School. Slipping her phone from her back pocket, she saw that the text that arrived earlier was from a number she didn't recognise. She tapped on it.

V it's me

A surge of searing pain burned through her body. It was Dan, it had to be, he often calls me V in text messages. *Oh God, let it be Dan. Please let it be Dan.*

Her hands shook uncontrollably, so much so, she couldn't make them work to phone the number back. Wiggling her fingers and counting to twenty, she took deep breaths in an attempt to lower her heart rate. What was happening here? Was Dan really sending a text message from someone's phone. If that was the case, why wasn't he saying where he was. Taking her mobile in her hands, she breathed in through her mouth, out through her nose, and pressed the button to call the number back. The call was answered after four or five rings.

'Hello', came a polished voice. 'Can I help you?'

Victoria held her breath and said nothing.

'Hello, hello. Is there anybody there?'

The male on the other end of the phone gave an exasperated sigh before ending the call.

Victoria's mind began spinning frighteningly fast. Dizziness enveloped her, making her limbs feel powerless. She would have to call the police immediately and then she would call Al. She wasn't entirely certain, but she had more than a strong suspicion that the voice on the phone belonged to Mr. Bancroft-Hain.

Chapter 30

On the phone call to the police, Victoria desperately tried not to stumble over her words as she explained all the new information and the text message she had received. Slowly and clearly, she read the digits of the phone number to the police officer. Officer Weeks listened to everything she had to say, writing it down as she said it. He then read back the information and phone number for her to confirm. It was all correct and Victoria agreed to that. She was informed that they would be able to trace the owner of the phone with reasonable haste, giving them good leverage to possibly bring in Mr. Bancroft-Hain for questioning. This was great news to hear, for now she felt like she was being taken seriously. Things were moving forward in the right direction and, above all, she had solid evidence that Dan was alive.

She called Enid first to give her the latest development. Enid was a stoic woman, but Victoria could see that she was beginning to show cracks in her strength. No wonder, this was her son that had vanished, how could she be at any level of peace when she knew he was out there somewhere.

The news lifted Enid greatly. Something was now happening that could bring her boy home. He was alive and now the police were going to find him. He wasn't home yet, but an unbearable weight had been removed from her shoulders. She could now focus more on keeping Bob safe and helping with Artie.

'Victoria, this is great news,' Al said. 'The police have to act on this. You must feel so relieved that he is alive. Whatever you do, don't send a text back and don't answer your phone if you don't know the caller. If this is Bandy Bain's phone, he may notice that a message has been sent. Don't alert him to anything.'

'Yes, yes, you're right. I nearly did send a message back, but I thought better of it, that's why I called instead. Al, I can't be sure that it was Bancroft-Hain, but he had a similar pompous tone. I had a feeling that he was somehow involved in this. There is no other explanation.'

'Amanda and I have an appointment to visit the school tomorrow at six. All the staff will have gone home by then, I'm sure. I will find out what I can. Make a call to my mobile at half past six to enable me to get away from Bandy.'

'How's the disguise going?' Victoria asked, with a laugh.

'Not bad. I have a few days hair growth on my face, and I found a pair of glasses in the box of my aunt's stuff in the attic. I also found a short blonde Twiggy-style wig for Amanda in there too. I'm going to wear a suit and tie; Bandy Bain will never be able to imagine the Al he knows in a suit. It's been at least seventeen years since he's seen us, so I'm hopeful that we can pull it off. I really want to check the list of names in his ledger.'

The gratitude Victoria felt was immeasurable. Al had to be one of the most special people she had ever known. Dan was a complete stranger to him, and yet he cared so much about finding him. Every time she had called him, he had been there for her at a moment's notice.

'I can't tell you how thankful I am for everything you've done for me, Al. I don't know how I can ever repay you.' Her heart was full to bursting.

'You can't!' he joked. *Unless you could be mine one day.*

That night, Victoria slept the sleep of a newborn. She knew the net was closing in on Bancroft-Hain and it wouldn't be long before Dan was back home.

After dropping Artie at school the following morning, Victoria headed home to do some desperately needed housework. When she pulled up outside the house, the Amazon van drew up behind her. *That will be Artie's animals. I hope they're good. He won't want them if they are not the same as the ones he has.*

She brought the package into the house and gently peeled the seal in such a way that it could be resealed. Artie knew a parcel was coming and she had promised him that it was his to open. He remembered things like that, and he didn't respond well to broken promises. The animals inside were individually wrapped in bubble wrap. The sellotape was fairly accommodating when it came to peeling it back. The moment she took the elephant in her hand, she knew, she just bloody knew. *He is going to hate these animals,* she thought, opening the others. *He will notice that they are lighter, poorer quality and badly proportioned.* Gathering up the animals and their many wrappings, she headed to the wheelie bin outside and dumped them in. She felt cross with herself for not taking the time to walk up to Flamingo when she had arrived in Cheltenham. Pondering the thought for a moment, she impulsively took out her phone and ran through to Artie's room. His two animals were standing side-by-side on his bedside cabinet, so she kneeled in front of them and took a photo close up and further back. After checking that the pictures were decent, she sat down on Artie's bed and sent the photos to Al, explaining where they could be purchased.

Sorry to ask for yet another favour, but could you buy me three of these. You'll be able to find the time between all the other favours you're doing for me. I won't forget to call at 6.30. Good luck and thanks again. By the way, don't buy the giraffe, horse or mouse.

A reply came instantly.

No problem. I'll head along now to get them. Send me your address.

The recurring thought once again entered her head, *Al, you are the best, my hero.*

Chapter 31

Al was in the kitchen when Amanda appeared downstairs wearing her 'disguise'. What a difference a change of hair style and colour could make. Her tight curls were tucked away snugly in a blonde, bobbed wig; she was unrecognisable. The flowery dress was a complete contrast to her usual jeans and sweatshirt. Al clapped as she gave him a twirl.

'If Bandy Bain recognises you, it will be a miracle. I honestly think *I* would pass you by in the street. Actually Amanda, you look great, that look really suits you. What's the name of our daughter again?' he asked, feeling concerned about their cover story.

'Her name is Sophie; she is nine years old. Now, go and get changed, we'll need to leave soon. I've got butterflies on speed in my stomach.'

'Thanks for putting yourself through this. You really are the best sister in the world.'

Amanda gave a wolf whistle when Al appeared back in the kitchen, transformed. A sharp suit, crisp shirt and a silk tie gave him movie star good looks. His normal tousled hair was slicked back with gel, which strangely made him look like a real somebody. They looked at one another and laughed.

'This is the most nervous, excited and buzzed up I've felt in years. I am loving every minute of this undercover stuff,' Al told her.

'I can't say I'm feeling that way, I just want it over with.'

They set off in Amanda's car, just in case Bancroft-Hain had seen Al's car outside the day he brought Victoria to see him. He knew that was a long shot, but it was always better to be overcautious. There were no cars in the car park when they arrived. Either Bancroft-Hain didn't drive, or his car was locked up in one of the two garages that could just be seen at the back of the school. Al reached for Amanda's hand as they walked to the main door. He could feel her anxiety through her taut but trembling fingers.

'We're not doing anything wrong here, you know,' he whispered to her. 'We are just checking things out, that's all. Pretend you are in a TV drama, playing a part. You'll be great.'

They were met immediately in the hallway by an imposing blast from the past figure. Apart from the curly hair around his ears, which had turned grey, he looked exactly the same as he had done back when they both knew him. His tweed suit had been new, several decades ago. There was not a shop in England that would sell such an item. The fabric, the cut and the overall style gave it the look of costume and yes, true to form, the starched collar had given him angry red scores on his neck where it had chaffed.

Before offering a greeting, Bancroft-Hain stared from Amanda to Al, Al to Amanda, which was highly unnerving. A strange tension could be felt in the air and, for a moment, Al began to panic, just like he had done all those years ago when he had been left alone with the man. He knew he had to take the reins and do something, so he thrust out his hand, adopted a plummy accent and introduced himself.

'Mr. Bancroft-Hain, I presume? Tristan Whittaker, this is my wife, Tamara.'

Al's confident assurance appeared to humble Bancroft-Hain slightly and he dropped the mistrustful death stare.

'Yes, indeed, I am he. It is a pleasure to make your acquaintance. Now, let me regale you with the colourful history and successes of my charming school. We'll start with the classrooms on the top floor. Please, walk this way.'

Amanda squinted Al a look behind Bancroft-Hain's back. He presumed that she was experiencing the same feeling of surrealism as he was. They had travelled back in time to this place that the years had forgotten and met with a man who had been imprisoned in a bygone decade. The only positive thing that Al could take from this meeting was that he no longer felt quite so depressed about the way his own life had turned out. Compared to this man, he was a giant.

Bancroft-Hain strode ahead of them, pointing at various paintings and trophies as he went. This was his school, his birthright, his world and he was proud. He raised his hand to stop Al and Amanda in their tracks as they approached the full-length portrait of his father.

'What a wonderful painting. The artist has captured you to a tee,' Al gushed, knowing full well that it was Bancroft-Hain's father in the picture. He used over-exaggerated hand gestures to point at the painting, then to Bancroft-Hain.

Amanda successfully stifled a laugh at her brother's acting skills.

'Ha, ha, ha,' Bancroft-Hain guffawed, 'That is where you are wrong, my man. You see this is not me, it is my late father, founder of the school and, dare I say, a legend.'

'Well, I'll be...' Al shook his head in fake dismay.

'Let us continue,' Bancroft-Hain said, looking smug.

They headed up the main staircase with its familiar mahogany carved bannisters. Amanda noted it was the same red carpet on the stairs that she remembered and for some reason it brought back unhappy memories; perhaps she hadn't looked up much in those days. As she was closest behind Bancroft-Hain, she caught a whiff of mothballs emanating from his tweed suit. She realised that she had buried all memories of the place and now walking around it, hearing Bandy-Bain's voice and smelling his unpleasant odour, it felt like the door to the crypt was slowly creaking opening. It was nerve-wracking enough being on a secret mission, but this was taking her down a dark road which she knew had some ugly twists. All she wanted now was for this to be over. She glanced at her phone behind the old man's back, just to check the time. It had occurred to her that she was going to left alone with him when Al answered his phone call. It was twenty-seven minutes past six and Victoria would be phoning any moment.

Right on cue, Al's phone rang loudly, as he had deliberately turned the volume to its loudest setting.

Bancroft-Hain was obviously perturbed. Stopping the tour, he turned his head to glare at Al.

Making a big show of looking at the name of the caller, followed quickly by a shocked expression, Al apologised profusely to Bancroft-Hain, telling him that he absolutely had to take the call.

'Just go ahead without me. I'll catch up with you.' As he answered the call, he cut it off and began speaking urgently to no one.

Amanda nervously followed her old headmaster further upstairs to the classrooms at the top of the school. A sick churning began in her stomach.

Al kept talking in a loud and frantic voice as he ran full speed down the staircase towards the office. He needed to see the ledger.

Amanda had to applaud her brother's genius as she heard him in the distance shouting phrases such as, 'I can hardly believe he said that... We are going to have move into action to stamp this kind of behaviour out...' The forthright, anger-fueled expressions just kept on coming. Had she not felt so uncomfortable in the situation she was in, she would have laughed.

Sliding his phone into his back pocket, Al kept talking loudly, shouting about some horrific, imaginary situation he was in. His hand closed around the office door which he willed to be unlocked. It was. Still talking, he entered the unlit office which was just light enough to see his way around. Victoria told him which drawer the ledger was kept in, so he was able to head straight to it. He was very aware of time, and he knew that he had to get back upstairs very soon, or Bandy Bain's suspicions would be aroused. The drawer was locked, but as excellent fortune would have it, the old fool had left the key in the lock.

Now, what is the purpose of that, Al thought, as he shouted, 'This time he's gone too far and he's going to pay for that! Do you think we should involve the police?' The ledger was sitting face up as he slid the drawer open; well, he was pretty sure it was indeed the all-important book as it was exactly as Victoria had described it. He flicked through it until he found a page containing the heading, Candidates for Headship. Bingo!

Everything about Amanda's body language looked like she was listening with interest to Bancroft-Hain drawl on and on about the importance of early years development, but it was a façade, she was crumbling inside, and she wasn't quite sure why. The sound, smell and sight of the man was triggering something that was suppressed within her. Beads of sweat formed on her forehead and in her armpits, and the room behind Bancroft-Hain began to spin; no, not spin, sway, like the cheese-cutter swing at the playpark. Her mind was throwing up flashes of memory that she wasn't sure were hers, but she suddenly became aware that the old man had stopped talking. Focusing on his face, she saw that he was staring uncomfortably at her.
'What has happened to your spouse, madam?' Bancroft-Hain asked.
Amanda made a nervous, face-twitching response, 'Oh, I'm sure he'll be up in a minute. It's a very important call that he had to take.'
'Who called him?' Bancroft-Hain asked.
Feeling faint and flustered, Amanda tried to think of a name but then panicked that Al would say a different name when he returned. 'I don't know.'

'You seem convinced that it is a very important call and yet you have no idea who is calling. Hmm, odd, don't you think?'

For a few moments, Amanda became the same frightened schoolgirl who had once stood speechless before this man.

Reaching for his phone whilst still shouting his *important* conversation, he photographed the relevant pages on the ledger. He then returned it to the same position he had found it in. The small key in the lock dropped to the floor at the same moment he heard Amanda shouting his name. He knew this was her way of warning him that they were coming. Scrambling on his knees, he felt around for the key which had settled under the desk. Multitasking with fake conversation was no longer an option in this mission, his full attention was focused on getting the key, locking the drawer and getting the hell out of the office…fast.

Bancroft-Hain refused to be disrespected in his own school. He had been incredibly accommodating towards this young couple by fitting them into his busy schedule, after hours, and now with one of them absconding and the other staring blankly at him like a cretin, he had seen enough. As he led the way back downstairs, with the woman behind him, he stopped suddenly and stared at the wall beside him. Something in the framed alumni photos, dating back to the 1950s, caught his eye. He bent his knees and stared along at the various decades of young people who had attended The Bancroft-Hain School.

An icy chill tightened across Amanda's scalp. She knew exactly who the man was looking at. When he moved his gaze to yet another photo, she knew that Bandy-Bain was searching for her. Shuffling past him, she said, 'I think we had better head off now. We have an appointment at another school. Thank you for your time.' She gamboled her way down the flights of stairs. Her legs felt weak as she tried to move faster, but she was aware that Bancroft-Hain was following closely behind her.

'Tristan, Tristan!' she shouted, keeping up the pretence. 'Remember we have to be at the other school.'

Al slipped out the office door just as Amanda appeared. Fortunately, Bandy Bain missed the scene by a microsecond. Not quite sure of his next move, Al addressed the headmaster with apologies for the untimely phone call and then moved on to how grateful he was that they had been fitted into his full schedule.

Bancroft-Hain made no acknowledgement of Al's comments, he simply walked past them to place himself in front of the door to the school. Whether it was a gesture of barricading, Al wasn't sure, but an atmosphere of menace became obvious in the air around them.

'I know who you are,' he said, with a steely stare, 'And I know who you are,' he told Amanda, who would not look him in the eye. 'What I don't know is why you are really here.'

Al wasn't going to be pushed around by this ridiculous man. The troubled sixteen-year-old kid full of angst was long gone and he now stood before Bandy Bain, man to man. There were a few seconds of a stare off, then much to Al's relief, his old headteacher stepped aside to allow them to leave. Gripping on to Amanda's hand, they left the building. They hurried to the car and before getting in Al glanced at the doorway, only to see the old man standing there with fury burning red in his face. To his left, he noticed the two lock-up garages around the side of the school and made a mental note that they had to be investigated.

In the kitchen of Al's home, he sat with Amanda, studying the photos he had taken of the candidates' page of the ledger. There it was, obvious to see, the name Dan McKelvie, scored out several times. Bandy Bain had attempted to remove it with ballpoint pen, but the letters could be seen clearly underneath his scribblings. Surely the police would be interested to hear why the old headmaster denied all knowledge of Dan McKelvie; he certainly was.

'Amanda, look at this. You can see it. Dan McKelvie's name is on the list.' Looking across the table at his sister, he saw her silently crying, holding herself with her arms.
'What's wrong?' he asked, walking around to comfort her. 'What is it, Amanda, what's happened?'
Full blown sobs broke forth. 'I don't know what happened to me all those years ago, but it was something bad. I felt it. I've obviously buried it deep but as soon as I walked past the girls' toilets, some kind of jumbled memories came back to me. Al, I never want to see that man or his dreadful school ever again.'

Like a caged lion, Victoria paced the floor waiting for news from Al. Acting normal in front of Artie was not easy as he seemed to have a second sense when things weren't right. He must have asked her at least twenty times if she was alright. When she tucked him up in bed, she assured him that everything was fine, she just missed daddy. After Stick Man and two songs, she turned out his light and wished him happy dreams. She then went to the lounge where she sat in the silence, willing the phone to ring.

It finally did.

'Al! I was so worried. How was it? Did you find out anything?'

'Yes, Dan was on the list. He was invited to attend an interview, and Bandy Bain went to reasonable lengths to remove his name. Anything from the police about the phone the text came from?'

Victoria said nothing until she had mentally digested the fact that Dan's name had been on the list the whole time. *Why had that terrible man lied to her? He had seen for himself how distressed she'd been and yet he lied to her face. Why?*

'No, nothing from the police yet. Thank you, Al, I will always love you for doing that for me.'

As though coming from the blade of a Samurai sword, the words seared through his heart.

Chapter 32

Two officers headed out to speak to the owner of the mobile phone that the text message had come from. The missing man, Dan McKelvie, allegedly sent a text message to his partner from a phone registered in Cheltenham. The police had taken it seriously and were making their way over to interview the gentleman to find out how this could have happened. Dan McKelvie's partner had heard the voice of a man whom she believed to be the headmaster of the Bancroft-Hain school, but the police search for the owner took them across town to a quiet street, several miles from the school.

Stuart Adams was buttoning up his shirt, getting ready for work when the doorbell rang. He was taken aback to see two police officers standing on his doorstep. His first thought was one of bad news and automatically his mind raced through members of his family who could have been hurt. Apart from his wayward brother in Thailand, everyone he loved in the world was inside his house. His two sons were having breakfast before getting dressed for school, his darling wife was frantically searching for her car keys and worrying that she would be late for her work in a lawyer's office.

'Hello, how can I help you?' Mr. Adams asked.

'We are looking for the owner of a mobile phone,' one of the officers told him, quoting the number from the pad in front of him. 'It is registered to William Adams at this address.'

Mr. Adams laughed, more from relief than anything else. 'That is the phone belonging to my twelve-year-old son.

We only bought it for him as a safety device when he was out with his friends. My wife and I wanted peace of mind that not only could he phone us if he needed picked up, but that we could track his whereabouts. He is not allowed on any social media platforms or anything like that.' Why was he justifying his good parenting to the police officers, he wondered.

'I totally understand,' the elder of the two officers agreed. 'I have a son around the same age and my thoughts on phones for children are akin to yours. Could we take a look at the phone please, sir.'

'No, I'm sorry, you can't. My son lost it about two weeks ago. We've told him that he is not getting another one until he learns to take care of his property.'

'I see,' the officer said, feeling disheartened at yet another dead end in the case. 'Thank you for your time, sir.'

'No problem.'

The officers left the property knowing that they were no closer to finding this missing man. Now, which one of them was going to phone the missing man's partner to tell her the disappointing news; they would do rock, paper, scissors, to decide.

Back inside the Adams' home, Mrs. Adams was leaving with her car keys in her hand.

'Come on boys!' she shouted, 'Get dressed.'

'Just you head off to work, darling. I'll get the boys to school on time. I'll see you tonight,' Stuart Adams told his wife, kissing her on the cheek so as not to smudge her lipstick.

William and George Adams appeared downstairs, dressed in their school uniforms. Mr. Adams admired how smart his sons looked, especially when they wore their burgundy, Bancroft-Hain School blazers.

Chapter 33

After the positive news from Al the previous night that Dan was indeed on the candidates list, the news from the police about the phone was devastating. It seemed as though she was taking two steps forward, three back. What she needed was solid evidence that the police could use to open an investigation into Bancroft-Hain. Where on earth she would go from here, she had no idea. Perhaps she would wait to see if Dan got a chance to send another text message. Al had told her that they would talk at length tonight, so it was possible that he had cooked up another plan. All she could do was wait for his call. *When Al calls, I must remember to ask him if he managed to get the animals from Flamingo.*

As the day progressed, Victoria found herself really looking forward to speaking with Al. They had so much to talk about, as he hadn't given any of the details of the visit to Bancroft-Hain's school. All he had told her was that it was a disastrous success. She decided that she'd help Artie with his homework, get him fed, watered and bathed, then an early night may be on the cards for him. It was always easier to talk on the phone when there weren't any little, flapping ears around. Artie was a hoverer who liked listening for details of adults' conversations, then worried away on his misinterpretation of them.

The house was quiet and, lately, that was the way Victoria wanted it. Television no longer interested her. Why would it? She was living out a more complex, baffling drama than she could ever tune into on Netflix. She cared nothing for watching the news because there was only one piece of news she was interested in. Where was Dan?

Her idea for an early night for Artie had been a good one, because the moment his head rested on the pillow, he was asleep. That took away any pang of guilt that she may have felt about ushering him into his bed to get him out the way. She would never do that, but guilt had a funny way of pointing the finger at an innocent situation. Joni Mitchell was singing quietly in the background as she sat back on the sofa with her head resting on the back cushion. Dan despised Joni Mitchell, so it was the perfect time to play her music because when he came home, she would never play it again. Rather than putting on her pyjamas after her bath, she had slipped into her comfortable tracksuit. There was just something not right about being in pyjamas at seven o'clock, pyjama hour was nine and thereafter, in her opinion. With her phone on the coffee table where she could see it, she stretched out on the sofa, dangling her legs over the armrest. She allowed her mind to explore the possibilities of what Bancroft-Hain had to do with Dan's disappearance.

Only when a loud knock came from the front door, did she realise that she must have drifted off into sleep. Who could be visiting at this time, she wondered. Feeling slightly groggy, she wandered through to investigate her late-night caller. When she opened the front door, she almost wept with joy. It was Al.

'Al! What are you doing here in Edinburgh?' she screeched.

'I'm the new delivery man for Flamingo Toys,' he joked, bringing out three beautiful wooden animals that collapsed when you pressed the base.

Victoria didn't know whether to laugh or cry. Her emotions were hard to fathom but she was indisputably thrilled to see him. After she brought him into the hallway and closed the front door, she folded her arms around his neck and held on tight.

When the embrace ended, Al held Victoria by the shoulders, a serious look dominating his face.

'All the way from Cheltenham, I have been rehearsing what I want to say to you, but now I forget what I remembered to say, if you know what I mean. So, I'm just going to say what I feel and I'm sorry if it comes out wrong.'

Victoria stood transfixed, unsure of what was coming next. 'Go on.'

'I am in love with you. I know it sounds incredibly cliched, but I have no other words for it. I love you and I have never felt like this before. You have turned my life upside down and back to front and I absolutely love it. I feel alive for the first time ever and I think of you every waking and sleeping moment of every day and night since I first met you. I know that you are not mine to have but I couldn't possibly have kept this information to myself, it had to come out.'

Unexpectedly, even to Victoria, she leaned forward and kissed him with a forceful passion. She explored his mouth until she found his tongue. They kissed and kissed with full blown, lustful hunger. When it became unbearably sensuous, she led him through to her bed where they ripped at one another's clothes and made wild, uninhibited love.

They lay together, naked and spent, and although what had happened between them was unplanned, it was not unsurprising. It was possible that they had both committed the act several times in their own minds before it had become reality.

'Al, I'm not sorry that this happened tonight but we can't allow it to happen again. Dan is alive and I have to find him. Being anything other than friends will complicate things so badly. Do you agree?'

Al lay silent.

'You do understand that, don't you?' she asked, staring up at the ceiling.

'Yeah, but just let me enjoy things for a minute before I have to accept that it won't happen again.'

Victoria would have liked nothing more than to ask Al to sleep beside her all night, but there was Artie to think about. If Enid ever found out that she had a man in her bed in her son's absence, she would never speak to her again.

As though reading her thoughts, Al said, 'Before you start worrying about me expecting to stay overnight, don't. I've booked a hotel near here. Can we spend the day tomorrow?'

She pondered the idea for a moment, no, less than a moment. 'Definitely.'

Before opening the front door, she kissed Al gently on the lips. Passion, once again built up between them as they gripped tightly to one another.

'Okay, stop. You really have to go. I am so happy that you turned up at my door tonight. After a six-and-a-half-hour drive, I hope it was worth it,' she laughed.

Al turned serious. 'You'll mock me for saying this, but every time I'm with you, it's the best time of my life. Tonight surpassed everything that has gone before. You don't need to say it or feel it back, but I love you. I love you with every fibre of my being. You are all I want in the whole world.'

Tears flooded Victoria's eyes. So many words ran through her mind, but she said nothing.

Al stepped out onto the doorstep to leave, but turned to say, 'Is this how you treat all your toy delivery drivers?'

Chapter 34

Since the visit to The Bancroft-Hain School, Amanda had experienced what could only be described as night terrors. Vivid, distressing dreams had tormented her through the night and, on occasions, she had woken with an urge to vomit. Al had headed off to Scotland leaving her in charge of Cocoa Bean and she was thoroughly exhausted. Being happy and sociable to the customers was not coming naturally to her, and she found herself forcing a smile. Deep down in her stomach, she was suffering a constant dredging sensation which was affecting her appetite. Rightly or wrongly, the only thing she could think of to do was to text her ex-boyfriend, the policeman. The thought of spending one more night alone with her nightmares was unthinkable.

Jack, her ex, seemed more than happy to come over and spend a few nights with her and she was so grateful to him. His infidelity had wounded her deeply but now it was time for him to protect her. Had she not still loved him, she'd never have called him.

Since the visit to the school her mood had spiraled down into a dismal place. So, what had happened and how could she have suppressed it so deeply that all memory of it was erased? All she knew was that it was something to do with the girls' toilets near the entrance. And now, she wished that she had never stepped foot inside that mausoleum of a school.

She sat in her apartment, waiting for Jack to finish his shift and come over so that she wouldn't need to be alone. The fear that she had been experiencing would creep up on her without warning, but when Jack was there, she knew that she was safe.

Victoria climbed under the duvet of the disheveled bed. The essence of Al still radiated from the sheets and pillow, and it was intoxicating. She sniffed around the bedding until she found the strongest source of Al's smell and she buried her face in, inhaling deeply. There was no way she was going to change the bedding straight away, it was too good.
So far, there was no heavy burden of guilt or regret. She knew, of course, that it would probably come later. It hadn't been an act of revenge. On the contrary, Dan's infidelity had not even entered her head. It had happened in a moment of passion, and she knew exactly what she was doing, and it had been wonderful. Now, she felt excited to join him for breakfast at his hotel and hear all about how things had gone at the Bancroft-Hain School. In the morning, she would drop Artie at school and then head straight over to see him.

The hot jets of water felt great on Al's chest and head. There was nothing to beat a powerful shower and he made a mental note to himself to, no pun intended, splash out on a new shower in his house. Resting both hands on the tiles in front of him, he allowed the water to pound the flesh on his back for a deliciously long time. What a night he had just had with Victoria, possibly the best night of his life. She was something special, beautiful, funny and suited to him in every way. He was under no illusion that she could ever be his, but for now he was grateful that he had been given the chance to make love to her. He wondered how many times he had played out the scene in his mind, imagining her naked, lying on top of her, moving inside her; too many times to count.

Once he had helped her to find Dan, he would walk away into the sunset, never to see Victoria again. It was agony to think about, but it was the only outcome possible, and he had known that from the very start. For now, they would have to forget what had happened between them and return to being friends. Anything deeper was only storing up pain for him in the future.

He slid under the crisp, cotton hotel sheets and relived the events of earlier, which caused a stirring within him.

Chapter 35

Artie rose early and ran through to his mum's bed, scrambling under the duvet beside her. His little fingers removed a lock of her hair that lay across her face.

'Mummy,' he whispered. 'Mummy.'

Victoria slept.

'Mummy, there's a funny smell inside your bed.'

The words cut through her dream, making her throw back the duvet and leap from her bed.

'Come on you, let's get your Shreddies. Oh, and I have something nice for you.'

Artie bounced through to the kitchen shouting, 'What is it? Tell me? Tell me?'

'As soon as I get your breakfast, I'll show you what the postman brought.'

Into the blue bowl, Victoria counted out thirty Shreddies, just as she did every morning. She then poured milk in slowly until it covered ever little cereal square. A teaspoon of sugar leveled off flat with a knife was next and Artie watched with a critical eye to make sure she did everything just right.

'Sprinkle it evenly,' he shouted, as he watched his mum add the sugar to his Shreddies.

As soon as the cereal ceremony was over and Artie was happily tucking in, Victoria brought out the paper bag with the word Flamingo on the side. 'Here you are, little guy. I hope you like the choice of animals.'

Artie laid his spoon in the bowl to free up his hands to open the bag. First out was an anteater, which he studied from every angle. In order to try out the button on the base, he said, 'Tell the anteater to faint, mum.'

'Faint!' she shouted, pointing at the creature.

The anteater collapsed beautifully. Artie laughed, sitting the animal in front of him; yes, it was a keeper. Next out was a puma. Turning it around to inspect all sides, he then gave his mum the command.

Puma was another keeper and, so far, Artie approved of all the proportions.

Third out the bag was his favourite. A panda, proportions perfect, and which collapsed perfectly.

He returned to his Shreddies one happy boy, with the three wooden animals on the table in front of him, in height order.

When the school gate routine was complete, Victoria was excited to drive over to the Apex Hotel where Al was staying. They had so much to discuss about the Bancroft-Hain School visit and what the next steps could be. She hadn't even mentioned to him about the police tracking down the owner of the mobile phone that Dan had sent the text from.

We mustn't mention what happened last night. It was a one-time only occurrence, and it will never, ever happen again. We'll go back to how things were, great friends involved in the same investigation. Finding Dan is all that matters.

The receptionist at the Apex tried ringing the phone in Al's room to inform him that his friend, Victoria, was waiting. There was no reply. He advised Victoria to ring him on his mobile phone.

The mobile rang several times, but there was no response.

The manager agreed to escort Victoria to the room to check if Al was there. She could feel her stomach tighten with tension. Where was he? He had told her that he wouldn't go anywhere until she arrived; after all, he had no knowledge of the city of Edinburgh.

The manager knocked on the door, whilst Victoria stood two paces behind him. There was no reply. Her heart thudded as she watched the manager reach into his pocket to retrieve his skeleton key card. He gave one last resounding bang on the door with his fist. They could hear the movement of someone approaching. The door was then opened wide by Al, who was bare chested, and with only a white towel around his waist.

'Hi, what's going on?' he asked, surprised to see the official looking gentleman with Victoria hiding in the wings.

'We were unable to contact you by telephone, sir. It was just to let you know that your guest had arrived.' He stepped aside to allow Victoria to enter.

'I might have known that she was the one making all the fuss,' he laughed. 'Come into my boudoir and stop annoying everyone!'

The manager was unsure if he was joking or not, so he turned to Victoria saying, 'Will you be alright?'

'Yes, of course. He always acts like that. He's pretty harmless really.'

The manager left, leaving Victoria in the care of a half-naked man that she had sworn to herself she would never have sex with again.

It took no longer than a few minutes before they were in the hotel bed, completely naked, carrying on from where they had left off the previous night. It was urgent and passionate, with moments of meaningful tenderness. When it was over, she lay in his arms, as he caressed the soft skin on her arm. It felt good and although she hated to admit it, it felt right.

'Al, we can't…'

'I know, I know, you told me last night that we can't do this again. I get it, we won't,' he told her, kissing her gently and starting the arousal all over again.

It was lunchtime before they left the bedroom of the Apex Hotel. Victoria knew that she should have felt embarrassed and even ashamed, but she didn't. A real urge came over her to take Al's hand as they strolled into the city, but she resisted. It was the only thing that she had resisted since he arrived in Edinburgh. The sunshine was hazy, and the city was a bustling colony of foreigners. It pleased her to know that Al was getting to see the place at its very best. Their destination was George Street which ran parallel with Princes Street, with the best view of the castle. She absolutely had to show him it before they had lunch. It was the prize-winner of Edinburgh, as were the gardens below that lay below it.

They stood at the gold and green Ross Fountain in Princes Street Gardens. She studied Al's face as he looked up at Edinburgh Castle, perched on the unforgiving, sheer rock above. He was impressed, she could tell, and she loved it. Leaving the gardens by the sloping path up to the street above, she led him across the main road before heading down a side street to get them to George Street, where they could have breakfast.

As they walked past a window, she decided that she liked the look of Brown's brasserie and bar. They went in and, as good fortune would have it, there was a spare table with a view out onto the busy street.

Whilst holding hands under the table near the window, Victoria told Al how grateful she was for the wooden animals for Artie. She explained how particular he was about size, dimensions and display options. This made Al laugh, which pleased her because his smile was so attractive.

Al went on to describe the details of the appointment with Bandy Bain. He reached for his phone to show her the names on the candidate list, zooming in on the scored-out name of Dan McKelvie. It was obvious to them both what had been done to it.

'When I drive back later tonight, I'm going to sneak into the car park and check out the two lockups around the side of the school. Dan's car has to be somewhere, and Bandy Bain doesn't strike me as the kind of guy who could spray paint it, change the plates before selling it to a dodgy dealer. Bandy doesn't do anything outside of his little kingdom. His food is delivered and cooked for him and, as you may have noticed, he wears all his father's clothes. The school is his work, his home, his world. If Dan's car is anywhere, it's in one of those garages. Now, tell me how the police got on with tracing the owner of the phone that you received the message from.'

Victoria shook her head. 'It was a dead-end. It belonged to some kid who lost it somewhere.'

Something out of the window caught Victoria's eye causing her to feel concerned. Standing up, she told Al that she had to go out for a minute and that she would be back soon.

Wandering past the window of Brown's was Dan's father, Bob, looking very troubled. He had crossed over the street before doubling back the way he had come. Victoria ran out into George Street and headed in the direction she had seen him walking. Following behind, she quickened her pace to catch up with him. She ran at full pelt when she saw him aimlessly strolling out into the traffic.

'Bob!' she shouted. 'Bob!' He stopped dead in his tracks in the middle of the road, horns peeping impatiently around him. 'Bob!' As soon as she reached him on the road, she guided him to the safety of the pavement. 'You're okay, Bob. Let's just stand here for a moment.' Her heart was thudding. 'I'm going to take you home to Enid.' As soon as she mentioned *Enid*, he appeared less confused and began nodding.

'Yes, I would really like to go home to Enid.'

'Sit there for a moment, I have to make a call.' She guided him down onto the doorstep of an Italian restaurant.

First call was to Enid to let her know the situation and inform her that he was safe but confused.

'Don't worry, Enid, I'll bring him straight home,' she explained. It was clear that Enid had been beside herself with worry.

She then made a second call. 'Hi Al, my father-in-law has gotten a bit lost. I have him here but I'm going to take him home. I'm sorry to leave you alone with all that food and the chek. I'll have to pick up Artie from school after that. Safe journey home and thanks for everything.'

'No worries,' Al told her. 'I was pretty hungry anyway. Must have been all that exercise. See you.'

Fortunately, she was parked on the street at the rear of Scotland's First Minister's house. With one arm around Bob's waist, she led him to her car, which was, in fact, his car. Once she had pulled on his seatbelt, she headed round to the driver's seat.

Glancing over at the elderly man, who had once been a successful businessman, she noticed that he was crying like a lost child. She hugged him and told him he'd be home soon.

The front door of Bob's home was wide open when they arrived, and Enid stood waiting, her face furrowed with anxiety.

'He's fine, Enid,' Victoria assured her. 'I saw him from the window of Brown's in George Street, and he seemed a bit lost. He's okay now.'

'Come on, you silly billy. You're going to give me a heart attack,' she told him, kissing his cheek.

Bob gave an impish smile.

Enid turned to Victoria. 'He set off for a walk around the block about four hours ago. I was getting sick with worry. It's sheer luck that you found him. What were you doing in Brown's?'

'I was just meeting a friend for lunch.' That nasty delayed guilt began to jibe at her conscience.

'How lovely. Thank you for bringing the old boy home.' She then whispered, 'Things are getting steadily worse.'

Before she left to go and pick up Artie, Victoria said her goodbyes to the McKelvies.

Bob turned to her. 'You could go back and eat the food with Al.'

Never underestimate the memory of someone with dementia. He must have heard my conversation on the phone. She gave a nervous laugh and a feigned expression of confusion. 'Okay Bob. See you soon.'

Chapter 36

The Long and Winding Road would have been a fitting song for Al's journey home had it not been straight motorway practically the whole way. All he could do was turn up the music and lose himself in his thoughts, thoughts of Victoria and the deep, true love that he felt for her. How was he ever going to find a life partner when his heart would be forever filled with her? It was a depressing thought, so he pushed it from his mind, dwelled a little on the passionate sex between them, before moving on to a new topic. The coffee shop was the next item to be dissected. It had to go, for many reasons. It wasn't making any money and because he had come to despise it. It was stealing his life and, for what? To prove to his dead father that he was a success? He wasn't even achieving that goal. This brought him onto the subject of his parents and their death. Tomorrow, he would send a message to Gadhar Banik and arrange to meet him in London. He may not learn anything new, but it was worth a try. For some reason, he felt quite excited about meeting someone who had been so close to his father. In fact, it would be a fair comment to say that his father respected Gadhar more than he ever respected him, which was fair enough. He was just a wayward teenager, after all. Vivid memories returned to him of his father and Gadhar whispering and scheming and even falling silent when anyone entered the room. His mother didn't have the same relationship with Gadhar, which made him wonder if she ever felt excluded from things. He'd never know his mother's feelings as, from memory, she had no friends. Therefore, there was no one to ask. Her family was the only thing she focused on except for work, so he realised it must have been tough when he and Amanda returned to England.

Being so lost in thought meant that Al's journey passed with relative ease. It had given him a chance to really think some undisturbed thoughts and from this he had made a few important decisions. It was time to plan a different course for his life. The one he was on wasn't making him happy. First, he would explore new job prospects and then he would contemplate building a social life. The lonely lifestyle he had, which was filled with coffee-drinking old folk, no longer suited his needs.

It was late when Al arrived in Cheltenham but, as planned, he did not drive straight home. The street where Bandy Bain's school stood was a classic, leafy suburb with no traffic and spread out streetlighting. The fact that every one of the regency houses around was in darkness made him think that the residents were probably asleep in bed. It stood to reason that if you could afford a home on this street, you had either inherited it, a bit like himself, or you were old. Old neighbours tended to retire early for the night, which was good because he didn't want to be seen. The flip side of elderly neighbours was that they tended to be nosey curtain-twitchers, which was not so good, especially the old Mrs. Marple type. He'd just have to take his chances.

There was a bend in the road after the school and Al decided to drive on past this, so that his car could not be seen from the school. He spotted a perfect hiding place to park in, which was a darkened section directly between two lampposts, which limited the light. Also, in this favoured position was a particularly leafy oak tree which gave the car even more protection from any super sleuths in the neighbourhood.

All he wanted was a quick peek inside both lockups, just to check for Dan's car. They were probably locked but if he could shine the torch on his phone through a gap in the wooden door, then he'd be able to see if there was a vehicle inside. If there was then he would obviously have to investigate further to discover the model and the colour. Should the garages be empty, then he could walk away and forget all about it. He just had to know.

Staying close to the high walls of the elegant houses, he moved with stealth back around the bend towards the school. The headlights of a car approaching caused Al's heart to palpitate loudly. *Calm down. You haven't done anything yet. It's not an offence to creep along a road hugging the wall,* he told himself.

Beneath the shadow of a large tree, he stood perfectly still until the car had passed. To his knowledge, the driver hadn't seen a thing. When he reached the half wall, half railings surrounding the school property, he had to figure out the best way to scale it. It wasn't the height of it that worried him, it was the spear-shaped black metal points that he didn't fancy getting impaled on. If he walked in through the gate, he was wide open to being spotted from a window.

After a moment of thought, he decided to enter the garden next door to the school then climb over the wall into the playground. This meant that he avoided any injuries from metal spikes. Adrenaline flowed in rapids through his veins and Al had to admit that it felt good. He hadn't experienced thrills like this since his school days and it appeared to be awakening the dead core within him.

Once over the wall, he stayed still in the shadows for a few minutes, surveying all of the windows in the school for signs of life. Only when he was sure that all was quiet did he make his way over to the lockups. As predicted, they were securely padlocked but he could see that the wood panels making up the door had, over time, shrunk slightly, probably due to extremes in weather. The widest gap between the panels was low down to the left of the padlock. He knelt with his phone torch on and shone it through the inch and a half of space. Yes, he saw that there was a car inside the garage, but the colour and model were not clear. Shining the light on the back wall of the lockup, he noticed a small window. He needed a closer look, and that window would do nicely.

One more quick check of the windows in the school confirmed that they were still in darkness, which gave him the all-clear to creep around the back of the garage. He was just tall enough to be able to look through the glass, but the years of ingrained dust and dirt on the inside had made it impossible to see through. After coming this far, he wasn't going home without a result, so he removed his jacket, wrapped it around his hand and punched the hell out of the dingy little window. It really hurt but it got him the result he needed because when he shone his torch into the glassless space, he saw it. A red Volkswagen Scirocco. There were no doubts now. Dan's car was at the school, and Dan had to be somewhere in there too. Now they had something concrete to take to the cops, at last. He photographed it several times to show Victoria. If the old duffer decided to move it before the police got there, he would have the photographic evidence to prove its existence.

Maybe, he'd seen too many movies.

Chapter 37

The Rainy Day in Cheltenham.

Dan McKelvie glanced over at his partner, Victoria, who was sleeping in the passenger seat beside him. It had been a hell of a long drive from Edinburgh to Cheltenham, but it would be worth it. This was the first time he had taken Victoria away, just the two of them, since Artie had been born. He was fired up for the job interview he was attending the following morning but, if he was being completely honest, he was more excited to present the engagement ring to Victoria over dinner and ask her to be his wife, it had been a long time coming. He hadn't deliberately held off asking her for her hand in marriage, he had been sure of his love for her since their very first date. Money had been the obstacle to his proposal, until he made the decision to sell the items his grandfather had left him in his will. It hadn't been an easy thing to do because his nature had always been to hold on to objects of sentimentality, but the day he sold them to get money for the ring was a day that he would remember always. The lesson to be learned from the whole thing was that sometimes letting go of things could set you free.

Now here he was, almost at Cheltenham, with a two-day booking in the luxurious Queens Hotel. Tonight, they'd have an early night to ensure that he was sharp enough to sell himself as the best person for the job. After the interview, he would head back to the hotel where he had made a reservation for dinner. That's when he would pop the question and take the ring from his inside jacket pocket. In the weeks leading to the trip, he had rehearsed over a hundred times what he would say and how he would say it. It crossed his mind that having the waiter bring the ring to her on a silver tray might be quite romantic, but he wasn't sure. It had to be right, no, it had to be perfect.

When the barricade lifted to allow them to enter the hotel car park, Dan drove through and into the nearest space. This was going to be a trip that neither of them would ever forget. If it all went according to plan, their future would be a rose-filled garden of joy, providing she said yes, but he was pretty sure she would.

There was no need for dinner at the hotel when they arrived because they had grabbed a snack at the service station on the motorway when they had stopped to fuel up the car. Besides, it was late and if they forfeited dinner in the restaurant tonight, they would be able to afford champagne to celebrate the following night. At this point, Dan wondered if it would be advisable to let the staff in on the engagement secret, just to help create a celebratory atmosphere with music, clapping and cheering. *I wonder what a good song choice for the occasion would be. I'll try to find out Victoria's favourite song ever.* A very exciting picture was beginning to build in Dan's mind, and he could imagine the look on Victoria's face, especially because he wasn't exactly the most romantic guy in the world. She was going to love every minute of it, and they would be talking about it for years to come.

The hotel room that he had booked was perfect. It was situated at the side of the hotel, and it overlooked a colourful row of independent shops. *Victoria won't be able to resist the dresses in Citrus Clothing, and I'll put money on it that she goes into Cocoa Bean for a latte,* Dan thought, as he stood looking out of the window. A young man in an apron was cleaning the tables in the coffee shop and it made Dan wonder if having his own business like a coffee shop would have been a preferable career to teaching. Working in schools had its pros and cons, but over the past few years the behaviour of pupils was growing steadily worse, and he had no idea why.

Laying his case on the bed, he unzipped it and took out his navy-blue suit which was still on the hanger when he packed it. He unrolled his red silk tie and wound it around the neck of the suit, then took his new white shirt from its wrapping. His interview ensemble was hung up ready for the morning.

'I think I'm going to have a long hot shower, then I'm going to bed. I feel exhausted,' he told Victoria, who was lying on the bed looking at her phone.

'Oh no, it's not even eight o'clock. Come on, let's have one drink down in the bar before we settle in for the night… please.' Tossing her phone to one side, she made a pleading face with her hands in a prayer position.

Dan laughed. 'One drink, promise?'

'Promise,' she told him, holding up her girl guide sign with her fingers.

One drink led to two drinks, which led to three, then four. It was quarter to one in the morning before they headed up to the bedroom, a little more than tipsy. Dan knew that he was going to suffer in the morning, but what the hell, it had been worth it. They had talked and laughed, and, in his opinion, they were just like they had been in the early days. It kind of laid the red carpet for following night's proposal, and not only that, he had also found out that she loved Gladys Knight's Midnight Train to Georgia.

Cuddled together in the super king-sized bed, Dan desperately wanted to caress Victoria and have sex with her in a way that only alcohol and hotel rooms can unleash. His hand reached for her naked thigh, and he began rubbing it with force.

Victoria's hand closed around his. 'You have your interview in a few hours. Get some sleep and we'll make a night of it tomorrow,' she whispered.

As always, she was right, it *was* way too late, but they were definitely going to make up for it tomorrow.

Chapter 38

The rattle of heavy rain on the window and the thirst of a man in the desert were the factors that prompted Dan to open his eyes. Where was he? The unfamiliar room, the enormous bed, the headache...the interview! He propelled himself, flea-like from the bed and ran to the bathroom to sort himself the best he could in the minutes he had left.

Victoria sat up in bed. 'What's going on, Dan?' she asked, rubbing sleep from her eyes. Checking the clock on her phone, she suddenly realised why he was so manic. 'Oh Dan, this is terrible.'

Leaving the laces in his shoes untied, he ran over to her, kissed her forehead and told her he'd see her around five or six. He leapt the stairs two at a time and ran from the lobby to the car park. *Oh shit, shit, shit. You need a fuckin' token to get the barrier to rise.* The car door was left wide open as he bolted back into the hotel where the receptionist was helping an elderly lady with her sightseeing plans. He shifted from foot to foot. *I'm going to be late. Hurry up, some of us have commitments here.*

The attractive young woman on the reception desk sensed Dan's unrest and pre-empted his situation. Whilst continuing her conversation with the tourist, she slid a token across the desk.

'Thank you,' Dan said, snatching it up and leaving. When he climbed into the driver's seat, he realised that he didn't know the location of the school. The satellite navigation system in the car didn't work and he twigged that he didn't have his phone. *Shit, shit, fuck, shit. I must have left my phone plugged in next to the bed. No time to get it.* With haste, he sped out onto the main thoroughfare and decided he would stop the lady who was preparing to cross the road. Rolling the window down, he shouted, 'Excuse me, can you tell me how to get to The Bancroft-Hain School, please.'

The middle-aged lady paused for a moment to get her bearings. 'Straight down that road,' she said pointing in the direction. 'Then second left and first right. You should then see it on your left-hand side.'

'Thank you,' Dan shouted, giving her a small salute, two fingers raised to his forehead.

Oh dear, the lady realised, walking on. *It's actually third left, then first right.*

It wasn't long before Dan found that the nice lady's directions were awry, and he had to circle round a few times before asking a man this time. It added valuable minutes to his journey, but he finally entered the grounds of the school, screeching to a halt in a visitor's parking space. Grabbing his suit jacket, he ran in the torrential rain towards the main entrance, where he met a suited man who told him that he had left something in his car. *Phew, there's some other guy just as disorganised as me.*

A woman of way past retirement age greeted him from the open office.

'Sorry I'm late,' he told her.

'Don't worry about it. Name please.'

'Dan McKelvie.'

The secretary checked the list of names, saw Dan's on it and told him to go to the far end of the corridor where he would see a sign for the gymnasium. 'There will be coffee and digestive biscuits laid on free of charge,' she told him. Delighted that he made it with moments to spare, Dan walked along the corridor, passing the full-length portrait of whom he presumed was Bancroft-Hain. *He looks pleased with himself,* he thought, as he took a moment to study the pompous expression on the headmaster's face. A gurgling noise erupted from his stomach at that moment, which he presumed was a result of the alcohol he'd consumed the previous night. Quite suddenly, he felt a desperate need to force his buttock cheeks together and hold on for grim death. There was no doubt about it, he needed to get to the nearest toilet, fast. Unable to run, he minced along the corridor until he saw a sign which read 'Girls' Toilets'. A handwritten message had been taped below saying that visitors' toilets were further down the hallway. He paused momentarily to debate whether or not he would make it further down the hallway. A sound resembling gun fire blew off within his lower belly, which answered his question. The girls' toilets were the only option.

The candidates milled around in the gymnasium, drinking coffee and introducing themselves to one another, or more accurately, comparing themselves with one another. On the surface it was a pleasant get-to-know-you half hour before the main talk from Mr. Bancroft-Hain. Some of the candidates felt like they were being analysed by the headmaster as he sat at a desk in the middle of the room with his laptop open. Many of them were curious as to what he was looking at on the screen. Was he watching how they interacted with one another?

The half hour was almost up, and all the men stopped mingling when they heard the screech of chair legs being moved on the gym floor. It may not have been obvious to everyone, but one of the interviewees, Ben Gibb, noticed that the colour had drained from Bancroft-Hain's face.

'I must apologise to everyone here, but an emergency has arisen, and I will need to attend to it. Talk amongst yourselves and I will be back with you as soon as possible.' He then snapped his laptop closed and ran like the school was ablaze.

Dan felt as though he had lost half of his body weight down the toilet. It had been horrendous, but he felt better for it. Before he left the cubicle to wash his hands, he decided that it would be good manners to check the underside of the toilet seat for… well, putting it politely, unsightly splashes. He attempted to lift the seat, which happened to have unusually strong sticking pads holding it down. Should he leave it, he pondered at this point. No, he had to be considerate to the young girls who would be using the toilet after him. Giving it a yank, he managed to release the seat from the china bowl. He stared in down in utter disbelief.

'What the fuck?'

He ran to the next cubicle, it was the same. Kicking open the stall door of the end cubicle, he saw the same shocking sight, yet again. Every toilet in the row had been fitted with pretty high tech, as far as he could tell, cameras. 'The old fucking pervert,' he said aloud, reaching for his phone to call the police. *Oh shit! I left my phone at the hotel. I'll make a call from the office.*

Bancroft-Hain made it into the girls' toilets, in what he would refer to as, the nick of time. The candidate was just leaving when he met him at the toilet door. The late interviewee had given him a vile stare, then started to say, 'I know what you've...' but a quick, unexpected jab to the neck soon solved that little problem. The synthetic opioid, etorphine, put him in a catatonic state quicker than he could have hoped. It was only the second time he had used the new drug, and he had to admit that it was way more efficient than previously used agents.

Dragging him to the basement had been physically exhausting; after all, he was a dead weight. It was also time consuming, time that he couldn't spare, because he had several men waiting in the gymnasium for their interviews.

The basement was accessed by a door in a walk-in cupboard, just off the main hall. When Bancroft-Hain opened the door to throw the intruder down the flight of stairs, he made a mental note to disguise the door with a unit of shelves, perhaps for storing cleaning products. Florence, the cleaner, would now be forbidden from accessing the cupboard without being accompanied by him. For security reasons, he had already taken on board all the toilet cleaning duties himself. It would just take for some busybody to do what the candidate had done and lift the toilet seat to discover his surveillance equipment. That simply wouldn't do.

Before heading back to the gym to introduce himself to the men and give them the history of the school, he hurried down to the foot of the stairs to where his captive lay. Thinking on the hop, he decided to take the precaution of binding and gagging the man. It had been a young girl he previously used the drug on, and the effects had lasted a fairly lengthy period; however, this was a full-grown man, and he may not be stay sedated for the duration of the interview process.

Chapter 39

When he regained consciousness, there was no part of Dan McKelvie's body that did not hurt. His mouth and throat had the texture of sandpaper making it impossible to swallow, although there was no available saliva to gulp down anyway. Searing pains shot through his head causing him to wince when he moved. In all of his life, he had never felt so painfully uncomfortable. Confusion muddled away at his thoughts as he tried to piece together why he was at the foot of a flight of stairs in a damp cellar, bound and gagged. His mind tried to line up the events leading to this conclusion. Running late, taking the wrong turn, entering the school, the painting, yes, the hideous full-length portrait, upset stomach, girls' toilets… Oh yes, now he understood, the cameras hidden within the toilet bowls. A bolt of fear mixed with revulsion shot through him when he remembered coming face to face with the man in the painting, Mr. Bancroft-Hain. That was the last thing he could see in his memory.

The cellar was lit, albeit poorly, not from electric lighting but by a small window encased in black railings. Dan could barely move, but he could see that the window was inches above the ground. He watched the torrents of rain outside bounce off the painted hopscotch markings on the tarmac. The window was no bigger than an A4 sheet of paper, but he was grateful for the glimpse of outside and the fact it kept him from darkness.

There was no way of telling time, but it seemed like hours had passed without a sound or movement outside the four walls of his prison. The discomfort of the tight ropes around his wrists and his raging thirst, which was exacerbated from the gag over his mouth, were almost unbearable for Dan to endure.

When a murmur of distant voices became audible, he awoke or gained consciousness again, he wasn't sure which. The muffled sound brought him to his senses, and he saw that it may be an opportunity to attract attention. Scanning around the spartan space, he saw tins of paint standing together in the corner. He shuffled over to them and began kicking at them furiously with his feet bound together. The cans were almost empty and made no more than faint tinny clanks as they hit off the wall. The cellar he was in was a concrete room clearly in the bowels of the building. He had been stupid to think that a few rattling tins of paint was going to bring forth a saviour. It emotionally crushed him to hear the voices becoming louder as they approached the space above him.

Then, because of the tiny ground level window, where he couldn't actually see cars leaving, he *could* hear the starting of engines. That could only mean people heading off in the direction of their comfortable homes and loving families. This begged the question of how long Bancroft-Hain intended to keep him from Victoria and Artie?

The concluding section of the interview had been a tour of the school for the candidates. Bancroft-Hain proudly led them round his own little fiefdom, boasting of the achievements gained by the pupils over the years. He paused at the portrait of his father, strategically placing himself in front of the Beavis and Butt-Head sticker on his shoe. Holding up his hand for the men to stop behind him, he gathered them around to give the well-worn speech that he had given to prospective parents over the years.

'The day would not be complete without me telling you about my beloved father, who had the vision to open this wonderful school. Without him, we would not be standing here in this spot today. Many years ago, he took the bold step of offering children something more than the mediocre education that was supplied by the state. It still stands firm today and should be the forefront of the mind of the new head who will replace me. Here at Bancroft-Hain ,we endeavour to give equality and respect to all...'

Bancroft-Hain continued talking about the path of greatness that the school had forged out through the years. It was twenty minutes of blowing the Bancroft-Hain trumpet loud and clear to his captive audience. During the course of the day, he had made a note of the candidates that he would like to return for a second interview.

'If I announce your name,' he told the men, relishing the power he held over them, 'then I would very much like you to join me tomorrow for a second interview. If your name is not called, then I'm afraid it's the end of the road and I wish you well.'

The men stood waiting to hear if they would be returning or if they had a one-way ticket out the door. They stood, nervously staring at their shoes. This was not like any interview process that any of them had gone through before. This was Bancroft-Hain's system, designed to either humiliate you or fill you with gratitude.

There was a deliberate pause before announcing the first name. Bancroft-Hain was extracting the last dregs of power from the situation and relishing every minute of it. Inside, he was scoffing at the faces of the promotion-hungry men, before putting them out of their misery.

The crest-fallen losers made their way out to the car park, knowing that they'd be going home to continue their search for a promoted post.

The remaining four candidates hung around for their next instruction. One of the men shook hands with Bancroft-Hain, thanking him profusely. The others followed suit, wishing that they had thought of doing that first.

Chapter 40

Blood oozed from the rope burns on Dan's wrists; the pain was excruciating. Dehydrated as he was, he still felt the need to urinate, although he was contemplating just letting it go. His thoughts switched from escape plans to the prospect of staring death in the eyes and then to his love for Victoria and whether he had told her often enough how he felt. What must she be thinking? Would she even look for him? Did she feel abandoned?

Being left to rot in a cellar was a terrifying thought and he wondered just how long it would take for him to pass away. His wounds were bleeding, but he wasn't losing enough blood to end his life. How many days could a human last without water, he wondered. The last liquids to enter his body were on the previous night, and that was alcohol which he knew was a diuretic. Hazarding a guess, he decided that he would live for around three or four more days. Victoria once again haunted his thoughts and the look on her face when he told her about his drunken betrayal. How could he have risked everything that was precious to him for an embarrassing fumble with a woman he didn't even find attractive.

'Victoria,' he said aloud, in the darkness of the stone room. 'Beautiful, perfect, Victoria. I didn't deserve you but if I live, I will cherish you forever.' The sentiment brought tears to his eyes, which soon turned to sobs, partially due to his vulnerable state.

Dan opened his eyes and lifted his head from the wall it was resting on. Was that someone coming to help him? A door nearby was opening and there were footsteps on the stairs leading down to where he lay; it was too dark to see. 'Hello,' he rasped from his shriveled voice box. 'Help. I'm down here.'

There was no reply from the person who was now at the foot of the stairs. Straining to see in the poor light which was now supplied by the streetlight outside the school railings, he could only make out the outline of his silent visitor. He knew without doubt that it was his captor. A chilling sensation spread from his scalp to his spine, and he felt certain that he was going to be murdered.

Bancroft-Hain stood with assorted items in his arms. Towering above Dan, he looked down upon the wreck of a man who believed it was acceptable to destroy his life. Had he not moved hastily, this apology of a human would have alerted the police, who in turn would have misread the situation. It would have been the end of him, the school, and the good name of Bancroft-Hain. His father's words returned to his mind, words he had never forgotten. Trust no one.

'Mr. Dan McKelvie, I believe. I am Mr. Bancroft-Hain, headmaster and son of the founder of this wonderful school. I believe you know why you're here and I'm sure that you will come to understand that I had no option but to detain you.'

Dan was now fighting for his life. 'If it's about the cameras you've installed in the girls' toilets then I can assure you that I won't tell anyone. You have my word on that.' His throat ached from saying the words; the metallic taste of blood flooded his mouth.

'Be that as it may, Dan McKelvie, I simply can't take a chance on that desperate promise. I noticed on your application form that you reside in Edinburgh, Scotland and you have no spouse, which leads me to believe that there may not be anyone looking for you, which is good.'

Dan tried to tell him that he was wrong and that there would be plenty of people looking for him, but he had no words left to come out. There was no saliva and his throat had closed. His head hung on his shoulders, his posture that of a beaten man. The wounds on his wrists and ankles wept, the pain was such that it wiped out the humiliation of his wet trousers.

'I'm no killer, Mr. McKelvie, you'll be glad to hear, but I have no problem with letting you die slowly from natural causes because, technically, I won't have murdered you, well not in the same vein as sticking a knife in you or shooting you. Let's just say that nature will decide your fate.'

Lifting his head slowly, Dan glanced at Bancroft-Hain. His eyes were adjusting to subdued light, and he could just make out the expression on the man's face. *He's a fucking nutcase. I am not dealing with a normal person here.*

'So, firstly, I have a cushion for you to lay your head on. I also have two sets of handcuffs, one for hands and one for feet. These ropes look terribly uncomfortable and I'm sorry for that, but you have to understand that I had not prepared for such an eventuality. It would be fair to say, my hands were tied.' He laughed heartily at this opportune little joke arising. 'Anyway, where were we, I have water for you, but I must ration it to one small bottle per day. I don't have any foody snacks as such because my meals are all brought in to me by Hildegard Koch. She has been my cook and helper for, oh, let me think, how long has Hilde been with me… it must be over twenty years. I can't believe it.' He looked down at Dan, who was struggling to cough, then swallow. 'Oh listen to me reminiscing when you look like you need a drink.' Unscrewing the lid of the water bottle, he held it to Dan's lips.

The water entering Dan's mouth was like the sweetest nectar. He desperately wanted to gulp down the whole bottle, but this would have been unwise after being told that he would only have one bottle a day. He held some water in his mouth to ease the dryness before swallowing; it felt really good, although insufficient.

'As I was saying, Hilde brings my dinner each night and you can understand that she would become suspicious if I asked for two dinners each night. That said, I can suggest that she bulks up her portions somewhat. My point here is, Dan, I'm afraid that you'll have to settle for my leftovers. That will be your only meal as I can't go smuggling food and sneaking around during the day when the children are around. It's the best I can do for you.'

Dan wanted to ask how long he was intending to keep him down in the cellar, but he couldn't bear to hear the answer. Instead, he thought he'd try a little psychology and probe as to whether he thought his father would approve of the cameras in the toilets. It was obvious that Bancroft-Hain held his father in the highest esteem, perhaps a small twang at the conscience might bring him to his senses. It possibly hadn't occurred to him that his father could be looking down with disapproval.

'Do you think your father would approve of you watching your pupils in an indecent way?' Dan managed to ask, now that he had been hydrated.

From nowhere, an unexpected fist flew into Dan's face, knocking his jaw from its hinge. His back tooth swung loose.

'How dare you mention my dear father. You are not fit to lick his boots clean. He would be proud of my initiative and savvy. When I was a boy, he showed me how to watch the girls in the toilet using a series of peepholes. How far I have come from that with the use of technology, in which, I might add, I am completely self-taught. Yes, my father would be in awe of how I have developed the school and brought it into the modern age.'

Okay, now I'm certain of what I'm dealing with here, a complete maniac. I will have to choose my words more carefully and befriend him if I want to survive.

A searing pain shot through Dan's jaw, travelling up his face, causing him to wince. 'Yes sir, I believe you're right and I apologise for my question, I was just curious.'

Bancroft-Hain looked down at the wet staining around Dan's crotch. 'I see you've had an accident. I may be able to supply you with some pyjama trousers belonging to my father. My apologies for not supplying a bucket but as I told you earlier, I had no time to prepare. We will try to figure things out as we go along and face each hurdle as it comes. Now, let's get these ropes changed, handcuffs are much more suited to the job.'

At this point, Dan realised that there was going to be a few minutes where his feet were untied, or his hands were free. Could he take Bancroft? He was a big guy, but he was at least thirty years his senior. Dan was strong, he coached the rugby team, but he was well under par at the moment. Free hands meant he could fight, but not run, free legs meant he could run but not fight. Bancroft may not, as he put it, be a killer, but he served up a hell of a right hook. It had left him, he believed, with a fractured jawbone. Was it worth another injury? He decided not, besides, he didn't have the energy to run and what if the door at the top of the stairs was locked. No, he would wait for his moment, after he had befriended his captor.

Chapter 41

Feeling grateful for small mercies, Dan had to admit that the handcuffs were much more comfortable than the tight hessian ropes. The pillow made sleeping a bit easier and the bottle of water was his lifeline. Teaspoon sips was all he would allow himself to drink and that was only when his throat burned with thirst. Bancroft's father's pyjama trousers had once been brushed cotton with a striped pattern; the brush and the stripes had been long since washed away. However, Dan was pleased to have a pair of dry trousers regardless of what they looked like. His evening meal of leftovers had consisted of a boiled potato, a cooked carrot and a piece of gristle which had once been attached to some type of meat. The vegetables were devoured but it stuck in Dan's craw to chew on another man's gristle, although he was open to the fact that it may come to that, but he wasn't there yet.

The smell of the rubbery piece of fat on his plate was making him feel nauseous, so he pushed it to the far side of the room. The salty vegetables had left him thirsty, but he was aware of how long he needed to make his water last. Just one sip, he decided, before he settled down for the night.

It was remarkable how appreciative of the trivial things you become when everything has been stripped away, he thought, as he lay with his head on the pillow, looking out of the small window which supplied just enough light to comfort him. Lying on the hard ground in pitch darkness would have been difficult to endure. Memories came to him of how much he hated the dark when he was a boy.

His father told him stories at night, and then his mum would lie next to him until he slept. It was so kind of her to do that, he reflected, although maybe she relished the ten-minute sleep before she sat down for the evening. Thoughts of Artie came to the forefront of his mind. Precious, little Artie, with his peculiar ways. *I need to spend more time with my son. As soon as I get out of here, I am going to take him places and teach him things and just hold him.* Dan broke down sobbing. His family were his world and all he wanted was to see them again and make up for the times he felt that he had failed them. Tomorrow would possibly hold an opportunity to escape, but it would be a case of careful treading.

The sound of car engines outside and the scraping hunger in his belly woke Dan from his sleep. His dreams had been of Victoria, Artie, and home, but the reality of his situation soon caved in on him when he sat up and looked around. Loud growls came from his stomach, so much so that he eyed the gristle on his plate from the previous night. Using his cuffed hands, he lifted the chewy article but promptly tossed it back onto the plate. He was still of the same opinion, he'd never eat another man's gristle. Instead, he settled for a sip of water.

It dawned on him that it must be the day of the final interviews. The thought of waiting until nightfall before getting food and water was a heavy yoke to carry. Peeing in the bucket, when you're handcuffed and you have a ridiculous little rope holding your pyjama trousers up, was another inconvenience. Fortunately, he was so dehydrated, he hardly needed to go at all.

Later in the day, he heard a car leave the grounds. Shortly after, another drove off, followed by another. He figured that the short-list was possibly made up of four men, certainly no more than five. Bancroft-Hain should be with the successful candidate by now and judging by the light outside, it was probably nearing teatime. What scraps would he be given tonight, he pondered. Truth was, he couldn't care what was on offer, he was ravenous. The pain in his jaw had worsened but it wouldn't stop eating whatever was put before him.

The sound of footsteps stirred him. There was an element of fear in Bancroft's visit because the man was most definitely unhinged. Strangely enough though, Dan found himself feeling excited to see him. The loneliness, thirst and hunger were affecting him, and it had only been two days. He prayed that the scraps would be plentiful enough to stop him feeling so faint. He wrestled with different thoughts that infiltrated his mind, thoughts that all led to one question. Was this to be his final resting place?

At the top of the stairs, the looming figure of Bancroft-Hain appeared. The man was a caricature of a bygone age. Although he assured Dan that he was not a killer, it did not stop him being a frightening, unpredictable human being. The hours that Dan had been left alone gave him time to think, and he had come to the conclusion that he probably wasn't the first person to be taken down into this abysmal space. Evidence of this was a small pink hair clasp that he had spotted on the floor near where he lay. It was also apparent that Bancroft's father was as much a deviant as he was; in fact, his father probably taught him all he knew.

Bancroft-Hain descended the stairs with a small bottle of water and a plate containing meagre scraps. The plate was laid on the floor beside Dan, the way in which an owner would set down food for a dog. He then thrust the water into his hand. 'Don't forget to make it last. Sips Dan, just take sips.'

Despising his gaoler with everything that was in him, he played the only game he knew could help him. 'Thank you so much. I had just finished the other bottle, so you arrived at the perfect time.' He smiled like he didn't have a care in the world.

'I have some very interesting news for you, Dan McKelvie.'

Dan's first thought was, *is he letting me go?*

'I was interviewing my short-list of candidates earlier, and what an impressive group of men they were too. Actually, it was difficult to decide as to who would be the best to take over my position…'

Cut to the chase you old bastard and tell me what the news is.

'I was completely torn between two outstanding young men. Anyway, that is all irrelevant now because I have decided not to retire at this present moment. I thought I'd wait until, well until, I no longer had this situation with you living here in my cellar.'

Is he saying what I think he's saying? Is he waiting until I die before he can retire? Fear-fueled adrenaline raced through his entire body, but he kept his emotions intact.

Bancroft-Hain continued with his story. 'Be that as it may, I wanted to tell you about this interesting, rather comical thing that happened during the interviews. An attractive woman came hurtling through the door of the gymnasium, shouting that her partner had disappeared. She was desperate, actually quite hysterical. We were all aghast. I led her through to the office and told her that there was no record of you ever having applied for the job. She left with the knowledge that you had lied to her and had probably left her to start a better life elsewhere.' Laughter erupted from his florid face.

This was more than Dan could stand. Inside, something broke. He wondered if it was possible to snap your soul in two, because that was exactly how he felt; broken-souled. His nonchalant act was becoming increasingly more difficult to keep up, but he stuck with it. That pig of a man was not going to beat him. Then he surprised himself by laughing along with Bancroft.

As soon as Bancroft-Hain saw Dan laughing, the smile dissipated from his face. 'Is this woman not your common law wife?' he asked in confusion.

Dan continued to laugh, a little too uncontrollably. 'No, she is just some woman that has been stalking me. Man, she follows me everywhere. I can't get free of her.'

A look of disappointment replaced the joy on Bancroft's face. He had been looking forward to giving Mr. McKelvie the news and now it was worthless.

'Thanks for not telling her anything. Maybe she'll leave me alone.' *This guy is one twisted fuck,* he thought, reading his crestfallen look.

Bancroft-Hain left the room shortly after this exchange, as it hadn't gone the way that he had hoped.

Dan reached for the bottle of water first. *Don't gulp, don't gulp,* he warned himself, because all he wanted to do was gulp. Next, he reached for his dinner, which had been at one time a plate of mince and potatoes. All that remained was a spoonful of mash and the carrots from the mince. He presumed that Bancroft wasn't fussy for carrots because they had been left for him two nights in a row. In all, he managed to scrape together three small forkfuls. It was cold and inadequate, but he thought it tasted hell of a good.

Chapter 42

The following morning, Dan awoke to the sound of children shouting and laughing. His dreams had taken him far, far away from the dingy cell where he now lived. Children were playing with a ball directly outside the A4 sized window and he hoped they would look in and see him. It was so bright looking out, but he knew that it would be too dark to see anything inside. Reaching for his fork from last night's dinner, he hurled it up at the window with his handcuffed hands. It struck the glass hard but not one child turned in response to the clatter. Then rearranging the paint tins into a pyramid shape, he climbed onto them, but as dizziness came over him, he lost his balance, crashing to the stone floor. His hip hurt from the fall, but he wasn't done yet. Hopping, with feet together, he bounced up the flight of stairs cautiously. Having his hands cuffed together meant that he had no way of holding on for safety. The plan was to force the door open by using his shoulder.

The regency school building was built around 1820, and it was built to last, even the heavy panelled doors. It didn't matter how many times he rammed himself against the door, it was only his shoulder he dented. He had to face the fact that unless he had an opportunity to overpower Bancroft-Hain, he was trapped in the room, with no escape.

The thought of his beautiful, loving Victoria coming to the school to look for him was overwhelming. Tears filled his eyes at the image of her running frantically into the gymnasium to ask about him, and all Bancroft-Hain did was laugh about it. The dark hatred he felt in his core for that dreadful man was nothing he had ever experienced before. His feelings towards the man were not for the treatment he had received but for the lack of empathy and compassion he had shown towards Victoria, a loving and loyal person.

The children played at breaktime, then left at home time. Meanwhile, he sat alone with his thoughts, sipping his precious water. He imagined icy cold, running water pouring from the tap and him drinking, drinking, drinking his fill. It was enough to make him pick up his bottle and sip another drop. The sky outside was still light, so he knew that dinner time was quite a way off. The sky had to darken before Bancroft would come to him. What would his scraps be tonight?

Bancroft appeared at the top of the stairs at his usual hour, in his usual manner. There was a deliberate pause before coming down. Was this a way of teasing Dan, knowing full well that he would be hungry, and his water would be finished. Yes, Dan believed it to be a power-pause, a way of announcing himself and the importance of his visit. Bancroft sat the dinner plate of paltry scrapings on the floor beside him. Dan stared at them ravenously. The bottled water was then placed into his hands. His stomach told him to get his face down into the plate and hoover up the leftovers, but his pride warned him not to touch them until the odious man had left.

He decided to make conversation, like nothing was going on here. 'So, Mr. Bancroft-Hain, any more visits from that ridiculous woman who appears to be following me?'

'Thankfully, no. I think we've seen the last of her,' Bancroft said, taking a seat on the bottom step.

He searched his mind for another question to ask the man. 'How do you feel about your decision not to retire? Are you disappointed or relieved?'

Bancroft-Hain stared at Dan.

Instinctively, Dan began to panic, had he offended him? Was that the wrong question to ask? He kept an eye on Bancroft's fist, it had a way of coming up and striking when least expected. Bancroft rose to his feet, making Dan feel nervous. The imposing figure of sheer madness hovered over him. Without saying a word, he stood for a few moments looking down upon him like he was some bothersome insect.

'It's only a matter of time, young man,' he said chillingly, before climbing the stairs, leaving the through the door and bolting it behind him.

Like the days that had gone before, Dan was left alone. He knew that it would be twenty-four hours before he saw the man again. *Forming any kind of bond with this nutcase was going to be impossible,* he decided, as he reached for his dinner. The evening's menu was fish fingers, minus the fish. There were only a few breaded casings left. As a side, to accompany the fish finger coatings, were some chips, not the kind of chips with potato in the centre but the black, crispy kind that have been lying at the bottom of the chip pan from a previous serving. Dan ran his finger along the orange-coloured juice on the plate, confirming what he had suspected. Baked beans had originally been there. The days that followed, saw Dan becoming quite ill from lack of food and a lack of cleanliness to the open wounds on his wrists and ankles, to say nothing of his suspected broken jaw which was causing him extreme discomfort. The handcuffs to his legs and wrists had made a difference but the areas of broken skin continued to weep. It would have been his heart's desire to pour cold water over the inflamed flesh, but it was impossible. His head throbbed from the dehydration he was suffering as it was. Water could only be used for drinking and basically keeping him alive.

Chapter 43

Even with the rope belt on Dan's pyjama trousers tied as tightly as he had the strength to achieve, they still fell to his ankles when he stood up. Weight was dropping off him day by day and he felt lethargic and weak. As he waited for Bancroft-Hain to bring him his food, he decided that he was no longer above eating another man's gristle. It was nearing the hour when his captor would arrive, and he listened intently to every sound above him. Was that distant footsteps, he wondered, propping himself up to enable him to hear with both ears. There were footsteps but they stopped, then after a few moments, they began again. It was definitely Bancroft's feet making the noise; after all, he had heard them often enough. Why had he stopped? Any change to the usual routine unsettled him.

The door at the top of the stairs opened and Bancroft stood, water bottle in his tweed jacket pocket, plate in one hand and something else in the other. The light was too dim to see what he had, but it was certainly intriguing him. Did he stop to pick it up in the corridor, Dan wondered. Bancroft-Hain studied the object as he made his descent and Dan tried to analyse the seemingly confused look on his face. Suddenly, the object illuminated, and it became obvious that it was a phone. Dan's spirits soared, his body felt temporarily regenerated and his mind focused on how he could get a hold of it.

Sniffing the air in the room, Bancroft screwed up his pompous face. 'What an unbearable stench,' he announced, setting the plate and phone on the bottom step. 'I can only presume that your bowels have moved since I last saw you.'

'Yes, Sir,' he said, trying not to look at the phone. 'It is the first time it's happened in here. I am finding the air down here quite intolerable and I'm not sure I'll be able to enjoy my dinner with the smell lingering around.'

Gazing down into the bucket, Bancroft-Hain shook his head. 'I find that cleanliness is one of the greatest virtues. It has been neglectful of me not emptying your toilet, although it is not a job I relish.' Lifting the handle of the black bucket, he turned his head away from the odour and headed to the stairs. So full was the makeshift toilet that it splashed a little as he walked. 'Darn it!' he shouted, every time this happened.

As soon as he left through the door, Dan reached for the phone, putting in Victoria's number. He checked the bars at the top of the phone and saw that there was no signal. A text would be the best way to make contact, he decided. It would get through eventually. He typed a short message, saying, 'V it's me', letting her know that he was alive, and then pressed send. The clicking of footsteps above him began as the old man was returning.

When Bancroft stood at the top of the stairs, he looked down and saw Dan ravenously scoffing the dinner of one boiled potato and pork chop fat. He returned the bucket to the spot under the window, handed over the bottle of water from his pocket and reached for the phone which lay on the step. As soon as he lifted it, it rang, giving him quite a start.

Showing no reaction, although his heart had now jumped into his mouth, Dan continued to chew on Bancroft's gristle.

'Hello,' Bancroft said, 'Hello, can I help you?'

Dan knew instinctively it was Victoria. *Please don't say anything. Please don't say a word.*

'Hello, is there anybody there?'

Good girl. I love you.

Chapter 44

The police took seriously the news of Dan's car being in a lockup at The Bancroft-Hain School. They acted immediately on the information and two officers headed straight over to speak to Mr. Bancroft-Hain. It was early afternoon when the police car parked outside the school. As the two officers walked across the playground, they saw happy children playing hopscotch and football.

It was noted by both officers that although Mr. Bancroft-Hain was surprised to see them, his feathers were not ruffled in the least. On the contrary, he seemed pleased to welcome them into his study for a chat. The elderly lady in the office was instructed to bring tea for them and a plate of digestive biscuits appeared on the tray beside the teapot. It was highly civilized, the female officer thought. Bancroft-Hain played mum with tea pot and offered the biscuits to both officers, ladies first.

'To what do I owe the pleasure of this visit?' he asked them.

The young male officer sat forward in his seat, with the china teacup and saucer in his hand. 'We wondered if we could take a look in the lockup around the back of the school?' he asked.

'Oh, yes, please do. I was meaning to call you about that. A couple of weeks ago, I found a car abandoned on my school property. It's not the first-time strangers have parked their cars out there, without permission, to go to the shops or restaurants nearby. I find it inconvenient and quite frankly annoying,' Bancroft said, feigning a little outrage.

'Yes, I can see how that would be irritating. Some people just don't think.'

'Well,' Bancroft continued, having thought up a story on the hop. 'I didn't do anything for a couple of days and then I thought to myself, right, if they are going to disrespect me and my school, then I will give them the fright of their lives. So, I pushed the car into the lockup where it couldn't be seen to ensure that the owner had to contact me to retrieve it. They didn't come back and if I'm being completely honest, I forget all about the damn contraption. You see, I myself am not a driver.'

'I see,' the male cop said, buying the perfectly plausible story.

'If you finish your tea, I'll take you out to see it. In fact, it would be very helpful if you could arrange to have it towed away. I need that lockup space for storage.' Bancroft knew without a shadow of doubt that they had completely believed his explanation.

The police left The Bancroft-Hain School having arranged for a tow truck to remove the car from the lockup. They thanked Bancroft for the tea and asked him to get in touch if the owner returned.

Using his last ounce of reserved energy, Dan shouted with all of his might for help when he saw Bancroft-Hain and two police officers walking past the window. They were so close at one point, he could have reached out and touched them, but they heard nothing. He dry wretched when he saw the animated, smiling Bancroft engaging with the cops. By the look on their faces, he could see that they thought he was nothing more than a quaint, old eccentric.

223

Chapter 45

Amanda was happy to have Jack living with her for the time being. Going to sleep at night when you're not alone, was a much-needed security blanket. Waking up traumatised and having someone to hug away your night terrors was comforting. Yes, he had hurt her, badly, but she needed him and that meant forgiving him. Perhaps if she asked him why he cheated on her when they were happy and in love, she would find some type of closure, but it hurt too much to talk about it. It was better buried. The past few days, whilst staying with her, had allowed him to work hard at building her trust and had adopt the roles of therapist, confidant, friend and lover. His sleep had been as broken as hers because when she screamed out in the night, he got up, put on the light and held her until it passed.

It was difficult to arrive at the root cause of the trauma she was suffering, but she knew that it was connected to the visit to The Bancroft-Hain School. Something had happened to her there, in her youth, but she couldn't find a memory of it no matter how deep she dug. All she knew was that when Jack came home each night, she felt better until he left the following morning.

Almost a week after moving in with Amanda, Jack was sitting with his colleagues at work as they discussed a case where the victim had erased all memory of the crime that had been committed against her. It had been suggested that she attended sessions with a hypnotherapist who specialised in regression hypnotherapy.

Jack immediately took great interest in the case and made it his business to read everything he could on the outcome of these hypnosis sessions. The results had been nothing short of remarkable and although the victim found it highly traumatising to revisit the attack, it did bring the events and the perpetrator's description to the forefront. In fact, so successful was the process, that the police were able to arrest the offender.

Driving home from his shift, Jack couldn't wait to tell Amanda all about the case. They had to try something because they couldn't go on the way they were going, with no sleep, night after night. The regression hypnotherapy sessions may not provide the answers that Amanda needed but the victim he heard about was not an isolated case. According to the records, many people had been helped.

Swinging by the local Chinese restaurant, he picked up take-away food for them. Neither he nor Amanda had the energy for cooking an evening meal, but maybe things were about to change. He felt truly excited about this idea and, if it worked, they could start building a new life together. Marriage, babies, the works.

Chapter 46

Victoria phoned Al in tears. She had just received a call from the police informing her that Dan's car had indeed been found in Bancroft-Hain's lockup, but it had been abandoned on the grounds of the school. Bancroft had spun them a yarn and they had believed it. There had been no formal interview or search of the premises, they had simply taken him at his word.

'I want you to phone them back and insist that they search the school. Listen, Victoria, I believe that Dan is in that building and the only way you are going to find him is if you kick off at them and make a fuss. Even if they just do it to shut you up then at least you'll get a result. Do it! Do it now,' Al told her.

'What's the point? They don't believe me,' she sobbed.

'Remind them a text was sent from a phone, and you heard Bandy Bain's voice. Also, the last place he was seen was at the school, and you know this because you spoke to one of the interview candidates. You don't need to tell them how you got their contact details. Then ask them why he had never come back for his car. You have to be assertive here.'

Victoria sniffed. 'You're right. I'll call them now. I'll let you know how it goes.'

'Good. Lastly, forgive me for saying this… I love you.' Al ended the call.

It was wrong and she knew it, but a warm glow burned within her when hearing Al's words.

After a few deep breaths, she called the police and did as Al had told her. She kicked up stink.

The police officer told her that they would get back to her. She held out little hope.

The sounds of talking came from Artie's bedroom. Sneaking through on tiptoe, she peered her head around the door. The little guy was on the rug playing with his wooden, fainting animals. Each one had been given a different voice and a full-blown conversation was taking place between them. Victoria heard the giraffe announcing to the others that Artie's mum was going to find his daddy soon.

Chapter 47

Al paced around the floors of his oversized, three-storey house. His head was full of thoughts of Victoria. He missed her, truly and utterly missed her. In fact, he pined for her like a little dog waiting for its master. In many ways, he wished she had never walked into his shop that morning because now he was in constant torment when he wasn't with her. On the other hand, she had made his life worth living and given him a purpose for the first time. He had no idea when he was going to see her again, and that was messing with his head. To take his mind off his torturous situation, he took out his phone and sent a message to Gadhar Banik.

Gadhar, great to hear from you. Let's meet up for lunch and a few drinks. How does next week sound? Possibly Friday.

A message came back from Gadhar within the hour. It was a plan.
In the kitchen, he asked Alexa to play Marvin Gaye. That was the music to best suit his mood. Then, surprisingly, he poured himself a Morgan's Spiced Rum in a tall glass with coke and ice. He wasn't hungry, but he fancied something, something sweet. What would hit the spot, he wondered, looking around the room as though the answer would magically appear. Ah ha, he decided, ice cream with chocolate chips in it.
Now, he sat alone in his kitchen, listening to the music, drinking his rum and eating ice cream from the tub. What would make his night a little better? Victoria, of course.

Reaching for his phone from the breakfast bar, he sent her a message.

Hey, did you call the cops back and give them what for?

A text returned to him immediately.

Yep, I did exactly as you told me. They are calling me back tomorrow sometime. What are you up to?

This was almost as good as having her around, Al thought, relishing the fact that she wanted to chat.

Nothing much, just listening to Marvin, drinking rum and eating ice cream. I'm going to London next Friday to meet an acquaintance of my father's, so that should be interesting. I'll tell you about it sometime. It wasn't the time to go into details about his quest for the truth about his parents. He just felt the need to share minute details of his life with this woman.

Victoria sent a text back. *That's very intriguing. I hope you find some answers and even a bit of closure. I think it's a good idea. Artie played with his wooden animals until bedtime. They are all set out on his chest of drawers. Thanks again for doing that.*

Al felt like the texting volley was wrapping up and he really didn't want that. He wanted to keep talking all night.

I could pick up more animals and deliver them to your door.

The memory of this made Victoria smile. *No, it's okay, you and I both know that delivering animals to the door can bring a whole lot of danger.*

It was Al's turn to smile. *The world can be a dangerous place you know!*

Victoria decided to change the subject. *How's Amanda?*

Did I detect a quick subject change there? Amanda is not good since we visited Bandy Bain. She has a feeling that something bad happened to her there. Jack, the cop, is staying with her, and he has organised a Regression Therapist. Apparently, it can unlock memories that have been suppressed. I have always been doubtful about that stuff, but anything is worth a try. She is having night terrors.

Victoria couldn't reply for a few minutes. This news had left her quite distressed. If something had happened to Amanda when she was in the care of Bancroft-Hain, it showed that he was capable of dark deeds. She also felt a sense of guilt involving Amanda in her search for Dan. Bancroft was a dangerous individual and this could be proof.

That's very upsetting news. Let me know how it goes. I'll get back to you when I hear from the police tomorrow. Goodnight, Al.

She no longer felt in a chatty mood. This information had really gotten to her.

Al signed off, feeling a bit disappointed that their conversation was over. Being connected to Victoria in some way, was the only time he was happy these days.

Chapter 48

It was 6.30pm and Bancroft-Hain had just 'disposed' of his dinner leftovers down in the cellar, although he had to admit that there were slim pickings left on his plate. Hilde had come in and cooked his favourite meal, good old sausage and mash. The way she mashed the potatoes then stuck the sausages upright in the middle of them, always made him smile. What a treasure she was, a golden, bejeweled treasure. What would she make him tomorrow night, he wondered.

Alone in his private quarters, he sat back in his armchair with his feet on the matching footstool, watching a quiz show. He couldn't be bothered with most of the rubbish that was on, but he did like Mastermind, which was his favourite.

The chimes of the old front doorbell rang throughout the building, giving him quite a start. No one ever came to the door of the school after hours, unless invited by him. Pushing his bunioned feet into his carpet slippers, he made his way downstairs to see what in the name was going on. Disruptions to his evening did not sit well with him.

Although he was a tad taken aback by a visit from the two police officers again, he welcomed them in like long-lost friends. The starched collar on his shirt began chaffing on his perspiring neck, but he acted completely normally. In fact, he even managed a smile. The news that they wanted to look around the property unsettled him, but if he told them to come back with a warrant, their suspicions would be aroused. Dan McKelvie's chamber was hidden securely enough to give him complete confidence that a search would turn up sweet nothing. That would get them out of his hair for good and he would be in the clear.

'How wonderful to see you both again, so soon,' he gushed. 'Please, do come in.'

'We are sorry to disturb you, Mr. Bancroft-Hain. If we can just have a quick look around your property, then we'll be out of your hair for good.'

Ha ha, she read my mind! Bancroft chuckled to himself. 'Of course you can. I would offer you tea to start but all the female staff members have left for the day and I'm afraid it's not something that I have mastered for myself.'

The male officer laughed, the young woman did not.

Bancroft led them to the foot of the staircase, pointing upward. 'Perhaps the best place to start is the top. It's all downhill from there,' he told them, hoping his little joke would endear him to them.

The woman, Officer Bentley, had already formed her opinion of him.

Bancroft waited downstairs for the police to complete their search. It was quite laughable to him how unthorough their so-called search was. He could have hidden an army of prisoners around the school, and they would never have known.

Sure enough, the officers returned to him within no more than fifteen minutes. For a cheap thrill, he walked past the cupboard which held the stairs to the cellar. 'Here, let me show you in here before you go.' He was firm in the knowledge that Mr. McKelvie did not have the energy to shout, or make any noise. It was only a matter of days for him.

Officer Bentley put her head into the walk-in cupboard and looked up, down and around.

She was about to walk away when she decided to ask, 'Is that a door behind those shelves?'

Panic swept through Bancroft-Hain's body, but he managed to conceal it, just. 'Oh no, no, no,' he flustered. 'There are false doors like this one all over the school. I believe it has a stone wall behind it. There must be a key somewhere to unlock it, would you like me to look for it?'

Officer Bentley's colleague answered no, but she desperately wanted to say yes, just to gauge his response. There was something about this man that didn't feel right. 'Perhaps you could look for the key, in case we have to come back,' she bluffed.

Her colleagued turned to stare at her but said nothing. He had learned over the years to trust her responses and go with them.

What happened to all that talk about 'out of my hair for good'. Nosey, interfering bitch. If she'd come alone, she would soon find out what's down there. She'd be keeping Mr. McKelvie company. 'Yes, that's a good idea. I'm pretty curious myself as to what's behind the door.' He made an attempt at a fake laugh, but he really wasn't feeling it. 'Just as a matter of interest and I'll totally understand if you can't tell me, but what exactly are you looking for?'

'A missing person,' she answered.

Bancroft-Hain made an attempt at a shocked face, but he suspected that it was unconvincing. The woman cop had really knocked his confidence. 'Oh dear, is this anything to do with the man who said he had an interview at my school?'

'Yes, it's everything to do with him. It's quite strange that his car was found abandoned on your property, don't you think?' *No harm in rattling the old geezer's cage a bit.*

'When you put it that way,' Bancroft answered, feigning confusion. 'Yes, it does seem a trifle odd.'

Chapter 49

Victoria received a phone call from Officer Sue Bentley, informing her that they had visited the Bancroft-Hain School and completed a brief sweep of the property. They had found nothing.

Officer Bentley must have detected the disappointment in Victoria's response because she then told her that, for what it was worth and confidentially, she sensed the old gentleman had something to hide. She also told her that they had Mr. Bancroft-Hain on their radar and if anything else turned up, she wouldn't be afraid to seek a warrant. It wasn't the news that Victoria had hoped for, but it confirmed to her that she was on the right path that would surely lead to Dan. If he were alive, she'd find him; if he were dead, for that matter, she'd find him.

Before collecting Artie from school, she drove round to Enid's house to give her an update on the case and to check on Bob. It had occurred to her that not only was Enid's only son missing, but her husband, as the man he was, was also disappearing fast.

Fate must have prompted Victoria to go to her mother-in-law's house because when she arrived, she saw that Enid was in crisis.

'Enid, what's happened?' she asked. 'What's wrong.' Enid looked like she had reached the end of the road. 'Is it Bob?' It was not just Bob that was the problem, it was everything, Enid told her. The worry and grief for her missing son was getting pushed to the back of her mind because she couldn't keep a lid on what was happening in the house.

'Bob and I sat watching television last night and it felt so normal. He was just like his old self and for the first time in several weeks, it seemed as though he was back, you know, the real Bob. We laughed and talked and even made plans for the future. I took the opportunity to tell him about Dan and explained all about the breakthroughs that you had made in your search for him. He was very distressed and although that pained me, it was good to talk to someone who loves and cares for Dan as much as I do. I shouldn't have been so selfish.' Unfettered tears flowed, as she apologised for being so weak.

Feeling thoroughly heartbroken for the wonderful lady sitting beside her, Victoria reached out her arms and held her whilst she sobbed. Enid told her that sometime, in the early hours, Bob had written a note and left in search of his son. She had no idea where to begin looking for him.

Victoria immediately phoned the police to report that an extremely vulnerable person had gone missing.

They both knew that he would be found, but they had also resigned themselves to the fact that it couldn't go on like this and that he may have to go into some kind of care facility. Neither said as much, but they knew.

Chapter 50

Jack had made an appointment for Amanda to see the therapist that he'd heard so many good reports about. He had already arranged to swap shifts with a colleague to ensure that he could go with her. After late night discussions with Amanda, he was beginning to think that Bancroft-Hain had been no more than a bogeyman that she had blamed for her recurring feelings of trauma. Losing her parents in such a brutal way when she was only a young teen was a far more likely explanation for the night terrors. The case had never been resolved, and no one had been held accountable, so he believed that it was possible that her subconscious mind had unfinished business which played out when she was sleeping. It was just a theory based on one of the cases he had read about. Visiting the school where she had been so unhappy could have been the trigger that set off her nightly episodes.

When Jack shared his thoughts about the night terrors with Amanda, she had been adamant that it was nothing to do with the loss of her parents, but was indeed Mr. Bancroft-Hain himself who had set her world spiraling downward. But the more he reasoned and explained, the more probable the theory became. At work, using his phone, he even photographed relevant paragraphs of the case file that had turned him to this way of thinking. That evening, he read the information to Amanda, and she began to feel persuaded. What he also noticed was that as soon as Bancroft-Hain was eliminated from the picture, the terrifying episodes during the night lessened. It made life more tolerable for both of them as there were some nights where they slept through until the morning, although these were rare.

On the morning of the appointment, Amanda asked Jack to cancel as she felt that she couldn't go through with it. In her opinion, plenty of people lost their parents and they just had to move on and get over it. Her problem was that she tended not to open up about her feelings, so perhaps everything had been bottled up inside. Just talking through things with Jack over the past few nights had already started her healing process, she was sure of it. Going through some kind of hypnotherapy was only going to open old wounds and stir up hurts.

There was no discussion to be had on the subject, as far as Jack was concerned, she was going even if he had to drag her kicking and screaming. This would be good for her, good for both of them.

Knowing full well that she was beaten at the first hurdle, she sat next to Jack in the car saying nothing. Deep down, she was incredibly touched that he truly cared. She wouldn't have blamed him if he'd run a hundred miles in the opposite direction that first time he had experienced her night madness.

The therapist invited them both into her room, which was a tasteful space with calm, muted colours on the walls and soft furnishings to match. The sessions would be with Amanda only, but the doctor wanted to give them both an explanation of what the Regressive Therapy entailed.

The voice of the therapist was commanding yet her words were spoken softly. When she talked, you simply had to listen as you somehow felt drawn into the sound. This was difficult to explain unless you had experienced it.

'So, Amanda and Jack,' she looked from one to the other as she said their names slowly. 'Let me explain a bit about what happens here. Regression Therapy centres around the negative areas in a patient's life so as to isolate the cause of certain behaviours or emotions. By identifying the root cause, it should allow the patient to address and deal with unhealed issues.'

Jack nodded his agreement to this opening statement. This woman filled him with hope that she could help Amanda. She continued. 'We simply start with a method of deep breathing, which should help you to enter a state of relaxation. As part of the regression process, I will then guide you to speak aloud about past experiences. If this is successful you should be able to describe your feelings, your surroundings and even sounds that you may hear. We basically just take things as they come and see where they lead.' She finished talking with a wide, sparkling smile, looking from Amanda to Jack for a response.

The therapist's voice had been so mesmerising that both Amanda and Jack sat silently staring at her, almost willing her to talk more.

'Okay, there is no time like the present, so Jack if you would like to leave us for a while, you'll find a coffee shop in walking distance from where we are now. The receptionist will give you the details.'

Amanda lay along the leather chesterfield and awaited her next instruction.

Chapter 51

Mentally and physically, Dan was deteriorating. Most of his days were spent sleeping, at first to pass the time but latterly he was overcome with exhaustion constantly. The pain in his jaw, at times, was all consuming and began to inhibit the chewing process of the little food that he was given. When he least expected it, painful, dry sobs would burst forth from his throat, making a sound that alarmed him. His movements were slow, and it had become increasingly more difficult to aim his urine into the bucket. If only he could get washed and shaved, he found himself thinking, as he scratched like a dog with fleas at his matted beard. All hope he had of ever leaving the cellar had long gone, he now wanted it to be as tolerable as possible. Watching the children playing games outside usually brightened his mood as did the visits from Bancroft-Hain with his scraps. The small bottle of fresh, cold water was his highlight, partly because his body craved it so badly. He took a certain sense of pride in the fact that he knew exactly how much to drink during the twenty-four-hour period, without running out or having any left over. The past few days, he had tried engaging in conversation with Bancroft to find out if there was any outside news that involved him. He was met with two responses, a fist to the stomach or silence. It was becoming blatantly obvious that the old man was getting bored with the responsibility of keeping a human alive in the cellar. It could only be likened to a child receiving a puppy for Christmas and losing interest in it by January. Happy times involving Victoria and Artie filled his thoughts when he wasn't racked with guilt over how he handled situations with them in the past. Being alone with only your mind made for torturous living as memories good and bad that you had forgotten existed, surfaced and taunted. If there had been the slimmest of chances that he was ever freed, he would do things so differently. Never again would he hurt the precious love of his life with his words or actions. It dawned on him that he had to be locked up in order to change his outlook on life. It was a case of being incarcerated to be set free.

The footsteps at the top of the stairs had a strange effect on him. The weakness in his body and the handcuffs that bound his ankles and wrists made him feel frightened of the man, but he was the caregiver, the one who kept him alive, so his appearance excited him. Dan could see his face when he was three quarters of the way down the stairs and the look in his eyes was thunderous. Something had happened and he could sense it.

'Are you alright, sir?' he asked nervously. 'You look upset.'

Bancroft said nothing, he simply sat the plate of scraps on the floor. Instead of lifting the dirty plate to take away, he kicked it, full force, causing it to smash against the wall.

This doesn't look like a good time to ask for a bucket of water to get washed in, Dan thought.

'This has gone on long enough!' Bancroft-Hain shouted. 'You have brought so much trouble to my door and now I have the worry of the police returning with a warrant. As I said before, I am no killer, but I need to speed things along a bit here. First, I had that crazy woman asking questions about you, then I had a couple who supposedly wanted a tour of the school. Did they really think I was stupid? Eh, did they? I recognised them straight away. They were a troublesome brother and sister act who attended my school years ago. I never forget a face and I remembered theirs as soon as they walked in the door. They came to snoop around. I checked my cameras, and the male imposter sneaked into the office to rummage around in my personal paperwork. What the blazes did they want?'

He was rambling now, throwing out some very private information. 'Now, I have that bitch from the police force intimidating me, making me feel small. I will not tolerate that. I'm afraid I'm going to have to cut your water ration down to half a bottle. It is the only way.'

On hearing the news about the water, Dan's throat instinctively became dry, and panic quickened his heart. The rush of blood through his veins brought on a fight or flight moment. Having nowhere to run to, he chose the fight option. With everything that was left in him, he threw himself at Bancroft, knocking him backward onto the stairs. Silence followed. Dan looked down at his captor, who lay motionless, blood oozing from the back of his head. He had done it! He had killed the old bastard. The police would see that it was a self-defense mechanism; kill or be killed.

He knew that the door at the top of the stairs hadn't been locked, it never was unless Bancroft was leaving the room. Unfortunately, Bancroft-Hain's body lay across the stairs making the climb to the top, or hop to the top, even more difficult. He decided to sit down on the stairs and bump his way up past the body. It was an effective, safe method so he kept going in the same bum-climbing movement to the very top. Had his hands been cuffed behind his back, he knew there would be no chance of opening the door, but they were frontward, and he grabbed the handle with both hands.

The last thing Dan remembered were two strong hands gripping his ankles tightly, yanking him backwards, then hitting his head on the stairs as he backflipped down, down, to the ground where he had lain before. The severity of the fall, the shock to the system and the pain from his injuries caused him to lose consciousness.

Chapter 52

The police car pulled up outside Enid's house. Bob had a look of bewilderment as he sat in the back seat, uncertain as to what was happening. The police had received a call from a concerned member of the public who had seen him wandering around the train station. After speaking to the attendant at the ticket office, a policeman managed to ascertain that he had asked about a train that would take him to Cheltenham. He was reported to have said that his son was in trouble and needed his help; however, he had no bank cards or cash to pay for a ticket.

Bob's condition had accelerated at an alarming rate, and it was suggested by his doctor that he go into hospital for an extended stay in order to carry out tests on his health. Victoria comforted Enid, who was distraught over the news as, apart from the day Dan was born, they had never spent a single night away from one another in their entire forty-seven years of marriage. For as long as Victoria had known Enid, she had been the strong matriarch of the family who stood steadfast in every challenging situation. Now, it was plain to see that she was crumbling under the extreme pressure of the past few weeks.

'Why don't you pack a bag and come to stay with Artie and me? I don't think you should be alone, Enid,' Victoria advised her, as her mother-in-law cried on her shoulder.

'Thank you, dear, but I don't want to leave my house. I want to be here. Would you mind if Artie came to stay for a few days? He gives me a focus and a purpose. I know it's a big ask but I would really appreciate the company.'

After a moment's thought, Victoria agreed to let him, but only if he wanted to go. He too was a homebird and keeping to an unwavering routine was his security. She also needed Artie and all of his peculiar little ways, but perhaps Enid's need was greater than hers.

When she collected Artie from school that afternoon, she waited until they got home before she posed the question of staying at his gran's house.

Artie sat up at the kitchen table with his glass of blue top milk and a chocolate chip cookie. He dipped and nibbled, dipped and nibbled, in his usual way. Victoria watched her darling little boy with his soft pudgy hands gripping the biscuit. She had to buy Maryland Cookies, no other brand would do, and he could detect a fake at the first bite. Once, she had brought Morrison's own cookies, which to her mind were identical, she had even hidden the wrapper. The memory of him nibbling it, then smacking his tongue on the roof of his mouth to test the flavour, made her want to laugh. He had identified the cookie as a fraud, then warned her, 'Don't buy anything different again, mum.' The biscuit was discarded, as was the rest of the packet. Now, seeing him enjoying his genuine Maryland Cookie, she had asked the all-important question.

'Yes!' he screeched, not having to give it the slightest thought. 'Can I go tonight?'

Victoria, although a little dejected, was delighted that he loved his gran so much. 'Of course you can. You'll be a great helper and good company. You really are the best boy in the world.'

Artie was dropped off at Enid's house, his little pull along suitcase dragging along behind him. Enid welcomed him in at the door whilst Victoria stood on the doorstep. Artie said goodbye without a kiss or cuddle; in fact, he didn't even turn around. Tears stung Victoria's eyes as she walked back to the car. No Dan, and now, no Artie.

The first thing she did when she entered her house was to pour herself a super-sized glass of red wine. She sat on the sofa and thought what her next move could be in the quest of finding Dan.

Chapter 53

The fact that Amanda wanted the therapist to find something in her subconscious was a positive in the process. If a patient attended under duress or harboured cynicism towards the therapy, a positive outcome could be hindered. Feeling nervous and a little awkward, she lay back on the sofa and adopted the deep breathing exercise as instructed.

The therapist was a woman in her fifties who went by the name Doctor Gail. She had been practising this type of treatment for many years and, had her line of work not been confidential, she would have had a few interesting stories to tell at a dinner party. She liked to think that her manner was forthright but gentle, friendly but professional. Amanda was responding very well to the breathing exercises and Doctor Gail could see that she was beginning to go into a state of hypnosis even though she was conscious. The questions she opened with held no heavy significance and Amanda answered them honestly. Doctor Gail continued by asking about her childhood and, again, Amanda opened up to her about life in Saudi Arabia, moving on to her departure to go to live in Cheltenham, then the news of the untimely death of her parents. Doctor Gail soothed her as the traumatic memory caused her to break down sobbing. This subject was explored fully, and it took most of the session to pull out the painful details of this time in Amanda's life.

Doctor Gail began to draw things to a close, feeling certain that the area to be focused on in the future was the loss of her parents and how she had felt like a small boat cut adrift in the vast sea. Before she finished, she asked Amanda whether her time at school had been happy. The response she received was like nothing she had ever seen before. Amanda became rigid with terror, her eyes were wide open and a howling scream escaped her mouth. Doctor Gail gently probed a little further although she was aware of the extreme trauma the session was incurring.

Chapter 54

Amanda started on her first day at The Bancroft-Hain School when she was fourteen years old. There was great comfort for her in the knowledge that within the walls of the imposing building was her much-loved brother, Al. She had come from the British School in Saudi Arabia and the work there had been set at a highly advanced level, which she managed to cope with by putting in the effort. The subjects at Bancroft-Hain school were a breeze compared to what she was used to, so she soon became the top student in every subject she studied. This either stirred jealousy among the other students or it drew them to her. The group of friends she chose to be with were hardworking, high achievers like herself.

Mr. Bancroft-Hain, the headmaster, had been very welcoming to her, telling her that she was a great asset to the school. On several occasions, he invited her and three of her friends to take tea with him in his study. In the beginning, this had made her feel valued and special.

After the tragic news of her parents' death, she returned to school within days. Her grades began to dip, and she distanced herself from everyone, including her friends. It would be fair to say that she had reached the lowest point in her short life.

Sitting in class one day, she experienced a wave of overwhelming grief which made her run from the classroom with no explanation given to the teacher, Mr. Brooks. In floods of tears, she ran to the girls' toilets in the main corridor. She stood at one of the sinks in the row and began splashing her face with cold water. The door opened and Mr. Bancroft-Hain entered and began comforting her. She felt no fear or sense of alarm, she was too distressed to analyse the fact that the headmaster had followed her into the toilets and now stood with his arms around her. There followed a sharp prick on the side of her neck, and a feeling of dizziness followed. She was conscious but unable to walk or speak. Mr. Bancroft-Hain lifted her into his arms, carrying her to the door. She was aware of him sticking his head out into the corridor to check that the coast was clear. He then carried her along to a walk-in cupboard. She soon became petrified with fear, but she was unable to shout out or fight for her freedom. He then opened a door in the cupboard and carried her down a flight of stairs, which led to a cellar with a small rectangular window.

Now, completely paralysed, Amanda was laid down on a blanket on the floor. Mr. Bancroft-Hain removed her clothes and fondled her, gently at first but it soon became frantic and rough. Although she couldn't lift her head, she could see him walk over to the corner of the cellar. He turned his back to her, faced the wall, before dropping his trousers to his ankles and relieving himself.

When Bancroft had finished in the corner, he turned and walked towards her smiling. She remembered his words to her.

'Come on, let's get you back upstairs. You are a good girl.'

He redressed her before taking her up to the matron, explaining that she was overcome with sorrow for her parents. The events that happened to Amanda that day in The Bancroft-Hain School were never spoken of to anyone. They were simply absorbed into her grief.

Amanda disclosed the facts of this crime to Dr. Gail, who documented everything.

Chapter 55

Victoria poured the last dribble of wine into her glass. There was no other way to describe how she felt other than drunk. Wonderfully, leglessly drunk and it felt so good. The past few weeks had wiped her out emotionally and now with her darling Artie out on loan, she felt isolated. Her phone lay on the coffee table and without a moment's hesitation she lifted it and called Al.

He answered immediately.

'Hello big guy!' she shouted. 'Whatyaupto?'

'Are you drunk, Victoria?' he asked, bewildered by the volume and lack of clarity in her speech.

'Yes, I'm bloody drunk, what are you going to do about it, eh?'

Laughter erupted from the other end of the line. 'Oh my goodness, you really are drunk. The question is, what are *you* up to?'

'I don't have my little Artie here for the next few days, so I thought, fuck it, I'm going to Cheltenham. Any objections?'

Al's heart felt like it had expanded with euphoria. Furthermore, he shocked himself by doing a few air punches. 'I have no objections as long as you're not going to be swearing and insulting people when you come to Cheltenham, it's a fairly posh area.'

'I'm going to drive all the way there without stopping, then I'm going to see that pompous big fucker, Bandy-Bain. I'm going to grab him by his tweed lapels and make him tell me where Dan is. That's my plan.'

'Hmm, sounds like a solid plan, Victoria. I wish you all the luck in the world with that. Phone me in the morning and we'll see if you still want to come. I do agree that we need to do something. I'm sure Dan is in there somewhere.'

In the morning, Victoria was sheepish to say the least. She called Al to apologise for her awful behaviour and explained that she hadn't sworn like that since she was a teenager; in fact, she didn't even swear back then.
'Are you still coming to Cheltenham?' he asked, thinking, *please, please, please.*
'Of course I am. I can't just sit here alone doing nothing. I'll be there by the evening. Prepare the blue room for my arrival,' she joked.
Al was under no illusions, Victoria was coming to Cheltenham to find Dan, not to see him, but did it really matter why she was coming, he was still going to have her by his side and under his roof. An extensive tidy-up ensued as he had neglected his home and himself since he saw her last. The motivation to shave, dress well and have an immaculate house suddenly returned to him with the news that she would be arriving early evening. A trip to the supermarket was a necessity because he had been living on cheese and crackers all week.
Victoria made a quick call to Enid to find out how things were going. She told her of plans to head to Cheltenham to confront Mr. Bancroft-Hain. Somehow, it was important to her to have Enid's blessing for the trip. Enid told her she would be praying for a guardian angel to protect her. This meant a lot to her, although at the back of her mind was the recurring guilt she felt about staying

at Al's house, especially now that they had blurred the lines of friendship by having sex several times.

The journey, as always, was tediously long. During the driving time, she made certain pledges to herself that she intended to keep.

She would keep her alcohol consumption to a minimum. This trip needed a clear head.

She would sleep in the blue room on the second floor, not in Al's room. All that had to stop.

Her relationship with Al would return to being a friendship, just as though nothing had happened. They would never speak of it again.

If she uncovered anything new, she would force the police into action. Her intended outcome for the trip to Cheltenham was to find Dan and bring him home.

It was always good to give yourself rules and boundaries, she decided, everyone needed to discipline themselves. If everyone just did whatever the hell they wanted, the world would turn to chaos.

Chapter 56

Al's phone rang when he was in the fruit and veg aisle of the supermarket. No one ever phoned him, so his first thought was, *Please don't cancel, Victoria.* Sitting his heavily laden basket down on the tiled floor, he reached into the inside pocket of his jacket to get his phone. The name Jack showed on the screen, which created a jolt through his system. They had each other's numbers, but they had never phone or texted, it had never been that type of relationship.

'Jack, hi. Is everything okay?'

'Not really, Al. It's difficult to talk about it over the phone but something pretty bad has come up. It's about Amanda.' Jack's voice was thin yet panicked.

'Is she sick, Jack?'

'No, but she is in a pretty distressed state. Could we come over tomorrow morning to talk about it?'

'Yes, of course. Come now if you want, although I'm actually in the supermarket.'

'No, she is too upset. We'll make it tomorrow around ten. See you then.'

Al's mind raced through every possible scenario about what could be wrong with his sister. Did she have cancer? Was she having a breakdown? Was the doctor going to commit her? Amanda meant everything to him. In fact, she was all he had. Apart from Victoria, she was the only human being to whom he was connected. There were no other family members, and he had no friends, so without his sister, his life would be an island.

He couldn't leave things like this until the morning, he had to know a few more details. He got Jack back on the phone.

'It's me again, you've got me wound up like a jack-in-the-box here. What the fuck is going on?'

'She will explain tomorrow. She's okay Al, she's not going to die or anything. She just needs time to process some stuff before she comes to speak to you. Push it from your mind until tomorrow. Everything will be alright, I'll make sure of it.'

'Thanks man. I appreciate what you are doing for her. See you tomorrow.'

Al drove home with his shopping in the back seat of the car. Amanda's behaviour lately had been a constant worry for him, as she had been so unlike her usual self. Then, when she explained to him about her recurring night terrors, he began to think that she was losing her mind. She did have serious trauma in her life and, as far as he could recall, she never really grieved over it. In fact, she never even talked about it. The subject of their parents never came up in any conversation, happy or sad, and that was not normal. At least now he had his meeting with Gadhar Banik, who may be able to give them both the answers that they desperately needed.

At home, Al unpacked his groceries, before putting the flowers in water and carrying them up to Victoria's room. She had been so pleased when she saw them the last time. Obviously, she had been the only person to sleep in the bed in the blue room, so there was no need to change the sheets. He lay down on top of the quilt and held one of the pillows in his arms. There was a faint scent of Victoria coming from the pillowcase. It was such a pleasing odour that she always, without exception, smelt of. He loved that about her. The past few nights he hadn't been sleeping well, and now lying on Victoria's bed, in the cool calmness of the room, he shut his eyes and drifted off.

Chapter 57

Bancroft-Hain would normally have to wait several hours before he could go down to the cellar to see his captive. This time though, he was pretty certain that it was all over. No more sharing his food, no more worrying that the police were going to find him, no more waiting for Dan McKelvie's light to snuff out. Had he not been such a decent human being, he would have finished Mr. McKelvie off on the first day, but it wasn't in his nature to simply take someone's life. His father had taught him that. The memory would stay long in his mind of the schoolgirl... what was her name, Betty Richmond. Yes, Betty Richmond, he remembered her well. Bancroft-Hain had been one year out of school and his father was training him to one day take over his position as headmaster. Those were the good old days when no teaching certificates in private schools were necessary.

He and his father had enjoyed watching Betty through the peepholes in the girls' toilets. Her breasts were large, her bra was lacy, and she unbuttoned her blouse low. Bancroft and his father often discussed the girls' attributes, then logged them in a ledger. What they did to Betty Richmond had been preplanned which, if truth be told, was one of the most exciting parts of the actual crime. The idea of taking Betty, in an unconscious state, down to the cellar, was keeping Bancroft awake at night, and his father admitted the same.

However, it hadn't quite gone to their careful plan. She had woken up as Bancroft-Hain watched his father removing her lacy bra. Oh, he would never forget those screams.

It had been an upsetting experience and now, standing in his study, remembering the details, he became distressed. His hands began to slap at his head, whilst involuntary moans escaped from deep in his throat.

The girl screamed the screams of a thousand limpkins, it had been deafening. Bancroft's father told him to run, and he would be right behind him. Through a gap in the door at the top of the stairs, he saw Betty's legs go from kicking frantically to lying straight and still and with her feet pointing outward. The screams had stopped.

'Did you kill her?' he asked his father.

'No, I simply calmed her down. Now we will leave her. Nature will work things out for us. We shan't utter a word of it again.'

Nature had indeed taken care of Betty, because by the following day, she was gone. His father had been right. Some years later, he heard two pupils discussing the disappearance of Betty Richmond and how she still hadn't been found.

With any luck, nature had taken care of Dan McKelvie and all he would have to do was bury his body in the old vegetable patch at the back of the school. As soon as Hilde left for the evening, he would eat his dinner then head down to see what was what. He felt no empathy for the man. After all, he had pushed him, causing a nasty gash on the back of his head where. Rubbing the wound with his index and middle finger, he felt it sting and the wetness around the area told him that it was still bleeding. Surely, he hadn't deserved that.

Chapter 58

Victoria pulled into the pebbled drive of Al's impressive house just after six o'clock. She rang the bell and a short time later, Al appeared at the door. She had half expected him to be watching at the window for her, but no, he didn't look ready for her at all. His hair was ruffled on one side and his eyes looked bloodshot.

'Are you okay?' she asked. 'You look dreadful, no offence.'

'I'm fine. I have just woken up. I nodded off on top of the bed and I must have slept for about three hours.'

'You must have needed it,' she told him, brushing his hair down with her fingers.

It's difficult to know what triggered it, be it longing, or simply the touch of her fingers in his hair, but without a word spoken, he had her in his arms and was carrying her upstairs to his room. There was no resistance from Victoria's side, so he carried on with a growing, ravenous passion. He laid her down on his bed and began removing his clothes. He watched as she removed hers. They then indulged in fast and furious sex which lasted no more than a few minutes. Al felt the need to apologise for the briefness of the act, adding that he couldn't help it.

Within five minutes of her arrival at Al's door, she had broken one of her golden rules. Why did she do that? Why did she find it so difficult to resist this man? Maybe she knew all along that she had no intention of keeping this promise to herself. No, she was sure that she really did intend to keep things on a friendship level. But now her guard was down, it was going to be very difficult to hoist it back up.

'Do you still want to sleep in the blue room?' he asked her.
'Yes, yes I do,' she told him, with her head resting in her hands. 'I had decided on the journey here that we should continue as good friends, but I fell at the first hurdle. It will be better if I have my own room. We can only call ourselves lovers if we sleep in the same bed, don't you agree?'

'Whatever you want, Victoria. If it makes you feel better to have your own room, then that's fine with me. I'm just really happy that you're here.' He took her hands in his, kissing them both on the palms. 'Let's just take things as they come. You are here to find Dan and I will help you with that. Please stop beating yourself up.'

Victoria headed to her blue room to freshen up. On entering the room, the person-shaped indentation on her bed caught her eye. Al must have fallen asleep on her bed before she arrived. It touched her that he would feel the need to lie where she had lain. It was the act of a love-sick romantic and it made her smile.

Carrying her toilet bag, towel and a dress she had brought with her, she walked across the hall to the bathroom. The smell of Al's cooking rose up the stairwell, as did the music of Otis Redding. A strange comforting feeling came over her because she knew that Dan was in the vicinity. The same could be said about being in Al's house because that's where he was, and she felt safe with him.

Victoria enjoyed every meal Al had ever made for her. He had a knack of putting the right something in his food to make it taste like a restaurant speciality. The whole vibe in his kitchen was relaxed but exciting in a peculiar way. It was simply great music, great food and great company. They talked about many things as they sat with their elbows on the table, their empty plates with cutlery pushed to one side. Al told her about his meeting with Gadhar in London on Friday. They were meeting at a gentleman's club called The East India Company. This led onto story exchanges of various trips they had each had over the years to London. The conversation moved on to reminiscing over Al's trip to Melrose. She was pleased when he told her that it was one of his favourite holidays. 'Talking of which,' he said, 'I was doing a bit of research on your man, Sir Walter Scott.'

'Really? You were doing research on him? Why?'

'I thought he was interesting. I read one of his plays called Marmion and I can even quote a famous line from it.'

Victoria sat back on her seat and took a sip of her wine. She was impressed and incredibly endeared. 'Go on then.'

'Oh, what a tangled web we weave, when first we practice to deceive.' He took a little bow.

'I didn't know that Walter Scott coined that phrase, I thought it was Robert Burns. Very good,' she told him, clapping. 'It is definitely a step up from Doctor Foster went to Gloucester.'

Al suddenly remembered to tell Victoria about Amanda, as he poured them both more wine. He told her that they would be coming over in the morning because she had something very upsetting to talk about.

Victoria was not only worried about her newfound friend, but she was also intrigued. Al had told her that her mental health had deteriorated since she had visited the Bancroft-Hain School. Could it be something to do with her visit, she wondered.

It was the small hours of the morning when Al and Victoria finally decided to call it a night. Al escorted her up to her room on the second floor. He kissed her passionately at the door and she instinctively pulled him over to her bed.

Chapter 59

Victoria was awakened by her phone playing its annoying tune; she had been meaning to change it. Her head felt fuzzy. *So much for me cutting down my alcohol consumption.*
'Hello,' she answered, glancing over and seeing Al asleep next to her, naked as a jay bird.
'Victoria Richards?'
'Yes.'
'This is Officer Calum Barnes from the Cheltenham Police Station. Your car is ready to be picked up.'
Until that moment, Victoria had forgotten all about the car. 'Did you find anything inside that would be helpful in finding my partner?'
'No, nothing. The driver's side window was smashed but the headmaster of the school where it was found had already admitted to doing that. It was the only way he could release the handbrake to be able to push the vehicle into the lock-up. Don't worry, he has offered to pay for the damage.'
Victoria screwed up her face and sat upright. 'You honestly think that's okay? The last place my partner was seen alive was at The Bancroft-Hain School, and there are witnesses to verify that. Then he vanishes,' her volume rising to a shout. 'His car is hidden away in Mr. Bancroft-Hain's lockup, and he tells no one. Now, he's off the hook because he has offered to pay for a window he broke whilst *hiding* my partner's car. Can you just clarify that you don't see anything suspicious in this situation?'
Calum Barnes babbled slightly, passing the buck onto the officers who had been dealing with the case. He did not

pick up on any of the points raised by her but, instead, went back to his original statement.

'So, as I said, your car is ready to be uplifted.'

Al who was now awake, reached for the bedding in a gesture of modesty. 'You told him, girl! Not that it did a blind bit of good.'

Her travel case sat unopened next to the bed, and Victoria reached for the zip to open it. It was the dressing gown that lay on the top that she was interested in. In the broad daylight, with the relaxed effects of alcohol gone, she felt a little embarrassed. It had been an extremely intimate night and the memory of it made her blush and avert her eyes from Al.

The chimes of the front doorbell rang throughout the house. Al catapulted from the bed. 'Shit, I nearly forgot that Amanda and Jack were coming over.' From the floor, he lifted his discarded clothes that lay in a trail from the door. The buttons on his shirt were still done up from the night before, so he pulled it over his head. With an absence of underpants, he pulled on his jeans before running down to unlock the front door to let them in.

When he saw his sister, he got quite a shock. She stood there on the doorstep, clinging onto Jack, her face ghostly, her frame tiny. Instead of her bubbly manner, she said nothing. Al led them through to the lounge because he suddenly remembered the state he'd left the kitchen in from the previous night.

'Can you guys just sit tight for a minute while I jump in the shower? Victoria arrived last night, so I'll tell her you're here. She'll be pleased to see you.' He reached down and kissed Amanda's forehead before leaving the room.

At the foot of the stairs, he made a dramatic show of shouting up to Victoria, as though he hadn't seen her since last night. 'Victoria! Are you awake? Amanda's here with Jack.'

Victoria pulled on her dress, before wrapping her hair up in a bobble. Her face was free from make-up, but she looked just as pretty without it. The only shoes she had with her were lying around the floor somewhere, but she decided that they weren't necessary and left the room in her bare feet.

When she caught sight of Amanda, Victoria was quite literally stopped in her tracks. She was unrecognisable from the rosy cheeked girl she knew. A simple hello would not suffice, Victoria decided, giving her a gentle but prolonged hug. Victoria had never met Jack before, so they introduced themselves and she thanked him for tracing the owners of the cars from their number plates.

Jack had to think for a moment. 'Oh yes, I'd forgotten that I'd done that. Was it helpful?'

'Very helpful, but I'm still at a loss as to what to do next.' It dawned on her that the visit wasn't about her and her search for Dan, it was about Amanda. 'Anyway, enough about me. How are you feeling, Amanda? Dan says that you are seeing a therapist. Is it helping?'

Jack stepped in to answer for her. He explained how the regression therapy worked and the fact that it involved hypnosis. Amanda had only been to one session, so the road ahead was still long.

Al entered the room and Victoria caught an appealing waft of his aftershave as he walked past her. In her opinion, he scrubbed up handsomely. A pang of guilt jabbed at her, not only because of the sexual relationship that she had found herself in, but how normal it felt to be a couple. There were so many things that she adored about Al, but his little-boy-lostness was the most loveable. He was, in many ways, still the young man waiting for his parents to return and that tore at her heart. She watched him pull up a footstool next to his sister, before reaching for her hand, so caring and attentive.

'Do you want to tell us what's going on, Amanda?' Al said softly. 'You don't mind Victoria being here, do you?'

Amanda shook her head.

'Would it be easier if Jack told us everything?' Al suggested, seeing how fragile she looked.

Again Amanda gave a nod and looked to Jack.

Al and Victoria listened in complete horror as Jack unfolded the details of what had happened to Amanda as a young vulnerable teenager, who was mourning the death of her parents.

Stars began to appear behind Al's eyes while his heart banged on his ribcage. His face burned with rage and his fingers curled their way into a fist without his knowledge. When he had heard the full story, he rose to his feet. 'I'm going over there to batter the fucking daylights out of that perverted bastard.'

'No Al, don't do that. There are other ways of handling this. I will put in a police report at the station tomorrow,' Jack said, in an attempt to diffuse the situation.

'The police!' he bellowed. 'The fucking police! Yeah Jack, that's a great idea. Victoria's husband has been missing for weeks now, and the police have done fuck all.'

As she processed the hideous crime that had been committed against Amanda, there was one part of the story that had whacked a gong in her head, and that was the cellar. She thought about Dan and how the police had done a brief search of the school and found nothing. Could that be because the cellar was difficult to find? Jack said that Bancroft-Hain took Amanda into a cupboard, then through a door which opened up to a flight of stairs leading to the cellar.

Victoria sat forward. She interrupted the conversation going on between Al and Jack, and blurted out, 'Dan is in that cellar. I know it, I sense it, I feel it. Let's go, now!'

Chapter 60

Dan managed to open his eyes a slit when he heard the key in the lock of the door at the top of the stairs. In the course of the night, he had seen Victoria and Artie standing over him. Victoria had offered him a tall glass filled with iced water and a slice of lemon. His hand had pawed at the air when he reached for it. In the light of the lamppost that shone through the window, he had seen his loved ones. Their smiling faces had been so clear to him and yet when he tried to take the water, there appeared to be nothing there. Just like a relentless carousel, his head spun around, rendering him unable to sit up. The injuries he has sustained from the fall down the stairs were swollen and bleeding. And now, Bancroft-Hain was coming. Dan no longer felt afraid of what was going to happen. The cruelty of the man had ceased to surprise him, he was unpredictable and thoroughly insane. Dan knew that his intention was to kill him without actually committing the act of murder. His mantra seemed to be that nature would take care of it, whatever the fuck that meant.

With great disappointment, Bancroft-Hain surveyed the scene at the foot of the stairs. There was movement, be it ever so slight, from the body on the floor. Why could this man not just die, he asked himself. No one should be able to survive such hardship. Bancroft wondered why he was unable to put the creature out of its misery. Perhaps it was his own goodness that stopped him from finishing him off.

'Don't bother looking up for the bottle of water,' he shouted, when he saw a pleading look in his prisoner's eyes. 'I told you before that I was stopping all the extras that I've been giving you. To be perfectly blunt, you are not worthy of it.' He made his way down the steps to get a closer look.

Dan waited until Bancroft-Hain was near to where he lay before reaching out with a half-hearted attempt to grab his ankles. There was no strength in his hands, and he only managed to brush the tweed fabric of Bancroft's trousers. A kick to the side of his head put him out cold.

Bancroft-Hain laughed aloud at the feeble effort to fight back. Staring down at the listless captive, he realised that he bore no resemblance to the man that he had drugged all those weeks ago. Nature seemed to be taking its time over snuffing out this one's life, but he felt quietly confident that the curtain was about to fall.

Chapter 61

As Victoria rose to her feet, strenuously announcing that she was going to see Bancroft, Al stood supportively beside her. His rage was for his sweet sister, but he had been involved in the search for Dan since day one and he suspected that Victoria was right about where Dan was. Whether he was dead or alive was another matter, but he knew that she could not do this alone.

Jack tried to calm the situation by explaining to Victoria that it was against the law to just barge into someone's property on a hunch. There were certain protocols that had to be followed if they were going to do this right.

'The first thing I'll do is give all of this information to my superiors and we can start the application for a search warrant. Now we have something that really points the finger at Bancroft-Hain and what he is capable of,' Jack explained.

Amanda sat with her hands on her face, saying nothing. The look in her eyes gave the impression that the light that used to shine brightly was dimming to an ember. It was more than she could deal with.

'How long does it take to get a warrant?' Victoria asked, walking over to lay her arm on Amanda's shoulders.

'It's difficult to say, it can take hours, it can take months. The court will decide on the evidence presented to them. I promise I will get straight on to it tomorrow.'

After a thoughtful pause from everyone present, Al said, 'Fuck this, Jack. There could be a dying man in that basement. I'm going in.'

'Me too,' Victoria added, following Al to the door.

'No, no, this is not the way! We could jeopardise everything. If you go storming in with tensions high, he will get advanced warning that we are on to him. Who knows what he could do,' Jack reasoned.

'No, Jack, we've suspected that old bastard the whole time and the police have done fuck all. I'm going to talk to him.' Al made it clear that he would not be shifted on this.

Following further discussion, a compromise was reached between them, and it was decided that later that evening, Jack would go to Bancroft-Hain's door with a calm, friendly manner. He would introduce himself as an off-duty police officer, then casually ask if he could have a look in the cellar of the school.

'I will say that my fiancé attended the school as a pupil, and that she has a vague memory of there being something frightening down there. I'll ask for a quick look around so that I can alleviate her fears. Well, that's the rough idea of it,' Jack offered.

'I think you should say that no one knows you're visiting. Be his friend, say you believe your fiancé obviously had a nightmare about the cellar and that it has haunted her ever since,' Al suggested. 'We will come with you, but we will stay hidden outside. Let him think you are alone, then he'll lower his guard.'

Ideas were birthing between them, some discarded, some taken on board. The desired option for Jack was to leave it to law enforcement, but he knew as soon as he left Al's house, he would go straight over to confront the old headmaster. Jack knew that he was the only man for the job.

Al rustled up another fabulous meal, which he joked was the last supper.

Chapter 62

Victoria travelled with Al in his car to the school. The gravity of what they were about to do wasn't lost on her. She knew that it was an all or nothing situation. Either Dan would be found dead or alive tonight, or they were no further forward in their search for him. In her heart, she knew that she was going to see him, but she pushed all thoughts of him being dead from her mind. The short journey from Al's to Bancroft-Hain's was travelled in silence, she was too tense to engage in conversation.

Al parked the car further up the street, making it invisible from the school.

'Here comes Jack,' he said, watching in his rear-view mirror. He saw Jack drive into the car park of the school, but from where they were parked, he could not get eyes on him entering the building. They would simply have to wait until he returned to his car.

If the truth be told, Jack was terrified. Sweat was forming on the back of his neck and beading up on his forehead. No matter how many times he told himself that Bancroft-Hain was only an old man, he couldn't alleviate the sense of foreboding. This was not the way to do things, and he knew it. Why had he agreed to it, he wondered.

The main door to the school was locked but he spotted the original doorbell which was set into the whitewashed wall. Holding his finger on the round ceramic button, he could hear the sound of the bell ringing through the building. He waited a few moments before he rang again, pressing even longer this time. Was that the sound of someone coming? He pressed his ear to the heavy door and listened, confirming to himself that there was a noise from inside. The banging pulse of his heart pounded in his ears and for a fraction of a second, he wanted to run back to the safety of his car. But it was too late, the bolts on the inside of the door were being slid back as he stood there, legs trembling.

Bancroft-Hain opened the heavy oak door and greeted him with a stern look across his face.

'I'm afraid these are out of hours for the school,' he told the young man, eyeing his rather scruffy looking attire.

Jack gave a nervous laugh which came unexpectedly from the back of his throat.

'Yes, I know,' he answered, giving a strange little bow of apology. 'I have a rather unusual request that you may want or not want to grant.' *That was a very stupid thing to say*, he told himself.

'I'm all ears, young man,' he said, folding his arms.

Oh man, why am I letting this old timer intimidate me. Take control of the situation, you're a cop remember. Stop shaking like a woosy. After his little pep talk to himself, he straightened his back, cleared his throat and adopted a new role of superiority.

'Would it be possible to take a look in your cellar, sir?'

'That's quite a random request. May I ask why?' Bancroft said, rather taken aback.

'It's a long story and it may sound fanciful, but my fiancé attended your school many years ago. She often experiences nightmares which involve something evil in the cellar here. She doesn't know I'm here, but I wanted to tell her that I have visited the place of her nightmares and that there was nothing to fear. Does that sound ridiculous?' He made eye contact with a smile. Feeling unsure if he imagined it or not, he thought he saw Bancroft's tension melt away and his body visibly relax. Of course, that could have been wishful hoping on his part.

Bancroft gave a loud guffaw. 'That is quite a story,' he told Jack. 'How could I refuse to help a young damsel in distress. I can show the cellar to you and if you wish, you can bring her round sometime and I will give her the guided tour myself.'

Jack couldn't have been happier with the way things were going. Sometimes being up front with people was the best way to appeal to their human side. So far, although a little self-important, Bancroft-Hain hadn't quite been the monster that Al and Amanda painted him to be.

He was instructed to follow Bancroft along the corridor, past the girls' toilets. Walking on a little further, the painted portrait of the old gentleman hanging on the wall caught Jack's attention. He marveled at the likeness of the man and the accuracy of his tweed suit, rounded shirt collar and tie. It crossed his mind to compliment Bancroft on the piece of art, but he decided to stay focused on the reason he was there.

Striding several steps ahead, Bancroft-Hain was like a man on a mission, walking towards the storage cupboard where the cellar door was concealed. 'Not far now,' he bellowed, without turning around. The cellar door key was in the pocket of his heavy tweed trousers, his fingers fondled them gently. 'Just round the next corner,' he announced to Jack, who was walking briskly to keep up.

'Here we are. The cellar is located through a door in this cupboard. No one would ever know that it was there.'

A flutter of nerves unsettled Jack at that moment. Perhaps it was the idea of no one knowing the door was there, or it could have been the air of excitement that Bancroft-Hain gave off in showing him the location. Once again, that voice within him prompted him to run, but he was there now, and he had to see if Victoria's missing partner was down there. As Bancroft pulled the key from his pocket, Jack stood warily behind him. He decided that this was a good moment to inform the old headmaster that he was an off-duty police officer.

The key remained unturned in the lock as Bancroft froze rigid at the bombshell that had just been dropped. He had to think fast. What should he do for the best, he wondered. Would the fact that he was a policeman affect his decision? For a moment, he couldn't decide, he had to think, quickly. No, he would keep to the plan, nothing had changed. Turning the key until it clicked unlocked, he reached for the handle of the door and turned.

'Go on,' he said, smiling. 'Be my guest.'

Jack took a few steps forward in order to peer into the semi-darkness.

'Feel free to take a closer look,' Bancroft-Hain coaxed.

Knowing that he couldn't leave without any answers, he took a few more steps until he was standing at the top of the flight of stone stairs. Electrifying shockwaves bolted through his system as he looked down at what appeared to be a human body on the floor of the cellar.

'What the hell is that lying on the ground down there!' he yelled. 'Is that a man?' He took two more steps down. His brain could not quite compute what he was seeing. 'Is that an injured man?' he screeched again at Bancroft.

'It is indeed,' Bancroft sneered, holding on to the doorframe to give him maximum power in his legs as he booted Jack in the small of his back.

The sound of Jack's skull hitting the stone stairs made Bancroft-Hain wince. 'Ouch!' he said, screwing up his face. 'Looks like that's the end of him.' Shutting the door of the cellar, he locked up and returned the keys to his pocket. 'Well, that was an unpleasant start to my evening,' he said aloud.

Chapter 63

Nearly an hour had passed before Victoria suggested that something had happened. The chances of Jack and Bandy-Bain chatting pleasantly over a cup of tea were slim to nonexistent. Jack didn't want to be there, so he would have gone in, checked the basement and left.

'Al, something's wrong. Jack would have been out by now. Can you ring his phone?'

Al tapped on the steering wheel, thinking what the next move should be. 'Okay, I'm inclined to agree with you, things aren't right.' His phone was resting on the dashboard. Staring at it for a few minutes, he tried to decide whether phoning was a good idea or not. It couldn't jeopardise anything, he debated, could it? No, he didn't think so. He reached for the phone and called Jack's number. It rang out. He tried once more, and it rang and rang until suddenly when Al was set to give up, someone answered.

'Help,' came the faintest whisper, barely there at all.

'Jack, Jack, are you okay? We're coming in.'

'Not Jack.'

The call was not cut off, but there was only silence from the other end.

'Is it Dan?' Al shouted into the silence of the phone.

Nothing.

Victoria took the mobile from Al's hand. 'If it's you Dan, I'm here, I'm outside and I'm coming to get you.' She passed the phone back and climbed out the car. 'I'm going in, Al.'

'Wait, wait. Let me think about this, get back in. Amanda had told the therapist that the door to the cellar was inside a cupboard located along the main hallway. I think I know where that is.' He shut his eyes in order to see a mental picture of the ground floor of the school. 'Right, let's sit tight for a minute, we are going to do this right. Now, let me think.'

Taking Al's lead on this, Victoria shut the car door and waited to hear the details of his plan.

'Right, I want you to stay in the car and phone the police. Explain everything and don't hold back. I've got a few tools for changing tyres stored in my boot, so I'll take a look at what might be helpful for getting in through the cellar door, it's bound to be locked. Hopefully, the old sod waits until he's going to bed before he puts the alarm on.' Al was basically thinking out loud at this point, trying desperately to come up with a plan that would get him into the building without Bandy noticing. 'I'm going around the side of the school to where the windows of the girls' toilets are. I can break one of them easily enough and climb through. I know how to get to the storage cupboard from there. I'll worry about the rest as it comes.' Leaning over to Victoria, he kissed her lips. 'I love you.'

'I love you too,' she told him. A crippling feeling of guilt took root in heart, but she dismissed it because it was true. She lifted the phone and called the police station.

Chapter 64

The window for the girls' toilets was too high for Al to reach. Looking all around him for something to stand on, he spied a small picnic bench in the infant playground ahead. He ran over to check the weight of it and as good fortune would have it, it was cheap, lightweight wood. It was easy to carry over to the window but now he worried if it would actually take his weight. With his legs apart to distribute his weight, he stood on the wobbly bench, reached up with his fist inside the sleeve of his jacket and walloped the pain of glass. It only cracked the first time but caved on the second blow. Again using his sleeve, he brushed away some of the splinters in the frame.

Once inside the toilets, a thought entered his head that made him shudder. His sister had stood inside that very room, heartbroken with grief for her parents and that perverted old bastard had drugged her and dragged her down into his lair to assault her. The hatred he felt for Bandy Bain was all consuming; in fact, he wanted more than anything else to kill him. It would be worth a stretch in prison to see that vile creature meet an untimely end. But that was something to think about later, now he had to get to the cellar to find Dan and now Jack.

Al knew that he didn't need to be silent because, from memory, Bandy Bain's private quarters were on the top floor. On his last visit to the school with Amanda, he had noticed CCTV cameras which could pose a problem. Bandy may be jittery after his visit from Jack, especially knowing he was a police officer. On the other hand, the old guy had probably been getting away with doing anything he wanted all these years, with no one to answer to. He would be relaxing in the knowledge that no one knew Jack was there. Anyway, who would suspect a sweet, eccentric old gentleman of any wrongdoing.

He made his way along the corridor, taking a quick look behind him, just in case. On his right, he passed the ridiculously extravagant painting of Bandy's father, which made him cringe. What kind of person commissions an artist to paint them in their finery, then displays it for everyone to admire. The Beavis and Butt-Head sticker on Bandy Senior's shoe tickled him greatly, because it showed utter disrespect for the man.

The cupboard was a little further along, on the other side, if memory served him correctly. Yes, he saw it. There was a small open area, and the cupboard door was tucked in there on the left. Glancing behind him once more, he tried the handle and found it unlocked. The door led into a walk-in storeroom with shelves of cleaning products and various random items that had probably been sitting in there since he was a boy.

Where now, he wondered, until he saw Bandy Bain's half-baked attempt at hiding the door behind shelving which was adorned with a display of paint cans. That was probably the least effective concealment job he had ever seen, but there again, Bandy was so arrogant, he would never dream that anyone would come looking. The slatted shelving unit was light to move once he had removed the paint. And there it was, the door down to the cellar. He reached into his jacket and pulled out the wrench that he had taken from the boot of his car.

After trying a few different ways to prize the door open, he soon realised that there were no gaps wide enough to wedge the wrench into for leverage. The door was solid, and it hung flush with the wall; it was impossible.

Tossing the wrench to the side, he searched the shelves of the cupboard, where he found a hammer. Using it to strike the handle several times, it soon became obvious that it wasn't even making a dent. His blood pressure rose with frustration, because he had come this far and now he couldn't get the ruddy door open. No, there had to be a way. For a few minutes, he stood thinking, waiting for a plan to dawn upon him. Eventually, he decided, *Fuck it!*

He took the best run possible, considering he was in a cupboard, and with his full weight, he threw himself at the door, shoulder first. It didn't work but there was a cracking sound from one of the hinges. Once or twice more may do it. He headed to the far side of the cupboard, counted to three before hurtling himself in an ungainly manner at the hinge side of the door. This was enough to loosen the screws of the lower hinge. Now, he needed to bust the top hinge. The pain coming from his shoulder was excruciating, so he decided to kick the door a few times to see if he could make an impact.

The booting continued for some time before he managed to swing the door open. It looked dark down the flight of steps and all that could be heard was a deathly silence.

'Dan! Jack!' he shouted, reluctant to climb down. A revolting smell wafted up to greet him. It was musty, damp and held undertones of human waste. Whatever was down there, Al knew it was bad, very bad. The muscles in his stomach tightened and the hairs on the back of his neck rose upward.

Chapter 65

Bancroft-Hain had watched Al entering the toilets by the window. His cameras were everywhere. He managed to pick him up again in the hallway. His eyes narrowed when he saw him standing smiling in front of his father's portrait. *Careful, sonny boy.*
There was a drawer in his bedroom that kept safe his recreational drugs and syringes. His paisley patterned pyjamas lay over the top of the medicine bottles. Removing the pyjama covering, he took out the first bottle from one of the neat rows. *This will soon put a stop to everything that has been going on.* The syringe bled the bottle almost dry. The dosage was too much, he knew that it was way too much, but that was his intention. There was no other way.

Chapter 66

Al stepped into the abyss with his sweatshirt pulled up over his nose. The smell was unbearable. It didn't take long for his eyes to adjust to the poor lighting which came from one source, the lamppost outside in the street. Jack lay face down, blood oozing in a halo around his head. The other body, presumably Dan, was curled in a kidney shape. Al stood, staring in disbelief. He couldn't quite get his head around the fact that Victoria's partner had been living like this for several weeks. Suddenly, a moan came from Dan, and Al immediately knelt down to hear his plea. It was obvious that he was in very bad shape; in fact, he was distorted with injuries.

'It's okay, Dan, it's over. Help is coming. Victoria has called the police. She never stopped looking for you.'

Dan seemed to lift a little with this news of Victoria, there may even have been a trace of a smile, but Al couldn't tell in the poor light.

Al turned to the motionless Jack to feel the pulse on his neck. There was no pulse, he was gone.

Al became overwhelmingly sad. He broke down, sobbing for a good man who hadn't wanted to deal with matters this way in the first place. His favoured option had been to apply for a warrant and take things down the right and legal route of the law. His sorrow was also for his sister. How was he going to tell her? She also didn't want us to take matters into our own hands.

The sound of a siren blared from outside in the courtyard. The room was filled with intermittent flashes of blue light.

Al ran to the front door to unlock the heavy bolts. Four police officers stood on the doorstep, while Victoria hung back in the playground.

'We will need a couple of ambulances,' he instructed the police team.

'Victoria! He's alive,' Al shouted with genuine joy.

Victoria fell to her knees on the tarmac. Her hysterical cries resounded around the grounds and building.

Two of the officers headed off to find Mr. Bancroft-Hain. They followed Al's instructions on how to find the headmaster's private quarters on the top floor.

'Be careful,' Al shouted after them. 'He is a dangerous man.'

Chapter 67

The two police officers entered the study of Mr. Bancroft-Hain to find that he had taken an overdose, the needle still hanging from his arm. They found him to be deceased, and yet another ambulance was called.

Dan was connected to a drip before he was taken out on a stretcher to the ambulance. He was barely conscious. However, on seeing his dear, sweet Victoria, he managed to reach out his hand for hers.

'I love you Dan,' she told him. 'I never stopped looking for. I'm going to phone Artie and your mum to tell them that you're going to be okay. We have all been so worried about you.' This poor soul of a man that she was talking to did not resemble her Dan in anyway. His battered face and body, his skeletal frame and the matted hair on his face, were so far removed from the Dan she knew and loved. It was heartbreaking and she could not imagine what he had been through and the suffering he had endured.

Dan gave her hand a squeeze, the tightest he could muster, but she didn't appear to feel it.

Jack left the Bancroft-Hain School in a body bag, as did the headmaster.

There were no words to describe the joy Enid felt when Victoria called to say that Dan had been found, and that he was alive. She totally understood that Victoria would need to stay by his bedside until he was fit enough to be transferred to a hospital in Edinburgh.

Artie came on the phone to his mum. 'Is it true, is daddy really coming home?'

'Yes, sweetheart, it is really true. He is too sick to travel right now, but as soon as he gets strong again, I'll bring him home to you.'

Enid took the phone from Artie. 'Victoria, you are an exceptional woman. You have singlehandedly found my boy. I'm so grateful to you for being a loving, faithful partner who never gave up.'

'Thank you, Enid,' Victoria said, squirming with guilt. Without Al, his sister Amanda and her boyfriend Jack, she wouldn't have stood a chance of finding him. *Faithful partner? That was definitely debatable.*

Victoria spent her days at Dan's bedside, her nights sleeping at Al's. She had promised herself, with great conviction, that she and Al would go back to having a platonic friendship. It was a promise to herself that she could not keep; if anything, the sex was more passionate than ever.

Later that week, Al left on the train to London to meet Gadhar Banik. Victoria missed him terribly and even took to sleeping in his bed whilst he was away. They kept in contact by text, but she no longer replied, *I love you too,* to Al's, *I love yous.* It somehow felt betraying to say the words.

It was so heartening to see Dan making small steps of recovery every day. He began to look more like himself. A shave and a haircut had worked wonders. There was no talk of what had happened to him, and Victoria didn't push for answers. When he was ready to tell her why he ended up in the cellar, then she would be ready to listen.

The police were also interested to hear from Dan about what had taken place at the school. In their search of the property, they had found a ledger which had originally been started by Bancroft-Hain senior, but his son had continued his work after he died. It listed attributes of many of the girls, some of which had a star drawn next to their names. The police believed that they were the girls who were drugged and abused in the cellar. It was only a matter of time before they traced and interviewed the girls in the book. The police were highly concerned about several girls who had the word NATURE next to their name. Rather than a star, their entry had a cross beside them. They now realised that the scale of the crimes committed over many years at the Bancroft-Hain School were way more extensive than had been originally thought.

Chapter 68

Al walked into the affluent East India Club and gave his name at the reception. He was told that Mr. Banik was waiting for him upstairs in the bar.

Before he arrived in London, he had researched the club and smiled at the irony of its description. 'A private members club which continues its tradition as a home from home for dynamic and sociable gentlemen.' He was neither dynamic nor sociable, which made him question whether they would even let him in the door. The girl at the desk did not seem to acknowledge his lack of qualifications for entry.

Gadhar was instantly recognisable. Apart from possessing a more gentlemanly air, he looked exactly the same as he had all those years ago. His smile was dimpled and warm, and his handshake was two handed and firm. Al liked that about him, it made him relax in his company. He marvelled at Gadhar's confidence in the way he beckoned the waiter over for drinks. Thinking back, he always had given off an aura of self-assurance. Perhaps that was why he had successfully elevated his position in life.

Gadhar shared fond memories of Al's father and Al soaked them up with interest. The few memories he possessed of his dad had sadly faded with time. Some of the stories involving his father surprised him. The image Al had always had of him was that he was a man filled with integrity. It was difficult to believe that he would be tied up in the somewhat shady deals that Gadhar described. Still, it was better to get to know the man he was and not the one he had created in his imagination.

Gadhar laughed at some of the backhanded 'business' that they had pulled off together, but Al found it difficult to see the humour, as the man being described was a stranger to him.

Gadhar sensed that Al knew nothing of his father's past and this prompted him to change the subject.

'So, Al, are you a family man?' he asked.

'No, I'm afraid I never got around to having a family,' Al told him, still feeling a little stung by the earlier revelations.

'Do you have a special lady in your life?' Gadhar continued.

'Yes, I have a special lady, but it is too complicated to explain, and I fear you wouldn't believe me if I told you.'

'Try me,' Gadhar pushed. 'Go on, we have all the time in the world.'

Al then surprised himself by opening up to Gadhar Banik about Victoria and how they met. Maybe he just needed someone to talk to. Having no parents, no friends, and a sister who had her own problems to deal with, he saw this man as someone who was close to his dad, which in turn made him a substitute for the real thing. Through tears and painful emotions, he explained everything about Dan's disappearance and how he helped Victoria to find him. It felt so cathartic to talk about his feelings and he realised that his whole life had been bottled up. Gadhar stayed silent, just listening and encouraging. He was just the right person, at the right time.

Al felt that if his father had trusted him, then so could he. For well over an hour, Al continued to describe the unexpected events that had happened in his life over the previous few weeks. He told him in detail the horror of what had happened to Amanda at the hands of the vile Bancroft-Hain. He wept when he described the scene in the cellar.

'I'm sorry, I don't know why I've off loaded all of this onto you, Gadhar.'

'Don't be sorry, it's been fascinating and as you said, quite unbelievable. What will happen now with you and Victoria?' Gadhar asked.

'Nothing. I think she cares deeply for me, but Dan is the love of her life, and they have a son.'

'Was there a time during the search for Dan that you wished him to be dead?' Gadhar asked bluntly.

'Hand on heart, I wanted him to be found alive. I didn't for one moment wish him dead. The love that I feel for Victoria is such that I want her to be happy. Dan being dead would have broken her heart. I couldn't have that.'

'You are a good man, Al. Your father would have been proud.'

This statement from Gadhar was the aloe vera for his troubled soul. His father had never been proud of him. In fact, he was justifiably ashamed. Gadhar Banik's seal of approval made him break down, but this time it was with relief, joy, pride and acceptance. In a way, it helped to release him from the time capsule that he had been trapped in for so many years.

Gadhar motioned for the waiter and they both ordered food and more drinks. Whilst they ate, Gadhar updated Al on the many routes that his life had taken since the death of his boss, Al's father. He told him all about his wife, who was English, and their daughter Isabella.

Al noticed the look of joy in Gadhar's eyes when he spoke of his family, and he felt strangely jealous. When it came to Al telling him all about his career, he did not sugar-coat it. He was honest about the Cocoa Bean and its slow decline. There was no shame involved, and he felt comfortable telling this man everything. Never before had he opened his soul to another human being the way he had to Gadhar.

Pushing his dinner plate to one side, Gadhar leaned forward to speak seriously to Al. His first piece of advice was to keep the shop, and not to sell. He became thoughtful thereafter, looking off across the male-dominated, Victorian style room. Then an idea burst forth in his mind, and he snapped his fingers in the air, 'eureka' style.

'Reinvent your shop. Turn it into the most fashionable cocktail bar around. Bar staff with dickie bow ties, live performers on a Saturday night, small and intimate with bookings weeks in advance. When people think they've found something exclusive, they will pay anything for it. The possibilities are endless for exclusive dining, a private speakeasy, functions...' Gadhar became lost in his own wild ideas.

Something in the way Gadhar showcased the idea of the shop reinvention, made Al start to visualise the cocktail bar with its high-class clientele. The idea of black tie and evening dresses at the weekends appealed to him, as did the hiring of top-class singers and musicians.

'Al, if you like the idea, I can help you plan it and invest money in the venture.'

'Let me think about it, Gadhar. You've certainly given me plenty to chew on. I have to think about Amanda and getting her better, but I am definitely fired up.'

'Well, when you're ready, just call me. Meanwhile, I'll start looking into the licensing process and I'll source various shopfitters. I think we could create something really special.'

It had been a surprising meeting with Gadhar, leaving Al feeling so grateful that he'd reached out. He had come for answers about his parents but ended up with ideas for his future. Shaking Gadhar's hand, he told him that he couldn't have paid for a better therapy session. It had been just what the doctor ordered.

'I actually wanted to meet with you to get some kind of closure about my mum and dad, but it doesn't seem so important now. The past is the past and it can't be changed,' Al explained.

'I knew that was what you were looking for and I anticipated that you would contact me one day.' Gadhar stretched down under the table for his tan leather briefcase. Reaching inside, he took out a folder and handed it to Al. 'Everything you need to know about who killed your parents is in this. The Saudis got the blame for their murder but they had nothing to do with it. The night they died, I was waiting outside in the car to take them home. I was approached by two men and told to leave. They informed me that they would drive your mum and dad home, but deep down I knew it wasn't going to end well. I had no option but to leave as they were armed.

All the details are in the file, and I think you'll be surprised who these men worked for. I have catalogued everything and there are photos. I have made no mention of myself in the findings, and I would be grateful if you would keep my name out of everything. There is enough information in there to take to the government to reopen the case, if that's what you want.'

A trembling weakness took over Al's legs as he held onto the file that contained everything he had ever wanted to know about the past. He could hardly wait to get to his hotel to start devouring the details. Gadhar may have felt guilty that night for leaving his parents alone with those men, but Al knew there was nothing he could have done. Perhaps guilt had driven him to compile a damning dossier of the murders.

In the taxi to the hotel, Al reflected on his lads' day out. It had been brilliant and had put him on an emotional high. In conclusion to what had been discussed at the club with Gadhar, he decided that the cocktail bar was a strong possibility, whilst approaching the authorities with the information needed to reopen the case was a definite.

Chapter 69

Back at the hotel, Al lay on the bed digesting the shocking information about who was involved in the murder of his parents. It was his mother who he felt the most upset about because she knew nothing of her husband's dishonest dealings. His father was aware that many of the so-called business ventures he was involved in would make him a lot of money or get him killed. Al wondered if he enjoyed the thrill of danger or if he just loved making money, regardless of the consequences. Either way, they didn't deserve to be brutally murdered, before being dumped on a stretch of wasteland. He owed it to them, Amanda and himself, to pursue this new evidence that had ended up in his hands.

Standing under the jets of the hot shower, he had so much to think about, but it was all overshadowed by the ache he felt for Victoria. She would be at his house right now and he wondered what she was doing. Fuck it, he was going to call her. There was so much to tell her about his day and the information he had just read about his parents. Taking the fluffy white towel from the stack, he wrapped it around his waist and lay back on the king-sized bed.
'Hi Victoria, I'm sorry for phoning you so late, but I have so much to tell you.'
'Oh, don't be silly, I've been waiting for your call. I would have been hurt if you hadn't phoned to let me know how you got on. Hold on, I'm just climbing into bed… actually, your bed.'

A rush of pure love for this woman filled his heart. *She has been sleeping in my bed to feel close to me while I'm away. Oh man, I love this woman too much. It's agony.*

'Right, that's me, I've scrambled under the duvet. Now, tell me everything,' she said, with excitement.

Chapter 70

The doctor gave the news that Dan could go home. Victoria was delighted because Enid and Artie were so desperate to see him. Oh, how she had missed Artie and the thought of being able to cuddle him. That morning, she had gone to Flamingo to buy some fainting animals, but there had only been one that would fit his proportion criteria. She had also taken a detour on the way to the hospital to see Amanda. She really did appreciate everything Al's sister had done for her in the search for Dan. Now, seeing her still so broken and without Jack in her life, she wondered if she would ever be well again. The therapy sessions that Jack had organised for her were helping, and that pleased Victoria. She wished her the very best and said that she hoped they'd meet up again one day, but she knew that the chances of this were slim.
Learning to live a life without Al was going to be extremely challenging. Victoria knew that she had to be all in or all out in her relationship with Al and, for obvious reasons, it had to be all out. No texts, no calls and no surprise visits, it was over. He had brought her so much happiness in her time of tragedy and yes, if she was being completely honest, she had fallen head over heels in love with the man. But real life wasn't like the stories in novels, it was about doing what was right for everyone involved. Al was only meant to be hers during her time of need and now she had to let him go.

Dan's return was emotional, even his father hugged him with tears in his eyes. Artie held onto his hand for the entire time until it was time for bed.
'Will you tell me a story, daddy?'
'Of course, what book would you like?
'Stick Man. All these terrible things happened to Stick Man, but he came back to his family at the end. What kind of things happened to you when you were away, daddy?'
Dark, desperate memories fell on Dan like a weighted cloak. 'I can't talk about it right now, son. I'll shout mummy up to read your story.'
As his dad hurried from the bedroom, Artie looked over at the Okapi fainting animal his mum had brought him back. Climbing out of bed, he went over to straighten it frontward and move it back a fraction of a centimetre. *There, that's better. I wonder what's upsetting daddy.*

A few weeks after his return home, Dan arranged for Enid to babysit Artie while he took Victoria out for dinner. He booked a table at their local restaurant, The Three Birds, which was walking distance from their house. It had always been a favourite eating place of theirs and they had spent many enjoyable nights dining out there.
As soon as Enid arrived, they headed off to eat. Victoria wore the dress she bought from Citrus Clothing that rainy day in Cheltenham and Dan donned his best blue shirt. The evening air was pleasant but cool and the days had begun to shorten. Slipping his hand in hers, Dan squeezed her fingers saying, 'Did I ever thank you for finding me?'
'Only about a hundred and twenty-four times, that's all,' she laughed. 'You would have done the same thing for

me. I knew that you had to be somewhere and there was no CCTV footage of you leaving the Bancroft-Hain School.'

The mention of the Bancroft-Hain school had an adverse effect on Dan, as they continued walking to the restaurant. A nauseous churning began in his stomach and an overwhelming need to go to the toilet came upon him. Quickening his pace, he whispered that he was sorry.

Panic gripped Victoria as she was unsure what was happening. All she knew was that Dan was behaving strangely, and she wasn't sure whether to keep walking or suggest that they head back home. It was probably too soon for Dan to be out and about after what he had gone through.

Every table in The Three Birds was full except the two-seater at the window. On entering, Dan ran straight to the gents, so Victoria motioned to the owner, *Is this our table?* by pointing. She could see that Jo, the owner, had more important things to do than greet her at the door, pull out her chair and flick her napkin onto her lap. Jo gave a thumbs up sign to let her know that she was grateful. The seat facing the window was the one she preferred to sit in. When she took off her coat, revealing the tangerine-coloured dress, she was aware of a lady to her left looking at her. *Why is she staring?*

She glanced over and the woman waved, and so she returned the greeting. It was Orla Francis, sitting with an older but distinguished looking man. *Of all the people to bump into on a romantic dinner. The days and nights I tormented myself over that woman and she turned out to be nice. I hope Dan doesn't notice her. Everything seems to upset him these days. I wonder what Al's doing?* she couldn't help thinking, just as she did several times every day.

'Sorry about that,' Dan said on his return from the gents. 'Have you ordered drinks?'

'No, I thought I'd wait for you,' she told him. Glancing up at him, she saw that he had spotted Orla. His manner became agitated and, at one point, she thought he was going to suggest leaving.

'Listen Dan, don't be nervous about Orla Francis being here. I had to go and have a chat with her when you first went missing.'

Dan's body stiffened, and his face adopted a grimace.

'It's okay, it was fine. At that stage, I was clasping at straws, and I didn't know if you two were in touch. I had to ask her if she knew anything and of course, she didn't. Dan, she's nice, I felt so much better about everything after speaking to her.'

This revelation didn't please him, but he took it well, relaxing a little. 'I understand that you did what you had to do.'

When Jo approached the table for the drinks order, Dan said, 'I would like a bottle of Bolinger Champagne if you have one, please.'

'I don't have Bolinger, but I have a lovely bottle of Moet et Chandon, if that would be acceptable.'

'Yes, that would be great,' Dan told her.

'Are we celebrating your return?' Victoria asked, shocked by his extravagance.

'We are celebrating more than my return,' he announced, slipping his hand into the inside pocket of his jacket and bringing out the small velvet box. Opening the lid, to reveal the diamond ring, he said, 'Victoria Richards, will you make me the happiest man in the world by agreeing to be my wife?'

He left his seat to kneel on the tiled floor.

This was all Victoria had ever dreamt of from Dan. She had imagined this moment so many times, visualising different locations and scenarios, and now, the moment had come. Of course she was going to say yes, but sadly there was there a lack of spark attached to the proposal. Looking around her, she could see that everyone in the restaurant was watching and smiling, even Orla and her partner. She pulled a wide smile up onto her face and answered, 'I'd love to.'

The diners in the restaurant cheered and clapped. There was even a wolf whistle.

The ring was gorgeous, the champagne went to their heads and the meal was incredible - as it always was in The Three Birds. In fact, it had been the perfect night.

Chapter 71

The wedding took a year to plan, and Victoria had become excited about the prospect of her big day. The venue they chose was the nearby Dundas Castle. Her dress was ivory with beaded detail at the bodice, suiting her shape perfectly. Having no parents and Dan's father in a full-time care facility, Victoria chose Artie to walk her down the aisle. The wedding was costly, but Enid had squirrelled money away in an account for such an event.
On the morning of her wedding day, Victoria slipped into her beautiful dress and as Dan had stayed at his mum's the night before, she called upon Artie to help her with the full-length zip.
She whistled when Artie appeared in the lounge with his little black suit, red bow tie and matching cummerbund.
'Artie, you are a handsome prince,' she told him.
'It feels tight and itchy,' he said, scratching. He had a problem with certain fabrics and his suit contained at least one of them.
'You'll get used to it. It's only for one day, sweet boy. I will bring something for you to get changed into at night.'
This seemed to appease him, as he left the room happy and headed through to his bedroom to play with his wooden animals.
The bridal car wasn't due for another hour, so Victoria hoisted up her gown and sat down to watch the television to sooth her nerves. She turned to the sky news in the hope of hearing the weather forecast. A headline streamed along the foot of the screen which caused her to sit forward, mouth open, heart thudding.

New evidence on the murder of two British Diplomats in Saudi Arabia 17 years ago. Case to be reopened.

The news threw her emotions into disarray. Tears flowed because it was a contact with Al and she still missed him, but there was a sense of joy that he would now be receiving the justice that he had been deprived of all these years.

Chapter 72

Victoria did not hear from Al again until one morning, around three years later. A text came through her phone whilst she was holding it. There were no words, only a photograph. The picture showed the Cocoa Bean premises, but it was no longer a coffee shop. In its place stood a high-class cocktail bar and restaurant called VICTORIA'S.